THE ASSET

Also by Mike Lawson

MIKE LAWSON

A JOE DeMARCO THRILLER

THE ASSET

Atlantic Crime
New York

FIRST EDITION

Printed in the United States of America

First Grove Atlantic hardcover edition: February 2026

Library of Congress Cataloging-in-Publication data is available for this title.

ISBN 978-0-8021-6700-2
eISBN 978-0-8021-6701-9

Atlantic Crime
an imprint of Grove Atlantic
154 West 14th Street
New York, NY 10011

Distributed by Publishers Group West

groveatlantic.com

26 27 28 29   10 9 8 7 6 5 4 3 2 1

To Gail

THE ASSET

1

Jenny stumbled walking down the steps of the diner and grabbed Noah's arm to stop herself from falling.

"Careful," he said.

"Shouldn't have had that last glass of wine," she said.

The diner was out in the middle of nowhere—a place where no one who knew her was likely to go and a place that didn't ask to see young drinkers' IDs—and although the food had been awful, the wine was good. But, like she said, she shouldn't have had the last glass. She wasn't much of a drinker to begin with, and three big glasses of wine had been too much—but they'd definitely put her in the mood. As if she needed alcohol to put her in the mood.

She said, "I can hardly wait to get you home."

He laughed.

Noah was the most beautiful man she'd ever known—and he was wrong for her in so many ways.

She was nineteen years old.

He was thirty.

He had a reputation for being a womanizer.

He was also her teacher.

And she didn't care.

———— ◆◆◆ ————

Noah was her creative writing professor, and he called her to his office one day to discuss a short story she'd written. She was shocked because he'd never paid any attention to her in class and when she'd tried to talk to him, he'd mostly ignored her. He told her the story she'd written was absolutely *brilliant* and how impressed he was by the way her mind worked. They talked for almost two hours that day—they talked about everything under the sun—and she was astounded by how much they had in common despite their age difference. He said they must be soul mates; he said that like he was making a joke, but it wasn't a joke.

A few days later, on a Saturday, he surprised her again when he called and asked if she would read part of a novel he was working on because she was so insightful and he wanted her opinion. But he didn't want to meet in his office. He said it was a beautiful spring day and he wanted to enjoy it, so he told her to meet him at a small park. She was delighted when she saw he'd brought a blanket and a picnic basket filled with finger food and a bottle of wine and real wineglasses. Cherry blossoms drifted down on them as they lay on the blanket and talked. It was like a dream. And when he kissed her—

As for sex, well, she finally understood it. She'd slept with only two men—boys, actually—before she slept with Noah. When she was seventeen, she slept with a guy she'd asked to the prom—he didn't ask her—and she only had sex with him because she wanted to lose her virginity and find out what she was missing. The act itself had taken less time than it took to brush her teeth and had been just about as satisfying. The second time was with a shy boy in one of her classes when she was a freshman at the university. He had a beautiful body because he was a gym rat but was dumber than a box of a rocks and sex with him was about as romantic as a painful yoga workout. And then along comes Noah and she finally experienced an orgasm she didn't give herself and learned why people made such a big deal out of making love.

———— ✦ ————

They walked across the gravel parking lot with her gripping his arm, not only because she was drunk but because she was wearing high heels. The diner was a jeans-and-tennis-shoes kind of place, but she'd worn the heels and the short skirt because she wanted to please him and her legs were her best feature. She'd been trying to figure out a way to get the money to pay for implants—nature could use a little help in that area—but she knew her parents, as rich as they were, wouldn't buy her new boobs.

She said, "I think you better drive."

"No way," Noah said. "I had more to drink than you did. Plus, I can't figure out where anything is in your car."

She drove a Tesla. A gift from Daddy. Normally they used his car, but he'd asked her to drive that night because his car wouldn't start, which wasn't surprising as the thing was so old you had to use a key to start it.

"Maybe we should Uber," she said. "If I get stopped, I'm gonna peg the meter."

"Uber? You think you'd get an Uber driver to come out here at this time of night? We'll be all right. It's mostly back roads to my place."

That was true. He lived in a house in a rural area and to get there she wouldn't have to travel on highways or busy streets. And it was almost midnight and there wouldn't be much traffic. The reason he lived where he did, out in the sticks, was because an old aunt of his owned the house and let him live there for free—which was good because he couldn't afford to rent in the city as half his salary went to his ex-wife. His ex had just totally screwed him when it came to alimony and child support.

He opened the door on his side of the car, but before he got in, he took out his phone, looked at the screen, and muttered, "Shit."

"What is it?" Jenny asked.

"A text from the fucking dean," he said.

She hadn't heard his phone ding for a text message and figured he must have had it set on vibrate.

"Why would she be texting you at this time of night?"

"Because she's insane."

"What's the bitch want?" Jenny asked. She knew he hated his boss.

"It doesn't matter," he said. He tapped on the phone, responding to the text, put the phone back in his pocket, and got into the car.

She got behind the wheel, put on her seat belt, and started the car. It would take about twenty minutes to get to his place. She put both hands on the wheel—ten o'clock and two o'clock like you were supposed to—and drove slowly, making sure she didn't cross over the lane markers. When they passed a twenty-four-hour convenience store, she looked over to see if any cop cars were parked there. Fortunately, there weren't any. Fifteen minutes later, she crossed a small bridge that spanned a narrow creek. She had only a couple more miles to go. Thank God.

"Damnit," he muttered, and took out his phone again.

"The dean?" Jenny asked.

"Yes." He tapped his phone and said, "That's it. I'm turning this damn thing off." He put the phone back in his pocket.

Then he reached over and put his hand under her skirt and started stroking her leg, his hand moving gradually, tantalizingly upward.

She said, "Stop that." She didn't want him to stop. "I mean it." She didn't. "We'll get into a wreck." She didn't care.

He kept stroking and said, "You better pick up the speed a little."

The speed limit was fifty and she was going forty.

He said, "A sure sign a drunk's driving is going way below the speed limit. Plus, I want to get you home and get you naked."

His finger slipped into her panties.

She moaned.

She stepped on the gas.

Ahead of her was a curve, one that turned sharply to the left. A sign said the speed limit for the curve was twenty-five. She didn't know how fast she was going and couldn't think with what he was doing to her. She rounded the curve without slowing down—and screamed.

A man was standing in the road, in her lane—and she hit him. He slammed hard into the windshield, then went flying over the roof of the car.

She stomped on the brake pedal and the car skidded thirty yards, almost going off the road before she could bring it to a stop. She killed the engine, undid her seat belt, flung open the door, and ran back to the man she'd hit.

He looked like a homeless guy, a street person. He was wearing a grease-stained army field jacket that was too warm for the weather, a black stocking cap, and jeans that looked as if they'd never been washed. And he only had one shoe on, like she'd knocked him out of the other one. His nose was big and red and pockmarked and looked like a beet. She could see his dirty, bearded face clearly thanks to a nearby streetlight that had probably been put there so people would see the speed limit sign for the curve. What in the hell had he been doing, standing on a road in a rural area after midnight?

She didn't see any blood, but he looked dead, his eyes half-open. She noticed his neck was at an odd angle and wondered if it had been broken when he hit the windshield or when he hit the ground after he'd gone over the car. She knelt next to him, the asphalt rough on her bare knees, and picked up one of his grimy hands and felt for a pulse in his wrist. There wasn't one.

Noah was standing about six feet away, like he was afraid to come any closer, looking down at her and the dead man.

She looked up at him and said, "He's dead. Oh my God, oh my God, oh my God." She sobbed as she said, "Call 911."

She saw Noah look around. There were grassy fields on both sides of the road, maybe pastures for cows or horses, but she didn't see any animals. There were no houses in sight and there were no other cars on the road.

Noah said, "No."

"What do you mean, 'No'?"

"Jenny, you're drunk. We're both drunk. And you were going over the speed limit. The cops will figure that out by the skid marks. If I call 911, you'll go to jail for vehicular homicide. You won't get off with just a fine. And I'll lose my job because it'll get out that I was with you and maybe I'll go to jail, too, for letting you drive."

"What are you saying?"

"I'm saying let's get out of here before another car comes by. There's nothing to be done for him. If he were alive, it would be different, but he's not. I don't want to see you ruin your life, and it wasn't your fault you hit him. Even if you were sober, you wouldn't have been able to avoid him. Let's go."

"I don't know."

"Jenny, I love you, but I don't want to lose my job. And I don't want to see you go to jail. Let's go."

2

Mahoney was the only white person in the restaurant—and he didn't feel the least bit uncomfortable.

John Mahoney was almost six feet tall. He had a substantial gut and was broad across the back and butt. His hair was thick and pure white—the only thing pure about him—and his eyes were blue and cunning. He was dressed in a dark blue suit, a white shirt, and a red tie; wide red suspenders matched the tie. The man sitting across the table from him was Black. His head was shaved and glistened as if it had been coated with baby oil. He wore a cream-colored suit and a royal purple shirt open at the collar. He wasn't one to blend into a crowd. He was taller and even more overweight than Mahoney—and his brown eyes were just as cunning.

The man Mahoney was having breakfast with was the Reverend Roland S. Calhoun. Roland had been named Ronald when he was born but had changed his given name because he considered *Ronald* too pedestrian. He was the pastor of a large church, one that televised its services, and he held his clerical position despite having sired two children out of wedlock. Because he had the upper hand, he'd insisted that Mahoney meet him on his turf, the restaurant being a block from the church where he preached and a place where people he knew would be impressed seeing him dining with Mahoney.

John Mahoney was the minority leader of the House of Representatives and the last Democratic Speaker of the House.

Mahoney was meeting with Calhoun because he was able to sway Black churchgoers with his rhetoric—he could talk the paint off a wall—and Mahoney wanted him to promote a marginal candidate running in a special election in Virginia for a recently vacated seat in the House. Mahoney wanted the politician elected because he was malleable and would do whatever Mahoney told him to do. And Calhoun was willing to endorse the candidate if he was properly compensated—which Mahoney, being the cynic he was, didn't find surprising or even unreasonable.

The problem was that Calhoun wouldn't come right out and say he wanted to be paid to promote the candidate. He had to go through a song and dance, rambling on about a charity that supposedly helped the downtrodden, and Mahoney had to act like he believed that the money being offered would go to the charity. They finally settled on an amount that wasn't outrageous, at least not outrageous in terms of what it cost to get people elected these days, and an investment in Calhoun was better than ads on television. The deal done, they shook hands and Calhoun left, patting people on the back on his way out of the restaurant. He stuck Mahoney with the check.

Mahoney dropped three twenties on the table—he couldn't afford to undertip and look like a cheapskate—and took out his phone to tell his driver to pull up in front of the restaurant. Before he could tap the number, a woman walked up to his table and took the seat Calhoun had vacated. The woman was white. Mahoney was facing the entrance to the restaurant, and he was certain he would have noticed her walking in because she was quite attractive; she must have come in through a back door. She was in her mid-thirties and had short blond hair and a trim figure. She wore a sleeveless white blouse that displayed well-toned arms and tight jeans that looked good on her. She was vaguely familiar.

She said, "Congressman, I have something important to tell you."

"Who are you?" Mahoney said, his phone still in his hand.

"You don't remember me?"

"No."

"I did some work for your chief of staff. You stuck your head into Perry's office once while I was meeting with him, and he introduced me to you. Anyway, my name's Diane Lake. I work for Vicount Analytics. Perry hired us to look into a guy named Ambrose running for the Wisconsin Seventh. We did our job and your guy won."

"Oh, yeah, I remember now," Mahoney said. Actually, he didn't remember meeting her, but he did remember the job Perry and the DNC had hired Vicount to do.

Vicount Analytics was a research firm. Corporate raiders used them before takeovers to make sure a company's financial statements matched reality. Wealthy people used them before they got divorced to find out if their spouses were hiding assets that should be community property. Corporate boards hired them to see if the guy they were about to make their CEO had lied on his résumé, like claiming to have graduated from Harvard when he hadn't. And politicians and PACs supporting politicians used them to do opposition research, and what Vicount Analytics did was dig in the dirt to see what nasty things were buried there.

Perry Wallace, Mahoney's chief of staff, had used Vicount to research a Republican named Baxter Ambrose who'd been running for a closely contested House seat in Wisconsin. Vicount learned that Ambrose, who frequently claimed to be a bullet-dodging combat veteran, had worked as a clerk in the heavily fortified Green Zone in Baghdad and the closest he'd come to combat was flying over the country when his tour was up. Vicount also learned that Ambrose, a multimillionaire, had paid no federal income taxes in the last ten years. But the biggest nail in Ambrose's coffin was the revelation that the wife of the supposedly pro-life candidate had flown halfway across the country and used a fake name to have an abortion—and her husband had accompanied her. He was captured on a security camera wearing a rain hat and sunglasses, the collar of his jacket turned up, and he looked like a bank robber—like a man praying he wouldn't be recognized.

Mahoney looked at his watch and said, "Yeah, well, nice to see you again, Diane, but I gotta get going."

He was about to press the button to call his driver, but before he could, Lake said, "Sir, what I have to tell you is more important than your next appointment. Believe me. It concerns Dutch McMillian."

Douglas "Dutch" McMillian was the Republican leader of the United States Senate. He'd served in the Senate for thirty-four years and had held the top job the last eighteen years. He was a brilliant, devious, ruthless politician, not unlike Mahoney in many ways, and he and Mahoney detested each other. Had Mahoney not been a Democrat, he and Dutch would have been best friends.

Mahoney put his phone down on the table. "What about Dutch? And how'd you know I'd be here?"

"I didn't. I followed you to see if I could catch you alone someplace."

Mahoney shook his head. So much for his security. He was lucky Lake wasn't some whack job who wanted to shoot him.

"And what I have to tell you isn't about Senator McMillian, at least not directly. It concerns his wife."

Dutch McMillian was married to a woman named Lydia Chang; she continued to use her maiden name after they were married. She'd been born in China and her parents immigrated to the United States when she was five with not much more than the clothes on their backs. Her father worked his ass off and became a successful businessman and sent his daughter to the best schools. Lydia worked even harder than her father and she was millionaire before she turned thirty. She was twenty years younger than Dutch and she was a beautiful woman, but Mahoney had the impression that ice water ran through her veins. She was aloof, almost haughty, and mostly stayed out of the limelight, but Dutch often said that he relied on her for advice more than anyone else in his inner circle—and Mahoney believed him.

"What about her?" Mahoney said. "And make it quick. I need to get going."

"I believe she's a Chinese agent."

"Oh, for Christ's sake," Mahoney said, and reached for his phone.

"Listen to me. I'm not some conspiracy nut. I saw Lydia Chang meeting with a man named Zhou Enlai. Do you know who Zhou is?"

"No."

"He's the second highest ranking intelligence officer stationed at the Chinese embassy in D.C. He's been here in the States about four years. He's young, he's bright, and he's ambitious. And if he's turned Lydia Chang and is running her, which I'm sure he is, it'll make his career."

"How do you know about Zhou?"

"I'm ex-CIA. I speak Mandarin, and when I was working at Langley, before I went to work for Vicount, I was an analyst in the China section. And the CIA knows almost all the Chinese intelligence officers working at the embassy, and that's how I know Zhou."

"And how did you happen to see Zhou meeting with Lydia? Were you following one of them like you followed me?"

"No. It was a total fluke. I saw them sitting together at Four Mile Run Park in Arlington. Four Mile Run isn't far from where I live, and I like to jog on the trail there next to the stream. Anyway, I was jogging and I recognized Zhou immediately from my time at the CIA. He's a striking man. But at first I didn't know who he was meeting with. Lydia Chang is also usually striking. But the woman with Zhou that day had on no makeup—and you never see Lydia Chang in public without makeup—and was wearing a hooded sweatshirt and she had the hood up. I guess that was the best she could do for a disguise. After I ran past them, I decided I wanted to know who Zhou was meeting with."

"Why?" Mahoney said.

"Because I'm an ex–CIA officer and Zhou is a Chinese spy and I felt it was my duty to find out. So I ran a little farther and then turned around and ran past them a second time and when I did, I took a photo of them sitting together."

Lake took out her iPhone and tapped it a couple of times and showed the screen to Mahoney. He studied the woman but couldn't be sure she was Lydia Chang—and he'd been in the same room with Lydia many times.

"Are you sure this is Lydia?"

"Yes. I thought it might be her when I looked at the photo, but I wasn't positive. So I found a place to hide, and when she left, I followed her to the parking lot and got her license plate number. It's her."

"But what makes you think Zhou is running her as an agent?"

"One, the place where they met. Why would Lydia Chang be meeting with Zhou alone in a park that's thirty minutes from where she lives in McLean? Two, the way she was dressed, the hoodie, no makeup."

"So, based on the fact that Lydia didn't have on her lipstick, you think she's a traitor giving Dutch's secrets to the Chinese?"

"Yes. There might be some other reason why she'd be meeting with a Chinese intelligence officer, but if there is, I don't know what it could be."

Lake didn't strike Mahoney as a crackpot, and if Lydia Chang was meeting with a Chinese spy, that had to be investigated.

"So why did you come to me with this?" Mahoney said. "Go tell the FBI what you think. It's their job to catch traitors, not mine."

"I don't want to become an FBI witness and get caught up in all the drama if I expose Chang. And because the FBI leaks like a sieve, I know my name would get out there, and I value my privacy. But that's not the main thing. I can just see myself showing up at the Hoover Building and saying, 'Hey, I'd like to talk to someone about Dutch McMillian's wife spying for the Chinese.' They probably wouldn't even open the door. And if I talked to the wrong agent, like someone whose politics are aligned with McMillian's, the agent might not do anything, or he might warn

McMillian. We both know that if you're the one making the accusation, it'll be a whole different story."

Mahoney didn't respond. He sat there studying Lake's face. When he didn't say anything after a few seconds, Lake said, "I know what you're thinking. You're thinking that this could be some kind of setup."

That's *exactly* what he was thinking.

"So what you need to do," Lake said, "is confirm what I'm telling you."

"And how would I do that?" Mahoney asked.

"By having someone you trust follow Chang, and that way you'll know I'm not lying. If Zhou's running her—and I know he is; I'm certain— he'll meet with her again. And then you can tell the Bureau."

"And you think I'd be willing to do that to hurt Dutch?"

"Yeah, maybe. You're not exactly best friends and I doubt it would bother you to cause him a major problem. But I think the main reason you'll tell the Bureau is because you're a patriot and you don't want the Chinese running the wife of the Republican leader of the United States Senate."

After another long pause, Mahoney said, "Text me that photo."

Lake said, "No. Get your own photo. That way you'll know I'm telling the truth."

———◆◆◆———

Mahoney, a tumbler filled with ice and bourbon in his big right paw, spun his chair around and looked out a window, in the direction of the National Mall and the Washington Monument. The sky was unusually dark for an early spring evening and filled with angry-looking red and magenta clouds, the lovely colors most likely produced by pollutants in the atmosphere.

After his encounter with Diane Lake, Mahoney had gone about the day doing what he normally did: browbeating those who needed to be beaten, cajoling those who needed to be stroked, dodging questions he didn't want to answer from the media, and sucking up to wealthy donors. But his conversation that morning with Lake was never far from his mind. He picked up his phone and called his chief of staff and told Perry to come to his office. "And bring DeMarco with you," he added.

Perry said, "Don't you remember? You sent DeMarco to Kentucky."

"Oh, yeah, I forgot about that," Mahoney said. "Well, see if he's back, and if he's not, tell him to get his ass back here right away. This is more important than Mookie."

3

"Where are you?" Perry asked. "Are you still in Kentucky?"

"No," DeMarco said. "Just got back. I'm at National."

Perry said, "That's good. He wants to see us both."

DeMarco said. "Now?"

"Yeah."

"Jesus, Perry, I'm exhausted. I've been traveling for six hours, not to mention spending two days in Bumfuck, Kentucky. I wanna go home. Can't this wait?"

"No. Oh, did you talk to Mookie?"

"No. He's disappeared and I don't know where he's gone to."

"Well, that's not going to make the man happy. Anyway, you need to come straight to the Capitol."

Joe DeMarco was a muscular man with dark hair he combed straight back, blue eyes, a prominent nose, and a cleft in a strong chin. He was a handsome man, but also hard looking, and he could be intimidating if he chose to be. His late father had worked for an Italian mob boss in

Queens, and DeMarco looked just like his father, meaning he looked like a guy who could have been cast as one of Tony's goombahs in *The Sopranos*.

DeMarco was John Mahoney's fixer, his troubleshooter. He was also his bagman, the one Mahoney sent to collect campaign contributions that some nitpickers might consider bribes. He had a law degree but had never practiced law, and he had an office the size of a tool shed in the subbasement of the Capitol. He wasn't listed as a member of Mahoney's staff. To give Mahoney deniability if DeMarco was ever caught doing something illegal, Mahoney had gotten him a civil service position in the legislative branch, where he supposedly provided legal services to members of Congress on an ad hoc basis. What this meant was that if some representative needed a free lawyer, DeMarco was available—although the only one he was really available to was Mahoney.

DeMarco had ended up in Kentucky thanks to a lady named Edna Cooper. Edna was short and stout; she looked the way Winston Churchill would have looked if he'd had a curly gray perm and a uterus. She was a dynamo with more contained energy than a nuclear reactor who would never quit and wouldn't take no for an answer. She lived in Salyersville, Kentucky, in Magoffin County, in Kentucky's Fifth Congressional District.

The Fifth Congressional District of Kentucky, based on the last census, is the second-most-impoverished district in the nation and has the highest percentage of White Americans in the nation. You're more likely to find a unicorn in Magoffin County than a person of color. It is also the most rural district in the United States, with 76 percent of its population living in rural areas. The district votes overwhelmingly Republican and its current representative to Congress had gotten 82 percent of the vote.

But in this bright red district lived the widow Edna Cooper. She raised funds for masochistic Democrats willing to be humiliated by running for state and federal offices. She put up posters; she organized phone banks; she mailed out postcards urging Kentuckians to vote blue; she stood on street corners passing out flyers that most of her fellow citizens tossed into trash bins. She harassed the DNC relentlessly, begging for money to support local candidates—and the DNC ignored her as it wasn't about to waste its money on the Kentucky Fifth.

Nonetheless, Edna, stubborn warrior that she was, fought on. At her own expense, she attended a conference in D.C. for political foot soldiers like herself where she managed to get a five-minute meeting with John Mahoney. The only reason a skeptical Mahoney agreed to see her was that she claimed to have information that could destroy Maggie Bower.

Maggie Bower was the congresswoman currently representing the Kentucky Fifth. She was a stoutly built blonde with a coarse complexion and a big mouth, and she'd run on a platform of wanting to dismantle the federal government—even though she was now part of it—and ending all forms of taxation—even though taxes paid her salary. She'd managed to graduate from high school without learning anything about American history or civics, had no apparent interest in governing, and had never sponsored a bill that actually became a law. But what she had going for her was national name recognition because she spent most of her time on talk shows and podcasts and social media sites espousing mind-boggling conspiracy theories that may have been absurd but were highly entertaining. One had to with the Deep State—whoever that might be—controlling the weather. Her current favorite was that extraterrestrials lived among us and the reason why they hadn't been exposed was because the people running NASA were extraterrestrials. She publicly insulted members of her own party who had the nerve to disagree with her and had done everything she could to topple the current Republican leadership in the House because they didn't support every outlandish notion she had. But her favorite target was John Mahoney. She disparaged him to the media on an almost daily basis, hurled obscenities at him and interrupted his speeches, and would follow him back to his office screaming at him as he ignored her.

Mahoney hated the woman passionately but had resigned himself to having to endure her antics as he had no hope whatsoever that a Democrat would replace her, and right now it looked as if she'd be reelected despite—or maybe because of—her outlandish personality and behavior.

But then Mahoney took a meeting he thought would be a waste of time with Edna Cooper. When Edna told him what Maggie Bower had supposedly done, Mahoney enveloped the short, round woman in a bear hug and immediately dispatched DeMarco to Salyersville, Kentucky.

The closest airport to Salyersville was the Huntington Tri-State Airport in West Virginia. It was a four-hour flight from D.C. to Huntington because of a layover in Charlotte, North Carolina, and then DeMarco had to rent a car and drive an hour and a half to Salyersville to meet Edna. He took Interstate 64 west out of Huntington along a brief stretch of the Ohio River, then turned south onto US 23, a four-lane highway running parallel to the Kentucky–West Virginia border for much of the way. The view was mostly of tree-covered, rolling green hills that he imagined would look magnificent in the fall.

When he reached Staffordsville, Kentucky, he turned off US 23 onto State Route 40, a two-lane blacktop going through the small towns of Barnetts Creek and Oil Springs and Falcon. He passed a woman driving a tractor down the road like it was a car. He wondered what people did for work in these parts, other than farming. He wondered if they still had coal mines in the region.

Finally, he reached Salyersville, the county seat of Magoffin County, also known as the "Gateway to Appalachia," according to one billboard he saw. The population was 1,546 souls. He put Edna's address into his phone's map app and passed a McDonald's and a Wendy's and a Taco Bell on the way there, which made him feel more at home. DeMarco was a city boy—he'd been born and raised in New York City and had spent his career in Washington, D.C.—and he felt as out of place in a rural setting as a duck in a chicken coop.

———◆◆◆———

Edna's house was a single-story brick rambler with a covered porch holding two weathered blue Adirondack chairs. A stately red maple tree took up most of the small front yard and the lawn was overdue for mowing. DeMarco concluded that Edna, like himself, wasn't into gardening or yard work.

He rang the bell. Edna opened the door, squinted up at him, and said, "You DeMarco?"

"Yep, that's me," he said.

Edna was dressed in baggy blue jeans and a T-shirt that had the outline of the U.S. Capitol over an American flag. A souvenir from her trip to D.C.? She offered him coffee and stale store-bought cookies—he would have preferred a beer after the long drive—and they took seats in her small living room, him on a brown couch made of fake leather, her in a matching armchair, her legs barely long enough for her feet to reach the floor. Off to one side was a dining table that obviously wasn't used for dining as it held a laptop computer and a printer and was covered with pamphlets and flyers and posters in progress. DeMarco figured that table was the headquarters for the Democratic Party in Magoffin County.

She said, "My son should be home soon."

The information that Edna had passed on to Mahoney had come from her son, who had obtained it from a man named Mookie. That's right: Mookie. DeMarco's task was to meet with Mookie, confirm he was telling the truth, and persuade him to talk to the media about what he'd witnessed.

DeMarco learned that Edna's late husband had been a coal miner—the job killed him—and she had three sons. The first was in the army, stationed in Germany. The second lived in Lexington and managed a Walmart there. Her third son, Bobby, worked at the local Ace Hardware and had just been booted out of his house by his wife for cheating on her and DeMarco got the impression that Edna liked Bobby's soon-to-be-ex-wife more than Bobby.

DeMarco learned all this because he spent an hour with Edna chatting and drinking coffee, waiting for Bobby to come home from work. Bobby was supposed to have been home at six but didn't arrive until an hour later because he'd decided to stop for a beer—or two or three or six—after work. When he arrived, smelling as if he'd been gargling Budweiser, Edna reached up, cuffed him hard on the ear, cursed him for his tardiness, then said, "Sit down and tell this man what Mookie told you."

Bobby was a foot taller than his mother. He had a shock of dark hair covered by a greasy red ball cap, long, hairy arms, and a prominent Adam's apple; his muddy-brown eyes were having a hard time focusing. He said, "Aw, Ma, do I have to? I'm beat. I just wanna eat and go to bed."

"You're not beat; you're drunk as usual," Edna said. "And, yeah, you have to if you wanna keep living in my house."

"But who's this guy?" Bobby said, pointing his weak chin at DeMarco.

"His name doesn't matter," Edna said. "Just tell him what Mookie told you."

So Bobby told him.

"Why did he tell you the story?" DeMarco asked.

Bobby said, "Because while we were havin' a drink together down at Shorty's, she comes on TV and starts running her mouth and Mookie says he'll never vote for that bitch again and hopes she dies. Then he told me the story."

"And you're sure he told you the truth?" DeMarco said.

"Well, yeah, I guess. Why would he lie about something like that?"

"How did Mookie happen to be there when it happened?"

"He was working for her," Bobby said. "She's got a farm, a good-sized place west of here, and raises some crops and a few hogs, and she hired

Mookie to butcher one of her hogs. That's what Mookie does for a living. He butchers hogs, turns 'em into bacon and chops, and he's good and he's fast. He butchers hogs for lots of folks in these parts."

And DeMarco thought: *Great.* The star witness against Maggie Bower is a hog butcher. That should play well on TV.

"How do you know Mookie?" DeMarco asked.

"I went to high school with him, although he dropped out sophomore year, and I see him every once in a while at Shorty's when I go there."

"Do you know where he lives?"

"He's got a trailer on the Mash Fork."

"'The Mash Fork'?" DeMarco said.

"Mash Fork Creek. I know that because he told me about his trailer getting flooded and almost washing away the last time the creek went over the bank."

"I need his address," DeMarco said.

"I don't know his address," Bobby said.

"Then what's his real name?"

"Beats me," Bobby said. "I've always called him Mookie. Everybody does."

"Well, shit," DeMarco said. "Someone must know his real name, like some of the kids you went to school with."

"Like I said, Mookie didn't go long and most of the kids I went to school with moved away from here as soon as they could. And high school was ten years ago."

DeMarco said to Edna, "I need your help. I need you and your son to start calling people, like kids Bobby went to school with, teachers, hog farmers, anyone who might know Mookie's real name and his address. Make up a story for why you're asking—like say a farmer you know has a hog that needs butchering and that's why you're trying to track Mookie down."

DeMarco couldn't believe he was talking about butchering hogs.

"You got it," Edna said. "Me and Bobby will start calling folks tonight."

Bobby said, "Aw, Ma, I gotta get up early for work tomorrow. We're movin' things around in the store."

"I don't want to hear any more whining from you," Edna said. "Go drink a cup of coffee and start calling people like the man said."

DeMarco said, "I'm going to find a motel here in town and in the morning—"

"There aren't any motels in Salyersville," Edna said. "But there's a nice Ramada Inn in Paintsville, about thirty minutes east of here."

DeMarco said, "I'll call you in the morning and hopefully you'll have a name by then and an address if you can get one. And Mahoney wanted me to let you know that if this pans out, he'll see if he can get you a seat at the next State of the Union."

"Really?" Edna said.

"Yeah, really," DeMarco said.

"Who's Mahoney?" Bobby said.

———— ◆◆◆ ————

Edna called DeMarco at seven the next morning, waking him up.

She said, "Mookie's real name is Marcus Morehouse. I had no idea he was one of the Morehouse clan. There's a whole passel of them outside of Lickburg, livin' in shacks in some holler, but he doesn't stay in touch with his family, and I couldn't get an address or a phone number for him. All his people knew was that he lives on the Mash Fork like Bobby said."

"Well, now that I know his real name, I can probably find him," DeMarco said.

DeMarco couldn't find an address for a Marcus Morehouse online using one of those people search engines, so he called Perry. "Get someone over at the IRS to give you an address for a Marcus Morehouse who lives near Salyersville, Kentucky, on Mash Fork Creek."

"'Mash Fork'?" Perry said.

While waiting to hear back from Perry, DeMarco had breakfast at a restaurant called Wilma's on Court Street in Paintsville. The waitress, a pretty but tired-looking woman about his age, asked how he wanted the grits that came with the bacon and eggs. "No grits," DeMarco said. He'd never been able to understand the appeal of grits, a product which you had to mix with something to make it edible, which meant it was basically inedible.

When the waitress came back with the check, he told her he had some time to kill and asked her if there was anything interesting to see in Paintsville. She said, "A lot of tourists visit the place where Loretta Lynn was born in Butcher Holler. It's only about fifteen minutes from here and it's kinda pretty there."

"Why's it called Butcher Holler?" DeMarco asked. He wondered what had been butchered there, humans or animals? Maybe it was the site of a famous massacre.

She said, "Because a family named Butcher owned the land."

"Oh," DeMarco said.

Perry called him back as he was leaving the restaurant.

Perry said, "Marcus Morehouse has never paid federal income taxes."

"Well, shit, Perry. There's gotta be some way—"

"Shut up," Perry said. "I called the governor." The governor of Kentucky was a Democrat, which was a political miracle because the state's two senators and five of its six representatives were Republicans. Perry said, "I figured Mookie probably has a driver's license and asked the governor to call the DMV and get an address for him. I'll text you the address."

———— ◆◆◆ ————

Mookie's trailer was only twenty minutes from Salyersville. It was one of three parked in a clearing above the north bank of Mash Fork Creek. The trailer was an old Airstream about thirty feet long. The aluminum was faded and the windows were opaque from grime. Mookie obviously didn't haul the trailer as the tires were flat and it was sitting on concrete blocks and there was a large white propane tank attached to the rear. Two sun-bleached green plastic lawn chairs sat in the weeds near the front door, close to a fifty-five-gallon barrel for burning trash. Off to one side was a pickup truck that appeared to have been cannibalized for parts as it was missing its engine, one front fender, and a door. The pickup was parked next to an unoccupied ten-by-ten-foot kennel that was made from chicken wire and littered with dog shit.

DeMarco knocked on the trailer door.

No one answered.

His string of bad luck when it came to Mookie continued.

DeMarco went and leaned against his rental car, trying to decide what to do next. It was only ten in the morning, and it was possible that Mookie was off butchering hogs somewhere. He could wait for Mookie to return home but it would probably be smarter to come back in the evening. But what the hell was he going to do all day in Salyersville while he was waiting? Maybe there was a golf course nearby where he could rent clubs.

Before he could check his phone for golf courses, a heavyset bald man with gray stubble on his cheeks and chin, wearing bib overalls and no shirt, came out of the trailer on the west side of Mookie's and walked over to DeMarco. He looked suspicious and unfriendly.

The man said, "You lookin' for Mookie?"

"Yeah. You have a phone number for him?"

"No. Never had no reason to call him. Why you lookin' for him?"

DeMarco remembered what Edna had said about Mookie belonging to the Morehouse clan in Lickburg. He said, "Mookie has an aunt over in Lickburg that passed away. I'm a lawyer and the executor of her estate, and she left a small amount of money to Mookie."

He waited for Mookie's neighbor to say: *You lyin' Yankee son of a bitch! Mookie doesn't have any aunts*—but he didn't. He said, "Well, I don't know when he'll be back. He took off a couple days ago, told me he had a job over in West Virginia, on one of the big pig farms there that needed some extra help. He took his dogs with him, so I'm guessing he'll be gone awhile."

DeMarco closed his eyes and exhaled. "Do you know which pig farm?" he asked.

"Nope. Lot of pig farms in West Virginia."

Jesus. DeMarco took a card out of his wallet, one that had only his name and cell phone number on it, and handed it to the man. He said, "When Mookie comes back, tell him to give me a call. It's not a lot of money, but it's his, and if I can't locate him, it'll go to the other relatives."

The man looked at the card and said, "Dee-mar-ko."

DeMarco got into his car and checked flight schedules. There was a flight leaving from Huntington to D.C. at one forty-five and he figured he could make it. No matter what Mahoney wanted, he wasn't going to hang around fucking Kentucky forever, waiting for Mookie to show up. If he'd brought his golf clubs with him, he might have waited a couple of days, but since he hadn't . . .

He called Edna and told her that Mookie was working in West Virginia and that he was returning to D.C. He gave her Mookie's address and said, "Edna, what I need you to do is drive by his place every couple of days—he only lives about twenty minutes from you—and when you see he's back—like, if you see a car parked in front of his trailer—give me a call and I'll come back."

The thought of having to come back to Kentucky made him want to weep.

He made the flight and Perry called him as he was leaving the terminal at Reagan National, telling him that Mahoney wanted to see them both immediately.

4

By the time Perry and DeMarco arrived at Mahoney's office, Mahoney was on his third tumbler of bourbon. It never occurred to him to offer Perry and DeMarco a drink. DeMarco thought Mahoney looked terrible: bags under his red-rimmed eyes, his face pasty from lack of exposure to sunlight. His big gut was stretching the red suspenders holding up his pants to their limit.

They sat down in the two chairs in front of Mahoney's massive desk. To the side of the desk was a wall filled with photographs of Mahoney posing with athletes and movie stars and politicians—politicians who DeMarco always thought of as the "unindicted co-conspirators." In stands behind the desk were an American flag and a Massachusetts state flag. The Massachusetts flag showed an Indian on a blue shield holding a bow in one hand and an arrow in the other, and above the Indian was an arm—just an arm—holding a sword. The banner on the flag read: *Ense petit placidam sub libertate quietem*. Perry had once translated the Latin for DeMarco and he knew the words meant: "By the sword we seek peace, but peace only under liberty." DeMarco had always thought that the state should hold a contest to come up with a better design.

Perry said, "So what's going on?"

Mahoney's chief of staff was an overweight, middle-aged white man whose hairline was rapidly retreating. He spent eighteen hours a day doing whatever was needed to keep Mahoney in power and he lived off Diet Coke and vending machine junk food and should have expired years ago from a massive heart attack. He was wearing a white shirt, an undone tie, and baggy suit pants, the shirt so wrinkled it looked as if he'd slept in it.

Ignoring Perry, Mahoney said to DeMarco, "Did you talk to Mookie?"

"No. He wasn't home and no one knows where he is."

"Well, goddamnit," Mahoney said. "How hard can it be to find a fuckin' guy named Mookie?"

"The thing is, Mookie butchers—"

"Never mind Mookie for now," Mahoney said. "He'll have to wait." Looking at Perry, he said, "You remember a gal named Diane Lake who works for Vicount Analytics? You hired her a couple of years ago."

"Yeah, sure," Perry said. "What about her?"

"What did you think of her?"

Perry shrugged. "Competent. Professional. I'd use her again."

"So she didn't come across as some kind of nut?"

"No, not at all. Why are you asking about her?"

"Because this morning she told me that Dutch McMillian's wife is a Chinese agent."

"You gotta be shittin' me," Perry said.

"Fuck me," DeMarco muttered.

DeMarco knew that whatever Mahoney was talking about was about to become his problem.

———❖———

After Mahoney finished telling them what Lake had said to him, DeMarco said, "Why don't you just sic the FBI on Chang *and* Lake.

Tell 'em what Lake told you about seeing Chang meeting with Zhou and that she has a photo of the meeting and let the Bureau take it from there."

Mahoney said, "There's no way in hell I'm going to accuse Lydia Chang of spying for the Chinese based solely on what Lake told me. For one thing, if I went to the FBI, it would get out that it was me who ratted on her, and it would stink of politics and of me trying to cause Dutch a problem. And if Lake is wrong about Lydia, then I'd *really* have a problem."

"You think she lied to you about seeing Chang with Zhou?" DeMarco said.

"No, I don't think she lied about that. I suppose, these days, the photo she showed me could have been photoshopped, but I don't think it was. But I just can't help thinking that there might be something else going on here. Lake could have gone to a dozen people with this thing, like people she used to work with at the CIA—assuming she really worked at the CIA—but instead she came to me, and I can't help but wonder if she's playing me in some way."

"Why would she do that?" DeMarco asked.

"Because this is fuckin' Washington and you can't trust anyone and everyone who works here has a hidden agenda. Anyway, the first thing I want you to do—"

Mahoney was looking at DeMarco, not Perry.

"—is see if Lydia is really meeting with this guy."

"What do you expect me to do?" DeMarco said. "Follow her twenty-four hours a day?"

"Yeah, if that's what it takes. And I want you to check out Lake. See if there's anything that's off-kilter about her."

"I'm going to need some help."

"If you're talking about your buddy Emma, forget it."

Emma was a former spy herself. She'd retired from the Defense Intelligence Agency, the DIA, and she had contacts in the Pentagon and the many other intelligence agencies headquartered in D.C. She could also be lethal if an occasion called for it. Unlike DeMarco, she owned guns and had no problem using them. DeMarco met her years ago by being in the wrong place at the right time and inadvertently saved her life when a couple of Iranians tried to kill her. Since then, if DeMarco asked for her help, she would usually lend a hand, and he suspected the main reason she did was not because she owed him for saving her life but because retirement bored her. The problem was that she despised Mahoney and didn't consider him fit for any public office and Mahoney didn't like her because he couldn't control her.

"Not Emma. She's still recovering," DeMarco said.

A few months ago, as Mahoney well knew, Emma had been shot while helping DeMarco on an assignment Mahoney had given him. The bullet broke her femur, which was bad enough, but following the surgery to repair her leg she got an infection that almost killed her, and she wasn't a hundred percent healthy yet.

DeMarco said, "I was thinking about a couple of guys that Emma and I have used before. I trust them."

"You sure these guys won't talk?"

"You don't know these guys, but they wouldn't talk if you wired their nuts to a car battery."

"Yeah, okay," Mahoney said. "But no one else. And you better be right about them being able to keep their mouths shut."

DeMarco said, "Let's say I'm able to confirm what Lake told you: that Lydia Chang is meeting with this Chinese spy. Then what?"

"I don't know," Mahoney said.

That was the *wrong* answer, DeMarco thought.

Mahoney should have said: *Then I'll sic the FBI on her.*

But with Mahoney, things were never simple.

And as he'd said, everyone in Washington had an under-the-table agenda, and John Mahoney had many.

5

Sergio and Javier were a couple of military trained killers originally from South America, and DeMarco's friend, Emma, knew them from her time at the DIA. She'd also helped them to immigrate to the United States when it appeared their life spans would be considerably shorter if they stayed in their homeland and, because of that, they would do anything for her. They now ran a detective agency in Miami that catered to Hispanic clients and mostly Cubans because, for whatever reason, Cubans seemed to have a lot of drama in their lives.

DeMarco met them when he and Emma used them as bodyguards to help protect themselves from a couple of corrupt FBI agents in Florida and they'd come armed with machine guns and silenced pistols and wearing body armor and comm systems and night vision goggles. DeMarco used them a second time, just recently, to protect two call girls—call girls who had slept with the president of the United States. That had been an assignment that DeMarco would never forget not only because Emma had been shot but because he'd also been shot and almost killed and then had been forced to kill a man who worked for the president. And it was only due to a stroke of dumb luck that he wasn't arrested for murder and didn't end up spending the rest of his life in prison.

DeMarco had called Javier after the meeting with Mahoney and Perry. He called Javier because talking to Sergio was like talking to a rock. Sergio acted as if words were gold and he hoarded them. He told Javier that he wanted to hire him and his partner, and they could charge whatever they normally charged. Or they could charge more than they normally charged. DeMarco didn't care how much they charged because the U.S. Treasury would be paying their bill. When he told Javier that the job would entail following someone twenty-four hours a day and he wasn't sure how long they'd have to follow the person—it could be days, it could be weeks—Javier said they'd drive up from Miami in a couple of vehicles they used for surveillance work.

The next morning DeMarco met them in a café in McLean, Virginia, that was close to Lydia Chang's home. They were already in the restaurant when DeMarco arrived. It was about a fifteen-hour drive from Miami to D.C. and they'd driven through the night but looked fresh and alert. DeMarco suspected they would have looked fresh and alert even if they'd walked from Miami.

Sergio and Javier were short, wiry men in their fifties with dark hair and cold dark eyes and looked pretty much alike except that Sergio had a mustache and Javier didn't. They were wearing jeans and faded T-shirts, and if you'd seen them doing yard work at some rich guy's house, you wouldn't think twice about it. You'd never guess from their appearance that they were as lethal as sharks.

DeMarco got a cup of coffee and sat down with them in a booth. He asked if they wanted breakfast, but they said they'd already eaten, which was too bad because DeMarco was starving.

He said, "The person I want you to follow is a woman named Lydia Chang. She's the wife of Dutch McMillian, the Republican leader of the United States Senate."

Neither man reacted visibly to this pronouncement. DeMarco wouldn't have wanted to play poker with either of them.

"You can go online to get a photo of Chang," DeMarco said. "And what I need you to do is see if she meets with a Chinese man named Zhou Enlai. I don't have a picture of Zhou yet but I'm trying to get one. If she meets with Zhou—or any other man who looks Chinese—I want you to get a photo of them together. The thing is, when she meets with Zhou, she might be wearing a disguise, so she won't look the way she does in any Internet photo you'll find. The last time she met with him she dressed down, didn't wear makeup, and wore a hoodie."

DeMarco took an index card out of his pocket and passed it to Javier.

"That's her home address and the address of her office in Reston. Her house is a couple of miles from here in a ritzy neighborhood because she and her husband are rich. You have to be careful watching her house. Her husband has a security detail and if they see you lurking about, the U.S. Capitol Police will take an interest in you. So don't get caught watching her."

"Why are we watching her?" Javier asked.

DeMarco hesitated, then decided to tell them the truth. Like he'd told Mahoney, he trusted them, and the more they knew, the more useful they'd be. He said, "Zhou is an intelligence officer working out of the Chinese embassy. And there's a possibility that he's running Chang as an agent and she may be passing on national security information to him. But I don't know for sure that she's doing that. All I know is that she met with Zhou once, and just the fact that she met with him is bad, considering who her husband is. Anyway, your job is to get me proof that she's meeting with Zhou."

DeMarco felt like doing his *Mission Impossible* impression at that point and telling them that if they were caught, the secretary would disavow any knowledge of them. Then he decided not to. Javier and Sergio, particularly Sergio, didn't have much of a sense of humor.

"What are you going to be doing while we're following this woman?" Javier asked.

"Me?" DeMarco said. "Probably nothing. I'm management."

That didn't get a smile out of either of them.

DeMarco said, "Actually, what I'll be doing is some research on the people involved in all this. Anyway, get on Chang. If nothing happens in a couple of weeks—I mean, I think it's pretty unlikely that she meets with Zhou very often—then we'll reevaluate and decide how long to keep watching her. Call me every day to let me know what she's doing and obviously call if she meets with anyone who looks like a Chinese spy. And like I said, if she does meet with him, I need a photo."

DeMarco stayed in the café and watched them drive away. Javier was driving a black van with no windows in the cargo box and DeMarco wondered if there was a periscope that poked up through the roof. Sergio drove a gray Toyota that would be ideal for tailing people. As soon as they were gone, he ordered breakfast. As he was eating the sausage that came with his breakfast, he couldn't help but think of Mookie.

The assumption was that if Lydia Chang was meeting with Zhou, she was passing on things she'd learned from her husband—things that weren't reported in the press. So while he was eating, DeMarco used his phone to go online and see what was happening in the U.S. Senate that might be of interest to the Chinese. And the answer was: a lot of things were happening.

There was a bill meandering its way through Congress having to do with providing more funding and advanced weapon systems to Taiwan—as if the Taiwanese had a chance in hell if the Chinese decided to invade their many islands. Another bill involved funding American companies to start manufacturing more of the things the Chinese made as it seemed prudent not to be relying on the U.S.A.'s number one enemy for about thirty percent of the products used by Americans. A third bill had to do with preventing the Chinese from buying more American real estate.

The Chinese owned about 380,000 acres of farmland—an area about the size of Rhode Island—and had invested six billion dollars in the U.S. housing market, and a few senators had decided they didn't want them owning more American property. And in the news was the usual hubbub about the U.S. Navy flexing its muscle in the South China Sea, about the competition between the United States and China to control outer space, and the Chinese government's unwavering support of Russia and North Korea and every other nation that the United States considered a threat to national security. And Dutch McMillian would know more about all these things than any *Washington Post* reporter because he was a member of the Gang of Eight. The Gang consisted of the two Republicans and two Democrats who led the House and Senate and the four ranking members from each party who sat on the House and Senate Intelligence Committees. These eight people were periodically briefed by U.S. intelligence agencies on serious and sensitive national security matters—and DeMarco could imagine Dutch talking to his closest advisor, his wife, about some of those matters.

DeMarco also looked at some of the online photos of Lydia Chang and her husband at various political and social events. She was a beautiful woman—tall, perfectly proportioned, a flawless, golden complexion. She was fifty-two years old but looked ten years younger. DeMarco couldn't help but wonder how Dutch McMillian had ever convinced her to marry him. Dutch was twenty years older than his wife and to call him homely was an understatement. He was shorter than Lydia, barely had lips or a chin, and was not known for his wit or his sense of humor. But he was a powerful, rich man and maybe that's what Lydia had found attractive about him, wealth and power being well-known aphrodisiacs. One article said they'd met at a private dinner party and ol' Dutch had charmed the pants off her, which DeMarco found hard to believe. But he must have gotten her pants off at some point, because they had one daughter, a sophomore in college, a girl named Jenny.

6

⸺◆⸺

DeMarco's next stop was a four-story building in Georgetown, on the banks of the Potomac. He wanted a photo of Zhou and he wanted to find out more about him and Diane Lake but figured a simple Google search wouldn't tell him what he needed to know. But there was a man in the building—actually, he owned the building—who could go way, way beyond Google.

The man's name was Neil, and he was a nonviolent criminal who belonged in a federal lockup and DeMarco had known him for years. Neil called himself an "information broker" and what this meant was that if an entity—an individual or a corporation—wanted data stored in computers protected by firewalls and cyber theft prevention programs, Neil could probably get the data the entity wanted. But DeMarco also knew that Neil, because he'd been doing what he did for so long, often didn't need to resort to high-tech thievery. He'd developed a network of people in banks and telecommunications companies and government agencies who he simply paid to give him what he wanted, as that was often quicker and less risky than getting the information the hard way. He should have been arrested years ago but never had been because he was a genius—and a lucky one—but lately, and ironically, he was no longer doing anything illegal. Neil currently had a contract with Homeland

Security to prevent people like himself from stealing classified information or holding American companies hostage with ransomware, and working for Homeland apparently paid enough that he didn't have to commit crimes. Either that or he'd just decided that doing honest work for once in his life was less stressful.

Neil's office, on the top floor of the building, had a view of the Pentagon and a seating area with a couch where he sometimes slept and a small kitchen with a microwave, a refrigerator, and a sink. Over the sink were shelves stocked with enough Top Ramen to last a month. The rest of the space was taken up by a long table holding three jumbo-sized monitors, and beneath the table were computer towers and black boxes whose functions were a mystery to DeMarco. On the floor were so many cables connecting all the hardware that the floor looked like a snake pit. On shelves around the room were more high-tech gizmos and manuals that DeMarco assumed provided DIY instructions for hackers.

Neil sat behind the table on a rolling stool, a can of Red Bull close to a keyboard he was playing like a baby grand. He was a stocky man who combed his thinning blond hair into a short ponytail and was dressed in a short-sleeved shirt, cargo shorts, and sandals. As it was May, his attire was appropriate for the weather, but Neil dressed the same way in the dead of winter. He apparently had some sort of metabolic disorder that caused him to overheat. Plus, he rarely left his office.

DeMarco had called Neil the day before and told him what he needed, and the first thing Neil showed him was a photo of Zhou Enlai at a party at the British embassy. Zhou was identified in the photo as being a *cultural attaché assigned to the Chinese embassy.* He was wearing a tuxedo, holding a champagne flute in his hand, and smiling down at the wife of the French ambassador, whose large, lovely breasts were practically falling out of her gown. Neil cropped Zhou's handsome head out of the group photo and texted it to DeMarco's cell phone and DeMarco forwarded the photo to Javier with a message saying: *Zhou Enlai.*

"Could you get any background info on him?" DeMarco asked Neil.

"Nope, not a thing," Neil said. "As you might expect, the guy's résumé isn't on LinkedIn. But if he's an intelligence officer, like you told me, and assigned to the embassy, he's almost certainly university educated, probably comes from some connected family, and is most likely ex-military or still in the military. But I don't know if Zhou is even his real name or if he's really Chinese intelligence."

"What about Diane Lake?"

"Diane Lake is thirty-five years old. She was born at Fort Lewis in Washington State. Her dad was army infantry, a noncom, not an officer. She graduated from West Point."

"Really," DeMarco said.

Women were first admitted to West Point in 1976, fifty years ago, but DeMarco figured going to school there still couldn't be easy for a woman. Diane Lake was most likely a pretty tough cookie.

Neil said, "She stayed in the army for six years, enough time to pay the army back for her education. She had postings in South Korea, Taiwan, the Philippines, and one in Virginia at Fort Belvoir at the U.S. Army Military Intelligence Readiness Command. She spent most of her military service with intelligence units, the kind of units that analyze troop movements and spy on folks with satellites while they plan the next war."

"She told Mahoney she spoke Mandarin."

"I didn't see that anywhere I looked, but maybe she does, and that's why she was posted to places close to China. Anyway, after she got out of the army, she was hired by the CIA and worked there for four years. But I don't know what she did there."

"She told Mahoney she was an analyst in the China section, which appears to make sense, considering her army background."

"You want me to try to confirm that?"

"No. Not yet, anyway."

"Good. Because if I got caught probing her employment at Langley, I could end up with my tit in a wringer. And I like my tit. Anyway, she quit the CIA a couple of years ago and went to work for Vicount, where they're paying her three times what she was making at the CIA. She's got a town house in Alexandria that's worth around eight fifty and that she's still paying the mortgage on, and, based on her tax returns, I'm guessing her net worth is about a million. So she's doing okay financially, but she's not super-rich."

"Has she recently come into a large amount of money?" DeMarco was wondering if someone might have paid Lake to pass on what she knew about Chang to Mahoney.

"Not that I could see," Neil said. "There've been no big deposits into the banks that provide the interest statements for her taxes or into her investment account at Ed Jones. But if someone wired money to an account in the Caymans, I wouldn't be able to see it unless I went deeper."

By going deeper, Neil probably meant hacking into Lake's personal computers.

"She divorced, married, single?" DeMarco asked.

"Divorced. Married a guy who went to West Point with her about a year after she graduated, divorced him four years later, and has been single ever since. Her ex-husband's name is Stephen Canfield and he's still in the army and stationed at the Pentagon. But she's not on Facebook or Instagram or any other social media sites, so unless I go deeper, I can't tell you if she currently has a boyfriend or a girlfriend or a cat."

"What about her job at Vicount?"

"Vicount was started by a former Wall Street quant named Clarence Peterman, who's some sort of math genius, and another guy, named Jimmy, not James, Wong and—"

"Wong? Is Wong Chinese?"

"Chinese American. His parents were born in the U.S. and so was Jimmy. Anyway, Peterman and Wong both worked for Jamie Dimon at JPMorgan Chase as analysts who'd feed stuff to Jamie to make him sound like a genius whenever he was talking about the economy. At some point they decided to leave Morgan Chase and started Vicount. Mostly what they do is corporate financial stuff but then they branched out into other kinds of research, like opposition research for politicians. The company's kinda like Fusion GPS, the outfit that got wrapped around the axle with Hillary Clinton and the Steele dossier, but they're smaller and have less of a profile than Fusion."

"Why would they hire Diane Lake? She doesn't sound like a finance person."

"Well, one reason could be that some of Vicount's clients are U.S. companies doing business in China. So maybe Lake was hired because she speaks Mandarin and with her previous jobs in the army and CIA she probably has a better idea than most folks about what goes on over there. But I can't tell you specifically what she does at Vicount. The company doesn't have an online org chart and it doesn't say who its employees are. The only reason I know Lake works for Vicount is because you told me she does and because I've seen her tax returns."

"The job she did for Mahoney didn't have anything to do with China," DeMarco said. "It was just straightforward opposition research on an American politician."

"So maybe doing China-related stuff isn't something she does full-time," Neil said. "Or maybe none of the time. You want me to go deeper on her?"

"No, not yet," DeMarco said.

Neil had confirmed that Lake had told Mahoney the truth about being ex-CIA and that it was plausible that she recognized Zhou based on her previous employment. And there wasn't anything to indicate she might have a political agenda when it came to either Mahoney or McMillian. Vicount worked for politicians, but the company wasn't biased toward either party; they were nonpartisan gunslingers for hire. It was still possible, however, that Lake had an agenda of her own that wasn't apparent when it came to Mahoney or McMillian, or she could be in cahoots with someone who had an agenda, but in order to find that out Neil would have to look at phone records and get into her personal computer to see who she'd been communicating with. DeMarco decided that before he asked Neil to do that, he'd wait to hear back from Javier and Sergio to see if Chang was really meeting with Zhou.

7

Sergio and Javier left the café where they met DeMarco and drove to Lydia Chang's home in McLean. As it was a weekday, they thought she'd most likely be at work and not at home, but they wanted to check out the house and figure out how to watch it without being seen. The fact that McMillian had a security detail complicated things. Javier parked the van a couple of blocks from the house while Sergio drove past it. There was no reason for both of them to drive by the house.

The house was a two-story brick colonial with shuttered windows and dormers in a steep roof. It had an attached two-car garage, and the grounds were well maintained. It was a large, expensive home but not as grand as Sergio had been expecting. He couldn't tell if anyone was home, but no one appeared to be. He didn't see anyone moving past the windows in the house or in the front yard.

Sergio didn't see anyplace on the block where they'd be able to park for long periods of time without being noticed, but on the next block over he saw a house that was being constructed or extensively remodeled. It sat on a small hill, on an elevation higher than Chang's home. The walls had Tyvek over the exterior plywood and clear plastic covering the openings where new windows would be installed. Sergio drove past the house and saw two pickup trucks and a plumber's van parked in front of the house and four men working. He figured that he and Javier could come back after the workers had left for the day and sneak into the house—which didn't have a front door—and watch Chang's home from the second story.

He called Javier and, speaking in Spanish, told him what he'd observed.

Their next stop was Chang's office in Reston, Virginia. Before going to the office, they went online and found photos of her so they'd know what she looked like. Her office was in an eight-story tower made of smoky black glass and wasn't identified by any signage other than the address number. Their plan was to watch the front entrance of the building and hope to see Chang leaving. If the building had an underground parking lot, then one of them would have to find a way to wait there without being noticed and try to spot Chang when she went to her car. As it turned out, locating Chang's car so they could follow her was easy. There were parking spots in front of the building, and one was prominently marked as being reserved for Ms. Chang, and in the parking space was a gleaming black E-Class Mercedes-Benz.

Sergio and Javier parked on the street in front of the building where they could see the entrance, their vehicles facing in opposite directions. They had to wait all day, sitting patiently, which wasn't a problem for either of them. With their former jobs as soldiers and their current jobs as detectives, they were used to long periods of idleness and boredom. While they waited, Javier received the text from DeMarco with a photo of Zhou Enlai. Handsome fellow, Javier thought.

At six, they saw Chang come out of the building. She was dressed in a black business suit and black high heels and was accompanied by an Anglo woman shorter than she was. Chang went to her Mercedes and the Anglo to a different car, and when Chang left the lot, Sergio followed her in the gray Toyota while Javier hung back as the black van he was driving was more noticeable.

Chang drove directly to her home, pulling her car into the garage. Javier drove to the home being constructed on the hill overlooking Chang's house. The workers were gone, and he didn't see anyone outside in nearby homes, but as it was still daylight, the people who lived in the neighboring houses would be able see him if they looked out their windows.

Javier was still wearing the jeans and T-shirt he'd worn that morning when they met with DeMarco. He reached into an aluminum box behind the driver's seat and pulled out a white hard hat and put it on. In the box were several changes of clothes for him and Javier that they kept there for surveillance work, including different jackets and hats and even one long-haired wig they could use to change their appearance.

Javier got out of the van, opened the back door, and grabbed a toolbox to complement the hard hat. The toolbox contained hand tools a person might keep in a vehicle—screwdrivers, pliers, crescent wrenches, duct tape—but also a set of burglary tools including lockpicks, lock rakes, a couple of small crowbars, and a glass cutter. He walked confidently and without hesitating into the house via the doorless front door opening, hoping that if anyone saw him, they'd think he was one of the workers who had an assignment that required him to work late. He would watch the house until it got dark and then drive away in the van and Sergio would sneak into the house and keep watching until Chang and her husband went to bed.

Half an hour after Chang arrived home, a black Chevy Suburban pulled into Chang's driveway. The driver, a man wearing a dark suit, got out of the Suburban and opened the back door, and Senator Dutch McMillian, also wearing a dark suit, stepped from the car and went into the house. The driver got back into the Suburban but didn't pull out of the driveway. Javier assumed the driver was part of McMillian's security detail; he couldn't see anyone else in the Suburban because the windows were tinted but he wouldn't be surprised if McMillian had more than one bodyguard.

Another half hour passed, and Lydia Chang and her husband came out the front door. Lydia was dressed in a red dress that hugged her figure and red stilettos that made her more than three inches taller than her husband. McMillian appeared to be wearing the same suit he'd had on when he went into the house. The driver of the Suburban got out and opened the rear door and McMillian and his wife got in, and a moment later the vehicle took off.

Javier called Sergio and told him the direction the Suburban had taken, and Sergio fell in behind McMillian's car while talking with Javier on the phone to let him know where he was. Twenty-five minutes later, the Suburban pulled into the driveway of the Four Seasons Hotel in Georgetown. A man—a second bodyguard—got out of the front passenger's side of the Suburban and escorted McMillian and Chang into the hotel. Sergio called Javier and told him where he was and what was happening.

Javier thought it unlikely that Chang would be meeting a Chinese spy in the Four Seasons while accompanied by her husband and his security detail, but he needed to see what they were doing and who they were meeting. Sergio couldn't go into the hotel because he was still dressed in jeans and a T-shirt and would look out of place. Also, Sergio wasn't good at schmoozing people. Javier found a place to park near the hotel and, taking clothes from the luggage he and Sergio had brought with them from Miami, put on a pair of gray slacks, a blue sport jacket, a white shirt, a tie, and dress shoes.

Inside the hotel, he quickly found the senator and his wife. They were in a large room with more than a hundred other people, standing and drinking champagne and eating canapés off trays borne by servers. He didn't see Zhou in the room. When one of the servers—a Hispanic man—left the room, Javier asked him in Spanish what the big shindig was. He was informed that it was a birthday party for a senator who'd just turned ninety, one of those guys who could hardly see, walk, or think and was a barely breathing advertisement for term limits.

Javier called DeMarco and told him where Lydia was and what she was doing, and DeMarco agreed that it was unlikely she was meeting with a Chinese spy. Nonetheless, Javier and Sergio hung around the Four Seasons until almost midnight and followed Chang back home.

8

For four days nothing happened.

DeMarco talked to Javier each day and it appeared as if Chang wasn't doing anything out of the ordinary. She went to a gym every weekday morning and her first stop after the gym was always her office in Reston. Her company owned and invested in commercial real estate, and she owned office buildings and shopping malls and industrial parks, and her activities appeared to be related to her business. She had lunches with other businesspeople and met at the offices of lawyers and bankers and accountants. One day she visited a worksite in Fairfax County where a ten-story tower was under construction. Javier and Sergio sometimes couldn't identify who she was meeting when she went into office buildings, but she was always accompanied by the Anglo woman they'd seen her with on the first day. She never met with anyone they saw who appeared to be Chinese.

Chang and her husband went to political or social gatherings three of the four nights Sergio and Javier were following her. The one night they didn't attend an event, Chang stayed in her house and never left it. In addition to the birthday party for the ancient senator, they went to a fundraiser at the Mayflower Hotel for a woman running for the Senate in Arizona and a ceremony at the White House. Javier, of course, couldn't follow Chang into the White House but he found out online that that evening the president was hanging the Presidential Medal of Freedom around the neck of a terminally ill singer who had given away most of her fortune to the disadvantaged. Mahoney and his wife were also there. The event at the White House made DeMarco shudder, thinking of the possibility of Lydia Chang wandering around the West Wing and planting a bug in the Oval Office for the Chinese. He knew that was pretty unlikely, but still . . .

Edna called once while DeMarco was waiting for something to happen with Lydia.

She said, "Mookie isn't back yet, but I got a phone number for him. There's two sisters here in town, June and July Wilson, and—"

"July?" DeMarco said.

"Yeah. They're, well, they're the town whores and everybody knows it. They're actually nice ladies and I like 'em. They're over forty now but a lot of boys in these parts got their cherries popped thanks to June and July—I wouldn't be surprised if my sons did—and it occurred to me that Mookie, being a single man, might avail himself of their services. It turns out he's sweet on June. Sometimes he pays her with slabs of bacon if he's low on cash. Anyway, she told me that Mookie has a cell phone, and she had the number, and she gave it to me. The problem is, Mookie thinks the government uses cell phones to track people and he keeps his phone in one of them special bags, those Faraday bags, so his phone can't be tracked."

"Why in the hell would he think the government would want to track a guy who butchers hogs for a living?"

"Because he's Mookie. June says he only turns on his phone when he's using it or expecting a call, like from June, to tell him she's available. I called the number she gave me and I got one of them messages saying the user hadn't set up his voicemail. But I thought I'd pass the number on to you and I'll keep checking to see if he comes home."

DeMarco called Mookie's number and got the same message Edna had received.

He felt like banging his head against a wall.

———◆◆◆———

On a Sunday morning, while Dutch McMillian was speaking at a conference in Aspen, Javier saw Lydia's Mercedes back out of the garage. He and Sergio followed her to a public park in Falls Church. Lydia got out of the car and Javier saw she was wearing jeans, a hooded sweatshirt, and sunglasses. She pulled the hood of the sweatshirt over her head and walked into the park and sat down on a bench near a bronze statue of a guy on a horse waving a saber. Five minutes later a tall, handsome Chinese man sat down next to her. It was Zhou.

Sergio had to slither through the trees in the park on his belly to get a clear photo of Zhou's and Chang's faces, which wasn't a problem for Sergio, whose former profession had required a lot of slithering through jungles in South America. He texted the photo to DeMarco.

———◆◆◆———

DeMarco didn't hear his phone ding that he had a text message because he'd left his phone in the cup holder in a golf cart and was busy lining up a three-foot putt—which he couldn't believe he missed. He didn't feel at all guilty about playing golf on a lovely Sunday morning. Why should he feel guilty? Sergio and Javier were taking care of business and didn't need any help from him. He saw the text just before he was about

to tee off on the next hole. When he saw it, he told the guys he was playing with that he had to return a call and that he'd catch up with them
as soon as he could.

He looked at the photo. Lydia Chang was wearing sunglasses and a
hoody but she and Zhou were both recognizable. DeMarco called Javier.

"How long was she with Zhou?" he asked.

"Fifteen minutes."

"Could you hear anything they were saying?"

"No. We couldn't get close enough for that."

"Did she give him anything? Paperwork, an envelope, a flash drive,
anything like that?"

"No. They just talked and he did most of the talking. And it looked
to me like he was chewing her out, wagging his finger at her, and she
had her head down, like you do if you're on the wrong end of a tongue-
lashing. When she went back to her car, she sat there for a while crying
before she took off."

"Huh," DeMarco said, thinking that was interesting. "Well, you guys
can go home. You got me what I needed, and I appreciate it. Text me
what I owe you and I'll get the money to you."

He'd have Perry take care of the bill. The money would come from one
of Mahoney's slush funds or Perry would come up with some devious
way to tap into the funds provided to operate Congress. Mahoney was
a master at getting the taxpayers to foot his bills.

The next day DeMarco said to Mahoney, "So now what?"

DeMarco had told Mahoney that he'd confirmed that Lydia was meeting with Zhou, that he had a photo of them together, and told him what
Javier had said about the way Zhou had acted toward Lydia and how
she'd cried in her car after the meeting.

The whole time DeMarco was briefing him, Mahoney didn't say a word, and maybe that was because he wasn't physically able to say a word. Mahoney was on a treadmill in the House gym, located in the subbasement of the Rayburn Building. He was wearing gray sweatpants, a sweat-soaked gray T-shirt, and brand-new, never-touched-dirt white running shoes. His face was the color of a boiled lobster. The treadmill belt was barely moving—if the machine had been a car, the engine would have stalled—but Mahoney was gasping for breath as if he were on the last mile of the Boston Marathon.

Mahoney did this periodically: went on a health kick to lower his weight and stave off a heart attack. These efforts usually lasting no more than a week before he went back to drinking a bottle of bourbon a day, smoking cigars, and eating bloody, rare steak. DeMarco hoped there was someone in the building with medical training and thought that Mahoney should have had electrodes pasted to his chest and connected to a monitor that would sound a loud alarm when he went into cardiac arrest.

Mahoney punched a button to stop the treadmill and put his head down on the handlebars. Finally, when he was able to speak, he raised his head and said to DeMarco, "There's no way Lydia Chang, as rich as she is, would spy for the Chinese for money. Nor would she do it for some ideological reason, like she's suddenly become a committed communist. Her attitude toward China is no different than her husband's. In fact, she's probably more anti-China than Dutch is, just to make the point that she may have been born there but she's now totally American. Zhou's making her meet with him. He's got something on her. He's blackmailing her. That's the only thing that makes sense. Maybe she's having an affair with some young stud and the Chinese got photos of her banging the guy. Maybe her company's doing something shady. So I don't know what's going on, but I'm willing to bet everything I own that the Chinese've got something on her and that's why she's meeting Zhou."

"You're probably right," DeMarco said, "but so what? Turn her over to the Bureau. Let the FBI find out why she's meeting with him."

"No. Not yet. I want to know what's going on before I do anything."

"Why?"

"Because I wanna know."

"But how am I supposed to find out her reason for meeting with Zhou? The only way I can think to do that is by asking her."

"So ask her. And you can tell her that I know about her and Zhou and I want to help her if she needs help."

"Do you really want to help her?"

"I don't know. Probably not. But I want to know what's going on. You can also tell her if she's not straight with you, I'll be forced to whistle for the spy-catchers. She'll talk."

DeMarco shook his head. Why couldn't Mahoney just do the straightforward thing, the simple thing? Why did he always have to make everything so fucking complicated?

Mahoney punched the button to start the treadmill moving and began walking, a grim, determined expression on his face.

DeMarco said, "You know, you can make that machine tilt like you're walking uphill, give yourself a better workout."

"Get the fuck out of here," Mahoney said.

9

———◆———

According to Javier, Lydia went to an upscale gym not far from her home in McLean every weekday morning. She'd leave her house at six, drive to the gym wearing a tracksuit and a baseball cap, pulling a carry-on bag, and, after doing whatever she did inside the gym, emerge at seven thirty dressed for work and head to her office.

Two days after she met with Zhou, DeMarco was waiting for her in the gym parking lot, standing by her car. When she saw him—a broad-shouldered man with an unsmiling, hard face wearing a dark suit—she hesitated briefly but then kept walking toward him. Lydia Chang wasn't a person who was easily intimidated.

DeMarco was again struck by how lovely she was—and again found it impossible to understand her marrying a man as homely as Dutch McMillian. She was wearing a navy blue suit that clung to her gym-toned body and matching high heels, the heels making her almost as tall as DeMarco. Her hair was black, cut short, and as shiny as vinyl; her lipstick was fire-engine red.

DeMarco said, "Ms. Chang, I need to talk to you."

"Who are you? If you're a reporter, contact my office."

"I'm not a reporter. My name's DeMarco and John Mahoney sent me. You have a problem and Mahoney wants to help you if he can."

"Help me? What are you talking about?"

"Ms. Chang, you've been meeting with a Chinese intelligence officer named Zhou Enlai who works out of the Chinese embassy."

Lydia was too stunned to respond. DeMarco could imagine the adrenaline surging through her body, prompting a fight-or-flight decision—and Lydia wasn't the type to take flight.

DeMarco said, "Mahoney believes that Zhou is forcing you to meet with him. He doesn't think you'd betray your country, and, like I said, he wants to help you if he can. But if you won't talk to me and tell me what's going on, Mahoney won't have a choice and he'll have to tell the FBI that you've been meeting with Zhou."

"That son of a bitch Mahoney would never help me. He hates my husband."

"Ms. Chang, if he didn't want to help, he would have already talked to the Bureau."

Another woman walked by at that moment on her way to her car. She looked over and saw Lydia talking to DeMarco and could see that Lydia was distressed. She called out, "Is everything all right, Lydia?"

"Yes, Mary, everything's fine."

Neither DeMarco nor Lydia said anything as Mary got into her car and drove away.

Lydia said, "There's a restaurant a couple blocks from here. It's never crowded. We'll talk there."

———◆———

They took seats in a booth at the back of the restaurant. As Lydia had said, the place wasn't crowded and there was no one sitting near them. They ordered coffee and said that was all they wanted. As soon as the waitress left, Lydia said, "Why should I believe you're trying to help me?"

"What choice do you have?" DeMarco said. "And like I already told you, if Mahoney wanted to cause you a problem, he would have already talked to the Bureau. And maybe there's some innocent explanation for you meeting with a Chinese spy, but whatever you're doing, and considering who you're married to, demands an explanation. And you can either explain it to me or you can explain it to the FBI."

"How do you know I met with Zhou?"

"Someone who knows him saw you talking to him at Four Mile Run Park in Arlington. And this person informed Mahoney."

"Who is this person?

"It doesn't matter," DeMarco said. "But it's someone who won't talk."

DeMarco saw no reason to identify Diane Lake. As for Lake not talking, he wasn't sure of that at all. She might tell her story to someone else if Mahoney didn't do something when it came to Lydia meeting with Chinese intelligence. But Lake probably wouldn't do that right away. He also didn't want to tell Lydia that he'd had the audacity to have people follow her and take her photo if he didn't have to.

"Now, tell me what's going on," DeMarco said.

Lydia looked down at the table. She was grasping the coffee mug so tightly that her knuckles were white. If she'd been holding a glass, it would have shattered. She didn't say anything for so long that DeMarco finally said, "Ms. Chang, if you don't—"

"He's using my daughter to blackmail me," she said.

"How's he doing that?"

"If I tell you, then you'll be able to destroy my daughter's life as well as mine and my husband's."

"I have no interest in destroying anyone's life. For the third time, I want to help you. Just tell me what's going on."

"Zhou sent me a text message with a video showing my daughter hitting a man with her car and then fleeing the scene of the accident."

"A video?" DeMarco said. *What in the hell is she talking about?*

"The text also contained a link to an article in the *Montgomery County Sentinel* about a man who was killed in a hit-and-run accident, and Zhou's text said that if I didn't meet with him, he would send the video to the police."

"Did your daughter hit a man with her car?"

Lydia hesitated. "Yes."

"How would Zhou have gotten a video of the accident?"

"I don't know for sure, but I believe that he orchestrated the accident and videoed it when it happened."

"I don't understand what you mean. Do you have a copy of the video with you?"

"Yes."

"Can I see it?"

After another long pause, she took her cell phone from her purse, tapped it a couple of times, and handed the phone to DeMarco. "Hit play," she said.

The video began with a bearded man standing on a two-lane blacktopped road. It was dark out but a nearby streetlight provided enough illumination to see the man clearly. He was swaying, as if he might be drunk, holding a bottle in one hand. Seconds later a car rounded a curve and struck the man, and he went flying over the roof of the car that hit him. DeMarco could hear tires skidding on asphalt as the car came to a stop.

A moment later a young woman with long dark hair, wearing a short dress, ran up to the man, knelt and felt for a pulse, and DeMarco watched her turn her head and speak to someone off camera. She said, "He's dead. Oh my God, oh my God, oh my God. Call 911."

"Is that your daughter?" DeMarco asked Chang.

"Yes, that's Jenny."

Whoever Jenny was talking to on the video said, "No."

It was a man speaking.

Jenny said, "What do you mean, 'No'?"

"Jenny, you're drunk. We're both drunk. And you were going over the speed limit. The cops will figure that out by the skid marks. If I call 911, you'll go to jail for vehicular homicide. You won't get off with just a fine. And I'll lose my job because it'll get out that I was with you and maybe I'll go to jail, too, for letting you drive."

"What are you saying?" Jenny said.

"I'm saying let's get out of here before another car comes by. There's nothing to be done for him. If he were alive, it would be different, but he's not. I don't want to see you ruin your life, and it wasn't your fault you hit him. Even if you were sober, you wouldn't have been able to avoid him. Let's go."

"I don't know."

"Jenny, I love you, but I don't want to lose my job. And I don't want to see you go to jail. Let's go."

The video ended.

DeMarco gave Lydia her phone back and said, "Who was she talking to?"

"Her boyfriend."

"What's his name?"

"I don't know. She won't tell me."

"Why not?"

"Because she's nineteen years old and she's in love with him and she wants to protect him."

"Who's the man she hit?"

"His name was James Harris. The article in the *Sentinel* said he was a military veteran with no fixed address, meaning he was probably homeless, and that he lived in D.C."

"Does your daughter know about the video and that you're being blackmailed?"

"Yes. But she doesn't know who's blackmailing me or what he wants. When I got the video, I went to see her. I had to know if the video was real. I had to make sure it wasn't some AI-generated fake. And I wanted to know if she was being blackmailed too. And I wanted to know if she'd contacted the police since the accident or if the police had contacted her. She was a complete basket case. She was crying nonstop and barely coherent and hadn't slept in days. But she didn't have any idea who took the video, and she wouldn't tell me her boyfriend's name. She said she didn't want to ruin his life. When I told her that I was being blackmailed—she thinks someone wants money—she said she was going to turn herself in, but I wouldn't let her."

"Why not? Her admitting what she did may be the only way out of this for you."

"Because I don't want her to go to jail. The maximum penalty for a hit-and-run homicide is ten years, and—considering who her father is—they'd probably give her the maximum to make the point she should be treated like any other citizen. So those are my choices, DeMarco. Either my daughter goes to jail or I spy for the Chinese."

"How many times have you met with Zhou?"

"Twice. The first time was at the park in Arlington. I met him a second time at another park in Falls Church a week later."

That was good. First, that she'd told the truth about meeting with Zhou in Falls Church and, second, that she'd only met with him twice. In two meetings, she couldn't have passed on much information, and Javier had said that she didn't give Zhou anything like a flash drive that could have held a lot of information.

"What did Zhou tell you the first time you met?"

"He told me that he was going to turn the video over to the police if I didn't agree to pass on what I learned from my husband on matters affecting the Chinese government. He had a whole list of things that he wanted to know about, Chinese-related defense appropriations, bills affecting the Chinese economy or Chinese businesses, anything to do with Taiwan, Navy maneuvers in the China Sea, and so on. Basically, anything China-related that wasn't reported in the press."

"Did he tell you he was Chinese intelligence or that he worked at the embassy?"

"No. I didn't even know his name until you told me, but it was obvious what he was, based on what he was asking for."

"What have you given him so far?"

"Nothing, really. I mean, nothing classified. When I met with him the second time at the park in Falls Church, I knew I had to give him something, so I told him the name of the admiral who's going to be put in charge of the U.S. Pacific Fleet—the admiral who would be directing China Sea operations. The admiral's name hadn't been given to the media yet. I told him that the current ambassador to China would be retiring soon and who was likely to replace her. And I told him that a second carrier task force would be deployed to the China Sea in a couple of months, something that was well-known in Navy circles but hadn't been reported in the press. But he wasn't satisfied. He told me that he already knew everything I told him—he probably has other sources of information—and started screaming at me that if I didn't provide him with something useful the next time we met, he was going to expose my daughter. I'm supposed to meet with him a week from today, when my husband is out of town again, but I don't know what I'm going to tell him."

"Do you have some kind of plan for getting out of this?"

"The only thing I could think to do was offer him a lot of money, which I did the first time I met with him, but he's not interested in money. So I have no idea what to do next, other than get my daughter the best lawyer that money can buy and have her turn herself in. But like I said, I don't want to do that."

"Let me see the video again," DeMarco said. Lydia handed him her phone and he played the video a second time.

DeMarco said, "I see what you mean about the accident being orchestrated. The video started before the accident happened, as if someone knew it was going to happen. And it's dark out. Why would Harris be standing in the road at night like he was? And he looks scared. I think someone was making him stand there. Maybe he had a gun pointed at him. And whoever was making him stand there was the one taking the video and that couldn't have been your daughter's boyfriend unless he had the camera set up on a tripod and he could start the camera remotely. But it's interesting how you can hear the boyfriend but you don't see him in the video. Like maybe he knew the scene was being videoed and he'd been told to stand back."

DeMarco handed Lydia's phone back to her and didn't say anything else. He just looked at her, studying her face. After a couple seconds passed, she said, sounding irritated and impatient, "So what do you plan to do next?"

Now, that was a good question—and the one he'd been thinking about. He'd accomplished the task Mahoney had given him—he'd found out why Lydia was meeting with Zhou—and what he could do was tell her that he didn't plan to do anything until he'd talked to Mahoney. And when he talked to Mahoney, he'd encourage him to let the Bureau deal with Lydia and her daughter. But he knew that Mahoney wouldn't be satisfied—that he'd want to know more before he did anything; like, he'd probably want to know if there was a link between the Chinese and the boyfriend. And, for that matter, DeMarco also wanted to know more, and even though he didn't find Lydia Chang particularly likable, he wanted to help her if he could, especially now that he knew that Zhou had used her daughter to compromise her.

He said, "We need to find out who the boyfriend is. That's our starting point."

"Starting point for what?"

"For maybe getting you out of this mess. Harris wasn't the victim of a hit-and-run accident. It wasn't an accident. He was murdered by whoever made him stand in the road. Your daughter may have been the one who killed him but that wouldn't have happened if he hadn't been forced to stand there. So maybe we can prove that Zhou essentially murdered Harris and that will give us something that can be used to get him off your back. Anyway, I don't know what comes next, but the first thing we need to do is find out who the boyfriend is and see what he has to say and see if he was directly involved in this thing."

"I'm telling you, Jenny won't give me his name. She's determined to protect him."

"Well, if she's that in love with him, then she's probably still seeing him or talking to him on the phone, and that means I'll find him."

"Then what?"

"Then I'll find a way to make him talk. Where's your daughter living?"

"In an apartment with another girl in Georgetown."

"Okay. Text me your daughter's phone number and her address."

"I don't want you talking to my daughter."

Choosing his words carefully, DeMarco said, "I understand. But if you give me her phone number, I know a guy who can see who she's been calling. And if that doesn't work, and if I have her address, I can follow her to see if she meets with the boyfriend." He wished then that he hadn't sent Javier and Sergio home.

Lydia hesitated briefly, then nodded and texted DeMarco her daughter's contact information.

"All right," DeMarco said. "It looks like we have seven days to figure this thing out before you meet with Zhou again. But in case we can't figure it out by then, you need to come up with something to tell him."

"If I give him classified information, then I'll really be in trouble," Lydia said. "So far I can honestly say that I haven't compromised national security in any way. I may have met with him, and I should have reported that as soon as he contacted me, but I haven't done anything illegal yet. But if I pass on something to him that is classified—"

"So you come up with something that sounds classified but isn't— something you might have learned from your husband. You invent something. You lie. Oh, I should have asked: Does your husband know you're being blackmailed?"

"No."

"Yeah, I didn't think so," DeMarco said.

As DeMarco was leaving, he expected Lydia to thank him for trying to help her.

She didn't.

She said, "I want you to know that I don't trust you, and I definitely don't trust Mahoney, and I suspect that Mahoney has some agenda and it's not helping me. But if Mahoney causes my husband or my daughter a problem, I'm going to tell people that he knew about the Chinese approaching me and instead of going to the authorities, he sent you. So you tell Mahoney that he's now complicit in this thing and I'll burn him if he does anything to harm my family."

"You're welcome, Lydia," DeMarco said.

10

Jenny McMillian lived in an apartment three blocks from the Georgetown University campus. DeMarco needed to speak to her in person but he couldn't just knock on her door because her roommate might be with her. So the morning after talking to Lydia, he was standing on a corner near her building, planning to follow her if she left and find an opportunity to speak to her when she was alone. He didn't know her class schedule but figured that classes would start about eight, which meant he had to wake up at six thirty to get there at seven thirty, and because of that he was feeling grumpy and out of sorts. Since he'd been there, he'd seen a bunch of college-age kids walking toward the campus. The girls looked bright and alert. The boys looked scruffy, hungover, and barely awake.

Lydia had told DeMarco that he wasn't to talk to her daughter and DeMarco had said, "I understand." As opposed to "I won't." And although he probably could have found Jenny's boyfriend by having Neil look at her phone records, he wanted to talk to her—not only because he wanted the boyfriend's name but because there were things about the accident that he needed to know. And he didn't care if this pissed off Lydia. She'd had her chance to do the right thing when Zhou first contacted her.

At eight fifteen, he saw the girl in the hit-and-run video walking toward him. She was by herself, which was good. She was wearing a gray GU hooded sweatshirt with the bulldog mascot on the front and jeans manufactured with holes in the knees. She had on a backpack most likely holding textbooks. She was moving slowly, the expression on her face morose, staring down at the ground as she walked.

Lydia Chang was a beautiful woman. Her daughter wasn't. She'd inherited Lydia's eyes and her lustrous dark hair, but she'd also inherited some of her father's facial features and the result was unfortunate. The most charitable way to describe her was *plain*.

She walked past DeMarco without looking at him. Or maybe she didn't even realize he was standing there as she was so preoccupied with her own thoughts. DeMarco walked up next to her and said, "Jenny, we need to talk."

Now her head jerked toward him, and he could see the fear in her eyes. DeMarco wondered if she thought he was a cop and suspected that ever since the accident she'd been expecting some cop to show up and arrest her.

She said, "Who are you?"

"My name's DeMarco. Your mother sent me."

Not true, but who cared?

"Why would she send you?" Jenny asked.

"Because I'm a lawyer and I'm trying to find a way to get you and your mom out of the jam you're both in."

"I don't know what you're talking about."

"Yeah, you do. You killed a man and fled the scene of the accident, and because of what you did, your mother is being blackmailed. I've seen the video."

"Oh, God," she said, and put her face in her hands and started sobbing.

Great, DeMarco thought. He was five inches taller than she was— she was shorter than her mother—and he knew he probably looked intimidating and as if he might be threatening her. He hoped some passerby didn't decide to be a hero and come to Jenny's rescue.

"Let's go sit in my car and talk," DeMarco said. He pointed and said, "That's my car over there."

"I'm not getting into a car with you. I don't know you."

"Call your mother. She'll verify who I am." The last thing he wanted her to do was call Lydia. "But ask yourself: How would I know about the accident if your mother hadn't told me?"

She hesitated, and before she could make a decision, DeMarco said, "Come on. I'm not going to hurt you. I'm here to help you." He took his keys out of a pocket, tapped the fob to unlock his car, then held the keys out to her. "I'll let you hold my keys so you don't have to worry about me driving off with you. And you can leave the car door open."

She didn't take the keys from him but she didn't resist when he took her gently by the arm and guided her over to his car. He took her backpack from her and put it on the ground near the front passenger's door and opened the door for her. She got inside the car but left the door open so she could run, and he went around the car and got into the driver's seat.

Before he could ask her anything, she said, "I've ruined my life."

DeMarco almost said, *Your life? You killed a man.* But didn't. Instead he said, "I don't know about that, but you're definitely in trouble and so is your mother. And if what you and your mother have done gets out, your father will also have a problem."

"What do you mean? What has my mother done? She's being blackmailed because of me but she hasn't done anything illegal."

"It's more complicated than that, Jenny."

"What does that mean?"

DeMarco ignored the question. "What's your boyfriend's name?"

"I'm not going to tell you."

"Jenny, I can get his name. I know a guy who can look at your phone records and he'll tell me who you've been calling, and I'll eventually figure out who he is. But that'll take time, and we don't have time to waste."

"No. I'm not telling you his name."

"Listen to me. You've created a huge problem for your mom and dad, and I don't have time to coddle you. And I think your boyfriend may be involved in what happened."

"What are you talking about?"

"What's his name? Like I said, I'm going to get it anyway, but the longer it takes, the worse it gets for your mother. Think about someone other than yourself."

He felt a bit bad about bullying a nineteen-year-old kid, but not that bad. The girl annoyed him, striking him as someone who had always led a life of privilege and was completely self-absorbed.

She put her head down and muttered something.

DeMarco said, "What?"

"His name is Noah. Noah Parker."

"What does he do? On the video, he said he didn't want to lose his job."

She shook her head, but before DeMarco could prompt her—or berate her—she said, "He's a professor at Georgetown. One of my professors."

DeMarco hadn't met Noah Parker yet but immediately decided the guy was a creep.

"I need to ask you some things about the accident," DeMarco said. "What time did it take place?"

DeMarco had read the article in the *Montgomery County Sentinel* that Lydia had mentioned. It said the accident had taken place on a road with the weird name of Turkey Foot Road outside of the town of Darnestown, Maryland, and asked the public to call the Montgomery County Sheriff's Office if anyone knew anything. But the article hadn't given the time of the accident, probably because the cops didn't know the time.

"A little after midnight," Jenny said. "I don't know, like, maybe twelve thirty."

"Why were you in Maryland at that time of night?"

"We went to dinner at a diner near Darnestown."

"Seems like an odd place to go for dinner. Darnestown's about an hour from D.C."

"The diner's close to Noah's house and we went there because we didn't want to be seen together and we were sure that no one who knew me would go there. I hit that man on the way back to his place."

"Does Noah know about the video and your mom being blackmailed?"

Jenny started blubbering. "No. He won't talk to me. I've been calling him and texting him, but he won't answer my calls or respond to my texts. I even borrowed my roommate's car and drove out to his place twice to see him. His car was in the driveway but he wasn't home. Or maybe he knew it was me and he wouldn't come to the door. And he hasn't been at school since it happened. A substitute's been teaching his class but the sub's an asshole and all he'd tell me is that Noah had asked for some time off."

DeMarco wondered why Parker hadn't been to work. Had the accident rattled him so badly that he needed to take time off? Was he playing hooky to avoid Jenny?

DeMarco said, "So you haven't told him about the video?"

"No, I just told you. I haven't talked to him since the night of the accident. And my mother told me not to tell anyone about the video. She said the video is evidence that will be used against me if anyone, like the cops, find out about it. But I haven't told Noah about it because he won't call me back."

"Well, your mother's right. You can't tell anyone about it." DeMarco was silent for a moment, then said, "Let me ask you something. When you left the diner, or when you were on your way to Noah's place, did he call or text anyone?"

"Why are you asking that?"

"Just answer the question."

"He texted his dean a couple of times. I mean she texted him, and he answered her texts. Anyway, he texted her when we left the diner and again a bit later."

"How do you know it was his dean who texted him?"

"Because he said it was."

"So he texted the dean when you left the diner. When was the second time?"

"I don't know the exact time. A few minutes later."

"Where on the road were you when he sent the text? Were you at an intersection or near some landmark?"

"I don't re—oh, he sent it when we crossed this little bridge that's a couple miles from his house. But why are you asking about his texts?"

"Just something I'm trying to figure out," DeMarco said.

"What are you trying to figure—"

"Was your car damaged in the accident?"

"Yes. The man hit the windshield hard and made a big crack in it. I was surprised it didn't shatter. Noah told me to take the car to a body shop and tell them I hit a deer. There're a lot of deer near his place."

"Has the car been repaired?"

"It's in the shop now. That's why I had to borrow my roommate's car. My car's a Tesla and the windshield's special—got sensors in it or something—and they're waiting for a new one to come in."

And DeMarco thought: *So not only did she hit the guy, then flee the scene, she tried to cover up what she did by lying about the cause of the damage to her car. Or that's the way a prosecutor would put it to a jury.*

"What am I supposed to do?" she said. "I told my mother that I should turn myself in, but she won't let me."

"At this point you don't do anything and you don't talk to anyone about what happened. Like your roommate. Have you told her about the accident?"

"No. She could tell I was really upset and kept asking what was going on with me, so I finally told her the guy I was seeing broke up with me, but I never told her who I was seeing or about the accident."

DeMarco could understand her not telling her roommate who she was dating because the creep professor, to cover his ass, would have told her not to tell anyone.

"Good," DeMarco said.

"What are you and my mom going to do?"

"We haven't figured that out yet. But stay away from Noah. Don't try to talk to him. Stop calling him."

"But I love him."

"Yeah, well, what can I tell you," DeMarco said.

All that did was make her start crying again.

DeMarco wasn't mentally equipped to deal with a lovestruck nineteen-year-old.

11

———◆———

"What do you want now?" Neil said, when he saw it was DeMarco calling.

"I need you to get me what you can on a Georgetown professor named Noah Parker. Like you did for Diane Lake."

"I'm busy, DeMarco. I'm—"

"You can pad your bill like you always do. This is important."

"It's always important according to you."

"Neil—"

"Yeah, all right. I'll get back to you when I can."

As he was near the campus, DeMarco thought about trying to find out why Parker hadn't been to work since the accident. But then he decided not to do that because he'd have to talk to Parker's coworkers and word might get back to him. He didn't want Parker to know he was coming for him.

He called Mahoney's office next to tell him what he'd learned, but Mavis—Mahoney's executive assistant and a woman who'd worked for him since he was a freshman representative—said he wasn't available and she didn't know when he would be. He was, as usual, already an hour behind schedule, and the day had barely started.

"Tell him to give me a call when he's got fifteen minutes to talk."

"Can I tell him what this is about?" Mavis said.

"He'll know what it's about," DeMarco said.

DeMarco found a place to have breakfast, and while he was eating he called Mookie's number again and got the same message about Mookie not having set up his voicemail. After that, he started looking at sand wedges online. The last time he'd landed in a bunker, one that had been deeper than a Kentucky coal mine, it had cost him two strokes and he was wondering if he should buy another sand wedge. Like the problem was his equipment and not his lack of talent. But the sand wedge he had was a 56-degree wedge, and he was thinking that maybe spending a hundred and fifty bucks on a 60-degree wedge would improve his chances of escaping from deep bunkers. But then Neil called, interrupting him before he could make such a momentous decision.

Neil said, "Parker is thirty years old."

And dating a nineteen-year-old, DeMarco thought.

"He's divorced, the ex-wife has custody of his two kids. And the ex, who must have had a good lawyer, is getting three-fifths of his salary, and the guy only makes about a hundred grand a year. He's got about fourteen cents in a savings account and next to nothing in his 401(k). He's living in a place out in Maryland—the closest city is Darnestown—and I'm guessing the reason he lives there is because the house is owned by an aunt of his who's in a nursing home and he's living there for free. One other thing. He was hit with a paternity suit from some woman a couple of years ago, but nothing came of that, so I'm guessing his DNA didn't match the kid's."

"Text me his address," DeMarco said. "And a photo of him if you can find a recent one."

"I can get one off the university's website," Neil said.

He thanked Neil, and a moment later DeMarco's phone dinged and he saw a text with a photo.

Noah Parker had curly blond hair, artfully disarrayed, and dimples in both cheeks when he displayed gleaming white teeth in a boyish smile.

He was absurdly good-looking and reminded DeMarco of the late actor Ryan O'Neal when O'Neal was young and dating Farrah Fawcett and he and Farrah had been one of the most beautiful couples in Hollywood. And the first thing that occurred to DeMarco was that a guy as good-looking as Parker could have had his pick from a litter of gorgeous Georgetown coeds. Why would he risk his career dating a girl as plain as Jenny McMillian? Her sparkling personality?

DeMarco left the restaurant a few minutes after talking to Neil, planning to head to Parker's place. Mahoney called as he was walking to his car.

Mahoney said, "What's going on? And make it quick. I'm late for a meeting."

Mahoney said this as if he weren't late for almost every meeting. And at his rank, meetings didn't start until he got there.

DeMarco told him what he'd learned from Lydia Chang and Jenny McMillian and how Zhou was using a video of Jenny hitting a man with her car and fleeing the scene to blackmail Lydia. He described how it appeared that the man who'd been killed had been forced to stand in the road and that Jenny had been with her boyfriend, who was also one of her professors, when it happened.

Mahoney said, "Jesus. No wonder she's meeting with Zhou. So what are you gonna do next?"

"Lean on the boyfriend. I think he might have been involved in setting up the accident."

"Why do you think that?"

"Because of some text messages he sent right before the accident. I think the texts might have been sent to tell whoever took the video that Jenny was on her way. The thing is, Parker's practically broke, so money could have been a motivator. He's also so good-looking that he could be dating the entire Georgetown cheerleading squad, and Jenny McMillian isn't cheerleader material. I'm wondering if Parker could have been paid to seduce her. Anyway, I'm gonna go lean on him."

"Yeah, all right," Mahoney said. "But what I'm thinking about doing right now is throwing Dutch McMillian and his whole fucking family under the bus. Did you see what that lying son of a bitch said last night on Fox about me?"

"Uh, no," DeMarco said, and then had to listen to Mahoney's tirade.

But he couldn't help but think: *So why don't you throw them all under the bus?*

DeMarco headed in the direction of Darnestown, Maryland, but decided that before going to Parker's place he wanted to see the scene of the accident and the route Jenny had taken to get there.

He called Jenny but she didn't answer, probably because she didn't recognize his number, so he left a message saying, "This is DeMarco, the guy you met with this morning. Call me back. Right away."

A minute later she called, and DeMarco said, "What's the name of the restaurant where you and Noah ate the night of the accident?"

"It's called Jimmy D's. Why are you asking?"

"Because I want to see the route you took to get to Noah's and the place where the accident occurred."

"Why?"

"Because I do," DeMarco said, and hung up.

Jimmy D's Bar & Grill was on the bottom floor of a badly weathered two-story, clapboard building that had a gravel parking lot that would hold maybe ten cars. On one side of the diner was a muffler shop and on the other side a Dollar General store. A red neon sign over the door displayed the name of the place and there were neon signs advertising Budweiser in two windows. Classy. Even taking into account Parker's finances, he should have been embarrassed to take a date there.

DeMarco plugged Parker's address into his phone's map app and the app led him to Turkey Foot Road. The road was a two-lane blacktop, and close to Darnestown there were large houses with large lawns surrounded by wooden rail fences, but before long he was traveling past woods and farmland, and few houses were visible and there was hardly any traffic. At one point he crossed a small bridge that passed over an almost empty creek and he noted the mileage on his odometer. Almost exactly one mile later he arrived at what he was pretty sure was the scene of the accident, the curve Jenny had rounded right before she hit Harris. There was the speed limit sign and the light pole he'd seen in the video.

He stopped his car and got out and looked around. He didn't see any indication that an accident had taken place there—no remnants of crime scene tape or marks on the road made by investigators and, obviously, no body—but he was fairly sure he was in the right spot. He noticed that on both sides of the road were pastures or fallow fields, and the grass and weeds near the road were knee-high and a drainage ditch ran along one side of the road. He supposed that whoever took the video could have hidden in the tall grass or the drainage ditch and would have been invisible at night.

He got back in his car and continued on, and a mile later he took a left-hand turn and then another left and headed down a one-lane, tree-lined gravel road and arrived at Parker's place. It was a one-story structure, less than a thousand square feet, and had peeling white siding and a moss-covered roof. The small front lawn was mostly weeds and didn't look as if it had ever been mowed; the dandelions were a foot high. Thanks to all the trees around the property and a twelve-foot-tall laurel hedge, none of his neighbors' homes were visible. On one side of the house was a carport with a plastic roof and an unwashed Ford Focus more than a decade old was parked under it. He hoped that meant that Parker was home, but Jenny had told him that the car had been parked there when she went to see Parker.

———◆———

DeMarco was convinced that Parker was involved in setting up the accident. Whoever forced the homeless man, James Harris, to stand in the road wouldn't have made him stand there all night, waiting for Jenny to hit him. And that's why DeMarco had asked Jenny if Parker had texted or called anyone. He believed that Parker had sent the text messages not to his dean, but to whoever was controlling Harris to tell that person that he and Jenny had left the diner and then texted a second time when Jenny's car was a mile away from the accident site so the video taker would know that Jenny was close to rounding the curve in the road.

DeMarco's plan was to force Parker to admit his involvement in the crime. He was going to tell him that, because of what he'd done, he was an accessory to murder and the only way out for him was to cooperate and identify the person he'd sent the texts to—who he suspected was Zhou or someone working for him. How Chinese intelligence could have gotten their hooks into a Georgetown professor, he had no idea. He'd find that out when he questioned Parker.

He knocked on Parker's front door but no one answered his knock, so he pounded on the door with his fist. The place was so small that if Parker was home, he should have been able to hear him. But no one came to the door. There was a picture window next to the door, but the blinds were closed and he couldn't see inside the house.

He walked around to the north side of the house and saw another window. This one didn't have closed curtains or blinds, but access to it was blocked by an overgrown rhododendron bush filled with pink flowers in full bloom. He had to brush away a large spiderweb, one containing a spider that looked big enough to eat hummingbirds, to get around the bush and to the window. While keeping an eye out for the spider, he peered through the window and could see Parker's living room: an old couch, a couple of end tables, and a recliner aimed at a television set.

In the recliner sat Noah Parker—and he had a black hole in the center of his forehead and the wall behind him was splattered brown with dried blood. He also noticed that Parker's stomach appeared to be bloated and his once handsome face was an unnatural dark red color and appeared to be melting, judging from the way the skin sagged.

DeMarco wasn't a pathologist, but it looked to him as if Parker had been sitting there for quite a while and his body was decomposing.

12

DeMarco knew that what he should do was call 911 to report finding Parker's body, but he didn't want to do that because if he did, they could use his cell phone number to identify him and track him down. He did *not* want to get caught up in a police investigation and be detained by the cops: they might even consider him a suspect as there was no way he could tell them why he came to see Parker or explain how he knew Parker. At the same time, he wanted the cops to investigate Parker's murder sooner rather than later to see if his death could be connected in any way to Zhou or whoever had orchestrated the accident. What he needed was a pay phone, but where do you find a pay phone in the third decade of the twenty-first century?

He thought about driving back to Darnestown to look for a phone but decided he'd have a better chance of finding one in Rockville. The population of Darnestown was a little under seven thousand, while almost seventy thousand lived in Rockville, and Rockville was only ten miles from Darnestown. He drove to Rockville and used his cell phone to locate the courthouse and found out there were four courthouses there. Why there would be so many, he didn't know, but he figured a courthouse was likely to have pay phones so impoverished criminals who didn't have cell phones would be able to call their lawyers and bail bondsmen. But as he headed toward one of the courthouses, he passed an Amtrak station and decided to stop there to see if they had one of the nearly extinct devices.

They did. There was a single phone booth occupied by a woman so large she couldn't shut the door and DeMarco had to wait for fifteen minutes, listening to her talk to someone named Myra about her good-for-nothing, piece-of-shit husband and her can't-get-a-job, pot-smoking son and her slut of a daughter who was seeing a married man. He stood outside the phone booth glaring at her and tapping his watch to indicate she'd been on the phone forever—and she acted as if he were invisible. Finally, the damn woman hung up and squeezed out of the booth and DeMarco was able to use the phone.

He closed the door and called 911, telling the dispatcher that a man named Noah Parker was lying dead in his home, the victim of an apparent gunshot wound, and gave the dispatcher Parker's address. When the dispatcher asked who he was, he hung up.

As he was driving back to D.C., he called Perry. He said, "The cops in Montgomery County are going to—"

"Which Montgomery County? There are Montgomery Counties in Virginia, Pennsylvania, Texas, Ohio, New York—"

Fucking Perry. What a show-off. But he knew that Perry not only knew the name of every county in the country—he was like that Steve Kornacki guy on MSNBC—he could also tell you how each of them voted in the last election.

"The one in Maryland," DeMarco said. "The cops that have jurisdiction there, which is most likely the county sheriff's office, are going to find a dead body in a house outside of Darnestown today." It occurred to him then that those same cops had probably investigated the hit-and-run accident.

"How do you know that?" Perry asked.

"Because I'm the one who reported the body," DeMarco said. "The victim's name is Noah Parker."

"Who's he?"

"A guy connected to the Lydia Chang thing. Look, I'll fill you in later on what's going on"—he'd told Mahoney about Parker but hadn't told Perry—"but I need to know as soon as possible what the cops find out when they do their investigation. Is the congressman who represents Montgomery County a Democrat?"

"Yes. And that would be Congress*woman* Shirley Barrett, you chauvinistic pig."

"Yeah, well, see if you can get her to call the Montgomery County cops tomorrow after the murder's been reported on the news or online. She should tell them that she wants them to keep her in the loop because Parker helped her on a campaign or she knows his mother or whatever. She should pretend she's rushing off to cast a vote, doesn't have time to talk, but a guy on her staff named DeMarco will be calling to get an update on what's happening. Do you think you can get her to do that?"

"Not a problem. Shirley's a natural-born liar and the only reason she still has a job is because of Mahoney. She'll do what she's told."

"But she can't know anything other than Parker's name."

"Not a problem," Perry said again.

"And I need to talk to Mahoney. Is he around?"

"The last time I saw him, he was headed over to the gym."

"He's going to kill himself," DeMarco said.

"That's what I told him. You know why he's started going to the gym?"

"No," DeMarco said.

"Because he's going to a black-tie event in a couple of weeks and he can't fit into his tuxedo and doesn't want to buy another one."

Mahoney called him thirty minutes later. He must have just finished exercising because he was panting, making DeMarco think of a hooked catfish flopping on a dock, gasping for air. He told him about finding Parker dead.

Mahoney didn't say anything for a moment, then said, "This fucking thing doesn't make any sense."

"What fucking thing?" DeMarco said.

"All of it. The professor seducing Dutch's daughter, the staged accident, the video, someone killing Parker. It's just too . . . I don't know what. It's just too much."

"Killing Parker makes sense," DeMarco said. "Whoever set up the accident didn't want him talking."

"Yeah, I know but—"

"It's time to turn this over to the FBI," DeMarco said. "Not only are the Chinese squeezing Lydia Chang, two murders have been committed."

"No, not yet."

"Why not?"

Instead of answering the question, after a long pause, Mahoney said, "Come to my place tonight about nine."

13

Mahoney had a condo in the Watergate complex. From the balcony, where his wife made him sit when he wanted to smoke a cigar, he could see the Washington Monument and the dome of the Capitol. Mahoney answered the door wearing worn Top-Siders sans socks, red sweatpants, and a New England Patriots T-shirt that had been signed with a Magic Marker by Tom Brady.

DeMarco asked, "Is Mary Pat here?"

Mary Pat was Mahoney's long-suffering wife. For more than forty years, she'd tolerated her husband's drinking, his many affairs, and his self-centered nature. She was a sweet woman—her character was nothing like Mahoney's—and DeMarco loved her dearly, but he had no idea why she stayed married to the man.

"No," Mahoney said. "She's up in Boston, seeing one of the girls."

Mahoney had three daughters, two of them lived in the Boston area, and Mahoney had a home in Boston.

DeMarco followed Mahoney through the condo to the dining room table where a man was sitting. The man was younger than Mahoney, in his sixties, bald and tan, short and trim; his nose was practically flat, as if someone had hammered on it repeatedly with a large, angry fist. He reminded DeMarco of the guy who'd been Rocky's trainer in the movie.

On the table was a bottle of bourbon, two glasses, a bowl filled with pretzels, a cribbage board, and a deck of cards; whoever was playing the blue pegs had a substantial lead. The man nodded to DeMarco, and he nodded back.

Surprisingly, Mahoney was gracious enough to ask if DeMarco wanted a drink. He said, "Sure."

Mahoney got a third glass, splashed bourbon into it, passed the glass to DeMarco, then said, "This is Mike McGuire. He retired from the CIA about a year ago. I wanted to get his opinion on this, this whatever it is."

DeMarco wondered how Mahoney knew McGuire but didn't ask. Nor did he ask if McGuire was a guy who could keep his mouth shut. If he wasn't, he wouldn't be sitting there.

"How much does he know?" DeMarco asked Mahoney.

Mahoney said, "He doesn't know the names of the people involved, with one exception. But he knows pretty much everything else. He knows that someone engineered a hit-and-run accident involving the daughter of a high-ranking politician and videoed it and the video is being used by a Chinese intelligence officer to blackmail the politician's wife. And he knows that one of the people involved in arranging the accident was killed, probably to keep him from talking." Before DeMarco could ask who the exception was, Mahoney said, "Tell him what you told me, Mike."

McGuire said, "This doesn't sound to me like something the Chinese would do. The Russians, maybe, but not the Chinese. Because Russian intelligence works for a maniac, they do things like kill people outside of Russia, poisoning them with polonium or tossing them off balconies. But in general, intelligence agencies don't go around killing people, no matter what you see in the movies. You kill people, particularly in this country, you get big investigations conducted by competent cops, and intelligence officers can get arrested. The other thing is, this is so complicated, getting someone to seduce the daughter, setting up the accident, getting the guy to stand in the road. I mean, there's just too many moving parts. Now, the Russians might do something like this because they all think they're fucking chess masters, but most outfits wouldn't." ⸱

DeMarco said, "Okay, but—"

McGuire said, "Do you know how intelligence agencies usually acquire assets? Well, it ain't normally using a honey trap like you read about in spy novels, where some hot-looking gal gets a potential asset to go to bed with her and then the asset's blackmailed. I mean, that's happened, but the way most assets are acquired is the asset *volunteers*. He calls up someone in an embassy or talks to someone he knows is an intelligence officer and says, 'If you pay me enough, I'll spy for you.' That's basically how the two biggest traitors in American history, Aldrich Ames at the CIA and Robert Hanssen at the FBI, were recruited. They offered themselves up for money; nobody had to do anything tricky to turn them into traitors. So this thing John says you're trying to figure out just doesn't sound to me like something the Chinese would do. They wouldn't put together something this complex; they wouldn't kill a couple of people. Mostly what the Chinese do—and they're very good at it—is acquire intelligence by hacking into computer systems."

DeMarco said, "That all may be true, but it's a Chinese operative that's squeezing—" He almost said Lydia Chang. "The wife of the high-ranking guy."

"Yeah, I know that," McGuire said. "But what I'm sayin' is that the Chinese most likely wouldn't have done the whole hit-and-run accident, video thing. Someone else did that and gave it to the Chinese. Or at least that's what I think."

"But why would someone do that?" DeMarco asked.

"I don't know. Maybe they want to damage the politician. Or maybe they knew the Chinese would be willing to pay a lot to compromise the guy's wife. I don't know, but my gut tells me that the Chinese weren't involved in setting up the accident."

DeMarco sipped his bourbon. It was good. Mahoney didn't drink cheap booze.

To Mahoney, DeMarco said, "You said you didn't name names but there was one exception. Who was it?" He thought he already knew the answer to his question, and it turned out he was right.

"Diane Lake," Mahoney said. "I wanted to see what Mike knew about her."

"I never met her," McGuire said to DeMarco. "I was mostly out in the field, and she was a house mouse."

DeMarco was willing to bet that McGuire had been one of those CIA officers who had been on the ground in Afghanistan after 9/11, hunting down Al Qaeda fighters before all the U.S. troops were flown in. He could picture McGuire, armed to the teeth, dressed like a native, creeping through caves in Tora Bora trying to find Osama bin Laden.

McGuire said, "I called a couple of guys when John said he was interested in her. Mostly what I got was that she's bright and super ambitious and she basically quit because she thought she should have been one of the people briefing the president in the Oval Office and not stuck behind a computer at Langley. But other than that, nothing really negative; just that she had a higher opinion of herself than her bosses did."

McGuire finished off the bourbon in his glass, poured another drink, then said, "But before I get back to whipping John's ass at cribbage, I'll tell you one other thing. I said the Russians were one outfit who I could imagine putting together something this complex. Well, there's another outfit that, on occasion, has done some overly complicated, convoluted, tricky shit. And that's the CIA."

14

The next morning DeMarco slept in until nine, scrambled eggs for break-fast, and, while eating, went online and confirmed that Parker's death had been reported. He decided to wait an hour before calling the Mont-gomery County sheriff, figuring that by then Congresswoman Barrett would have talked to him.

He took a shower, cleaned up the kitchen, paid a couple of bills that were almost overdue, then called the sheriff's office, telling the person who answered the phone that his name was DeMarco and that he was calling on behalf of Congresswoman Shirley Barrett. When the sheriff came on the line, DeMarco repeated the lie about working for Barrett, adding, "I believe she told you I'd be calling."

"Yeah," the sheriff said. "And I normally wouldn't tell you about an ongoing investigation, but since Shirley helped me get a chunk of that federal anti-terrorism money that I used to buy machine guns and body armor for my SWAT guys, I decided to make an exception. And because she's a ballbuster that would probably make sure I didn't get reelected if I didn't do what she wanted. Anyway, there's not much to tell. Someone shot Parker with a nine-millimeter bullet that my ballistics guy thinks came out of a Beretta M9, although he's not positive. There weren't any shell casings. There was no evidence that whoever shot him broke into the house, so maybe he let his killer in. Parker's wallet was found on the kitchen table and there wasn't any cash in it, but his credit cards were still there. The house was ransacked like the killer was looking for something specific or just looking for shit to steal. My guess is that whoever killed him somehow talked his way into the house, maybe he showed Parker a gun, killed Parker, and then went treasure hunting, although why he'd pick that particular house, I don't know. It doesn't look like a place where a guy with money or expensive things would live. The only thing we know for sure that the killer took was Parker's cell phone because we didn't find one in the house."

Without the phone, the sheriff wouldn't be able to see who Parker had been calling or texting, which was a good thing, because he wouldn't see that Parker had been communicating with Jenny McMillian. Unless, of course, the sheriff decided to get a warrant to get Parker's cell phone provider to show him their records—and DeMarco wasn't going to encourage the sheriff to do that. He'd have Neil look at Parker's phone records and hopefully he'd do it before the sheriff did.

"Do you know when he was killed?" DeMarco asked, wondering when Parker's death had occurred relative to the hit-and-run.

"No, we don't have an exact time or day. The body was too decomposed. But the pathologist figured it had been there at least a couple of weeks. We canvased the neighborhood, but his neighbors can't see his house because of all the trees, and none of them drove by and saw a strange car parked in his driveway. Most of his neighbors didn't even know his name except for one guy he borrowed a chain saw from one time when a tree branch came down in his driveway and the neighbor said he had to teach Parker how to use the saw. My detectives are talking to people over at Georgetown University, where he worked, to see if anyone knows if he had any enemies, and we fingerprinted the place and maybe we'll get a print that'll point to someone."

Oh, shit, DeMarco thought. They'd probably find Jenny McMillian's fingerprints. But then he thought, *Yeah, they might find her prints, but they might not be able to identify her.* It seemed unlikely that a nineteen-year-old would have her fingerprints on file unless she'd committed a crime sometime in the past. He'd have to ask Lydia if Jenny had ever been fingerprinted; if so, Jenny would have to come up with a story about why her prints would be in Parker's house. A private tutoring session? Nah, not likely.

"About the only other thing we're doing is leaning on the local addicts," the sheriff said. "One of them might have gotten desperate enough for money to kill Parker, but usually junkies don't kill, and they usually break into empty houses to steal and not one where someone is at home. So that's about it. Give me your phone number and if something comes up I'll give you a call, but don't go bugging me every day."

DeMarco gave the sheriff his number.

DeMarco had wanted to know what the sheriff knew about Parker's death to see if he had any information pointing to whoever had killed him—but it was obvious the sheriff didn't know anything. About the only useful thing he'd learned was that maybe Parker knew his killer and let the killer in.

He said, "Thanks for talking to me, Sheriff, and I'll pass on what you told me to the congresswoman. And I won't be calling you again, but please call me if there are any developments."

———— ◆ ————

DeMarco called Neil after speaking to the sheriff and asked him to see if he could get a peek at Noah Parker's phone records, something he should have asked the last time he talked to him. He wanted to know who Parker had been texting the night of the accident. Neil, of course, bitched about DeMarco interrupting his work, which made DeMarco wonder what Homeland Security had Neil doing that was keeping him so busy.

DeMarco decided that what he needed to do next was investigate James Harris, the man Jenny had killed. The person who'd set up the accident had forced Harris to stand in the road—DeMarco was sure of that—and this meant that someone had *selected* Harris to be the victim. And maybe there was a way to find out who that person was by learning more about Harris.

He went online and looked again at the article in the *Montgomery County Sentinel*, the one that had identified Harris as a homeless person and a veteran and asked anyone who knew anything about the accident to contact the Montgomery County Sheriff's Office. There was a phone number provided in the article.

But DeMarco couldn't call the sheriff and ask him about Harris because then he'd have to explain the link between Noah Parker and Harris, which he didn't want to do. So he'd have someone else make the call.

15

While flipping pages with one hand and using his other hand to stuff his face with Cheetos, Perry was speed-reading a bill coming up for a vote because Mahoney never read the bills he voted on. Perry read the bills—and told Mahoney what they said—and Perry actually read every word in documents that could be hundreds or thousands of pages long.

Perry's office was filled with paper. There were yellowing copies of the *Congressional Record*, studies generated by think tanks, glossy pamphlets packed with lies produced by lobbyists, and binders filled with statistics stacked on every horizontal surface: on his desk, on windowsills, on the tops of file cabinets, on the floor, and on two visitors' chairs. DeMarco removed a stack of manila file folders that was two feet tall off one of the chairs and sat down, and as Perry was wiping orange Cheetos gunk off his fingers, DeMarco filled him in on everything he'd learned since the initial meeting in Mahoney's office. Then he told Perry what he wanted him to do.

Perry put his phone in speaker mode so DeMarco could listen and called the number listed in the article on the accident. A woman answered the phone saying, "Montgomery County Sheriff's Office."

Perry said, "I need to speak to the detective investigating the death of James Harris, the victim of the hit-and-run accident that took place on Turkey Foot Road a little while ago."

"What's your name, please?" the woman said.

"My name's Perry Wallace and I'm the chief of staff for John Mahoney, the minority leader of the House of Representatives."

"Oh," the woman said, sounding impressed. "Just a minute."

A moment later another female voice said, "This is Detective Reynolds. You said you're Congressman Mahoney's chief of staff?"

"That's right. My name's Perry Wallace. If you don't believe me, look up the number online for Congressman Mahoney's office and call the number and ask for me."

There was a pause, then Reynolds said, "What can I do for you?"

"As you might know, Congressman Mahoney is a decorated veteran and has always been an advocate for veterans."

That was actually true. Mahoney had many faults: he was vain, he was self-centered, he was corrupt, he was a philandering alcoholic. But he'd served in Vietnam—had been wounded there—and the one good thing that could be said about him was that he genuinely cared about the people who'd served in the military and did whatever he could to make their lives better.

Perry said, "And when he learned that Mr. Harris was a veteran, he decided to make sure he was given a proper funeral at Arlington. But Congressman Mahoney also wants to know what's happening insofar as finding Mr. Harris's killer. He suspects that no one really cares about Mr. Harris, him having been homeless, but *he* cares."

"That's not true," Reynolds said. "I care. I care because I'm the investigating officer."

"Well, that's good to hear," Perry said. "Do you have anything pointing to the person who killed him?"

Reynolds said, "One thing. We'll be able to match tire tracks found at the scene to the car if we can find it because there's a defect on the tread of one of the tires that's distinctive. But there wasn't anything at the scene to identify the make or model of the car."

DeMarco needed to let Lydia Chang know that her daughter might want to get a new set of tires.

Reynolds continued. "There was no broken glass from a headlight or paint chips on the body—nothing like that. And there're no cameras where the accident took place, no nearby houses, the road isn't heavily traveled, and no witnesses have come forward. The only person that's called about the accident is you."

"Anything else?" Perry asked.

Reynolds said, "The way we ID'd Harris was from some paperwork he had in a wallet. He didn't have a driver's license but he had a Social Security card and another card that identified him as a veteran. He also had a card in one of his pockets for an addiction counselor at the Good Shepherd Mission in Southeast D.C. The mission provides food and shelter for the homeless and I called the counselor. I was trying to find out what Harris was doing in Montgomery County to see if that might lead to something. But the counselor said he didn't know Harris and that he'd never spoken to him. He said the staff at the mission gives his cards away to people who come there and that's probably how Harris got his card. So I drove over to the mission to see if anyone there knew anything about him and I spoke to the woman in charge. She also helps out on the food line. She didn't know Harris's name but she recognized him from the photo we took in the morgue, and said he hung out around the neighborhood where the mission is located and that he would come for meals most nights but he never slept there unless it was freezing outside. He didn't like to sleep around other people and he didn't like the rules about not drinking while he was inside the place."

DeMarco scrawled on a piece of paper: *What was the woman's name?* and held up the paper for Perry to see.

"What was the woman's name?" Perry asked.

"Just a minute. Let me look at my notes," Reynolds said. "Olivia Taylor."

"She tell you anything else about him?" Perry asked.

"Just that Harris was rapidly drinking himself to death and wasn't interested in getting treatment. And the autopsy showed that his liver and kidneys were pretty much toast. He was only forty-two, but when I saw the body, I would have guessed he was in his sixties. Ms. Taylor said she doubted he would have lived more than a couple of years, the way he drank and the condition he was in."

"Could she think of any reason for him being in Montgomery County? Like, did he have a relative living out there?" Perry asked.

"No," Reynolds said. "Like I said, she didn't even know his name. And the only relative of his that I could find was a sister in South Carolina and she hadn't spoken to him in years. I'm the one who told her he was dead. So I can't figure out what he was doing out here or even how he got here. He didn't own a car and the scene of the accident is forty-five minutes from the mission. A city bus wouldn't have taken him there and he probably couldn't have afforded a cab. I suppose he could have hitched a ride from someone, but why he would do that, I don't know."

DeMarco thought: *He didn't hitchhike. Someone picked him up and drove him to the place where he was killed.*

"So, I'm sorry, Mr. Wallace, but right now I don't have anything to go on, and the truth is, I doubt I'll be able to find out who killed him unless the driver grows a conscience and comes forward. But the case will remain open, and I'll keep working it."

Perry thanked the detective, hung up, then said to DeMarco: "Now, thanks to you, I'm going to have to make sure that Harris is buried at Arlington."

As DeMarco was leaving the Capitol, he saw Kentucky congresswoman Maggie Bower standing on the steps on the east side of the building, talking to a reporter holding a microphone and accompanied by a cameraman with a ratlike brown ponytail. In defiance of the dress code adopted by most lawmakers, Maggie was wearing a plain white T-shirt, and her broad hips were stuffed into a pair of too-tight blue jeans. On her blond head was a red baseball cap that had the words *Come and Take It* over an AR-15 rifle emblem. DeMarco walked over close enough to hear what she was saying.

Eyes blazing and filled with righteous indignation as she looked into the camera, she said: "I have indisputable proof, supported by eyewitness statements, that John Mahoney engaged in satanic rituals with members of his college fraternity and these rituals involved naked women and the drinking of human blood. I intend to present my evidence tomorrow on the floor of the House and propose that he be expelled if he refuses to resign. And I know that the good Christians of this country will support me."

DeMarco barked out a laugh before he could stop himself, and Maggie turned her head and glared at him.

DeMarco knew that Mahoney had attended Boston College about fifty years ago on the G.I. Bill after serving in Vietnam and got his law degree there—just barely. A minor scandal in his early years as a congressman was a story that he'd paid someone to take the bar exam for him. DeMarco suspected the story about the bar exam was true—Mahoney was no scholar—but it didn't damage him politically and was nothing compared to significantly more substantial accusations of corruption that came later that he also managed to dodge. As for Maggie's claim, her first credibility problem was that Boston College didn't have fraternities; it had "clubs"—none of which Mahoney had belonged to—but no fraternities. DeMarco could, however, imagine a young John Mahoney engaging enthusiastically in any activity involving naked women, although he probably wouldn't have drunk blood unless it contained a large percentage of alcohol. And he could hardly wait to see Maggie's eyewitnesses. He was willing to bet they all wore tinfoil hats to prevent government telepaths from reading their minds, and he figured it would be impossible for them to prove they had any association whatsoever with Mahoney half a century ago.

He thought for a second about calling Mahoney to warn him about Maggie Bower's one-reporter press conference but decided not to: if he did, Mahoney would ask why he still hadn't tracked down Mookie.

16

The Good Shepherd Mission was housed in a three-story brown brick building that looked more than a century old and that at one time might have been a school. It was on a block with rent-controlled apartments and run-down single-family houses, and nearby were fast food restaurants, warehouses, and small manufacturing outfits.

DeMarco went inside the building and briefly studied a few posters that advertised the various programs available to rehabilitate addicts and help them find jobs or get their high school degrees. He stopped a young woman walking by who was wearing a badge that identified her as one of the mission's volunteers and asked where he could find Olivia Taylor.

Olivia Taylor was a sturdy gray-haired lady who DeMarco thought looked like the grandma who would give you a hug if you needed one but who would also smack you on the back of the head if you misbehaved. She was a tough-looking old gal. She was standing in a room containing a dozen long folding tables where people could sit and eat, and behind her was a kitchen where DeMarco could see a couple of women wearing hairnets, preparing the evening's meal for those in need.

DeMarco said, "Can I speak to you for a minute?"

"Who are you?" Olivia said.

DeMarco took out his Congressional ID badge and showed it to her, saying, "My name's DeMarco. John Mahoney sent me here."

"Who's John Mahoney?"

"The former Speaker of the House."

"Oh, that guy," she said, the expression on her face transmitting her low opinion of Mahoney.

DeMarco said, "Yeah, I know, Mahoney has his faults, but he has a soft spot in his heart when it comes to veterans because he's a veteran. And I'm here because Mahoney wants to do the right thing for James Harris, a veteran who was killed in a hit-and-run accident. I believe a detective from the Montgomery County Sheriff's Office talked to you about James."

"What do you mean about Mahoney trying to do the right thing?" a skeptical Olivia asked.

"He's making sure that James is buried at Arlington, as is his right, but he's also trying to find some of his family members and people he served with so they can attend the service."

"I don't know anything about his family," Olivia said. "I didn't even know his name. I just recognized the photo that detective showed me because he'd come here for a hot meal."

"Did he have any friends you know about? Like someone who'd be with him or talk to him when he came here?"

"There was one guy. They'd stand in line together. He was a vet too. I know that because he had a Purple Heart medal he wore on his coat. I guess he could have stolen the medal, but I don't think he did. Anyway, I'd see him and James together sometimes."

"Do you know his name?"

"No."

"Can you give me a description of him? I'd like to talk to him to see if he can tell me anything about James's family or anything that could be said at his funeral."

"Why don't you ask the military about him? I'd think all Mahoney would have to do is call over to the Pentagon."

"I already did that," DeMarco said. "Harris was in the army, but his records are in a box in a warehouse in St. Louis and they haven't been digitized and they can't find the box."

Olivia looked like a lady with a built-in bullshit detector, and DeMarco hoped she didn't recognize that everything he'd just said was bullshit.

DeMarco said, "So can you give me a description of James's friend?"

"He's white, two or three inches taller than you, skinny as a rail. He wears a Washington Wizards stocking cap, one of them blue ones with the word *Wizards* on it in big red letters. The coat he pins his Purple Heart on is an old parka with a fur hood like someone who lives in Alaska would wear."

"You have any idea where I could find him?"

"No, but he's gotta be on the street somewhere close to here."

"Why do you say that?"

"Because he's like James was: drunk twenty-four hours a day and in such bad shape he can't walk very far. So he's gotta be someplace nearby."

"Well, I'll see if I can find him and see what he has to say."

Olivia said, "I gotta tell you, I'm surprised you're going to all this trouble." She frowned and said, "You better not be lying to me."

"I'm not lying," DeMarco lied. "And I'm only doing this because Mahoney's my boss and he wants it done."

"Well, I guess that goes to prove that there's some good in everyone, even someone like that rascal Mahoney."

Rascal. That had to be the most benign description of Mahoney that DeMarco had ever heard.

DeMarco got in his car and drove up and down the streets close to the mission. He spotted a number of people he suspected were homeless based on the way they were dressed, loitering in doorways, sitting on the ground with their backs against abandoned storefronts. One woman with untamed gray hair hanging down to the small of her back—like a down-on-her-luck Rapunzel—had a stolen shopping cart overloaded with all her worldly possessions. But he didn't see a man in a Wizards stocking cap. He again wished he hadn't sent Javier and Sergio home; he could have used them to track the guy down.

Twenty minutes later, when he was about to give up, he saw a man sitting near a dumpster in an alley behind a barbecue restaurant. The man was wearing the Wizards cap and the parka Olivia had mentioned. As it was sunny and over seventy degrees outside and humid, DeMarco figured he had to be baking inside the parka.

DeMarco found a place to park and walked over to him. The man was holding an almost empty wine bottle in one hand and his eyes were closed. His feet were inside worn tennis shoes and he wasn't wearing socks, and his ankles were swollen and red. Diabetes? The Purple Heart was pinned on his coat as Olivia had said, and DeMarco couldn't help but think that here was a man who'd once served his country and been injured in the line of duty and now he was living next to a dumpster.

DeMarco gently kicked his shoe and his eyes slowly opened. He looked up at DeMarco and DeMarco saw the whites of his eyes were the color of egg yolk.

DeMarco said, "I'd like to talk to you about your friend James Harris."

"Who you?"

"A guy who's willing to give you ten bucks if you'll talk to him."

"Talk about what?"

Jesus. "Your friend James Harris. He was a vet like you. You and he would have dinner together over at the Good Shepherd Mission."

"Oh, Jimmy. Haven't seen him in a while."

"Yeah, well, I'm sorry to have to tell you this, but Jimmy's dead. He was hit by a car."

"Oh, geez, that's . . . that's—"

"What's your name?" DeMarco said.

"Bob."

"Bob, do you know where Jimmy used to spend his nights?"

"Over there," Bob said, and pointed.

"Over there where?"

"Over there, by the warehouse."

"Which warehouse?"

"The one over there."

Christ. It was apparent that not many of Bob's brain cells were still firing.

DeMarco took out his wallet and handed Bob two fives. Bob took the money and pushed it into his parka and muttered, "Thanks."

DeMarco said, "If you show me the warehouse where Jimmy slept, I'll give you another ten."

"You will?"

"Yeah, I promise. Now, come on, get up and walk me over there."

DeMarco helped Bob to his feet, and when he did, Bob staggered and the bottle he'd been holding slipped from his hand and shattered. "Aw, fuck," Bob said. There'd only been a couple of ounces left in the bottle, but those ounces were precious to Bob.

DeMarco said, "You can buy another bottle as soon as you show me the place."

Bob was in such bad shape that it took almost ten minutes for him and DeMarco to walk a block and a half. When they reached an alleyway, Bob pointed and said, "Down there—the blue door. Jimmy liked it there because the roof over the door kept the rain off him."

"Thanks, Bob," DeMarco said, and handed him a ten-dollar bill. DeMarco knew that Bob was going to use the money to drink himself into a coma and he felt somewhat guilty about that, but Bob had been going down the path he was on long before today.

As Bob was leaving, shuffling off on his swollen ankles, most likely to the nearest store that sold cheap booze, DeMarco said, "Bob." Bob slowly turned to look at him with his yellow eyes and DeMarco said, "Thank you for your service."

———————◆◆◆———————

DeMarco walked down the alley to the blue door. It was covered with graffiti and the area near the door was littered with advertising flyers, fast-food Styrofoam containers, empty wine bottles, and crushed beer cans. All the windows in the building were covered with plywood. Across the alley was another building, a two-story brick one that was half a block long; iron bars covered the first-floor windows. On the corner of the building, under the eaves but plainly visible, was a camera pointing down the alley, and he wondered why someone would install a surveillance camera to overlook the alley.

DeMarco walked around to the front of the building that had the camera. On the ground floor was a company that sold plumbing supplies—copper and plastic pipe, fittings, valves, and so forth. Considering the neighborhood, the company was most likely a wholesaler who sold to contractors; do-it-yourselfers would go to a Home Depot or a Lowe's. DeMarco went into the building, where he found a middle-aged woman sitting behind a counter, squinting at a computer through reading glasses.

She said, "Can I help you?"

"I hope so," DeMarco said. "Can you tell me who manages this building?"

17

The property management company was located in an office complex near the Rosslyn Metro station and close to the Francis Scott Key Bridge. The director of the company was a man named Bruce Richardson, and when DeMarco walked into his office, Richardson was on the phone saying to somebody: "You get over to that building today—you hear me, *today*—and get that air conditioner running. You don't, I'm going to fire your useless ass and hire someone who gives a shit." He slammed the phone down and looked up at DeMarco.

Richardson was in his thirties and had short blond hair and the chiseled features of a matinee idol. He was wearing a short-sleeved shirt displaying heavily muscled arms and DeMarco suspected the muscles were partly due to the fact that Richardson used his arms to propel his wheelchair. On the wall behind his desk were a dozen photos and a couple of plaques. DeMarco didn't recognize any of the people in the photos; they were group photos and may have been people Richardson worked with. But there was one photo of Richardson that had been taken when he was younger. In it, he was standing with four other young men and they were all wearing camouflaged military uniforms, the kind of uniforms soldiers wore in Iraq and Afghanistan.

What DeMarco wanted was for Richardson to let him look at the video footage from the camera in the alley where James Harris had slept because he wanted to see if someone had picked up Harris on the night he was killed. He'd invented a plausible story about needing the video because of a lawsuit and a client he was representing, and if Richardson wasn't willing to show him the footage voluntarily, then he'd threaten him with a subpoena and promise to make his life miserable by doing all the nasty things that lawyers do. But when he saw the photo of Richardson with a group of soldiers, he decided instead to see if he could get his cooperation with a story that was almost true.

He said to Richardson, "My name's DeMarco. My boss is John Mahoney, the minority leader of the House."

Richardson raised an eyebrow but didn't say anything. At least, he didn't react negatively to Mahoney's name the way Olivia Taylor had.

DeMarco said, "Not long ago, a homeless veteran named James Harris was killed. I can't tell you exactly how this involves Mahoney, but, believe it or not, Harris's death has national security implications and Mahoney wants to find out who killed him. The cops involved don't give a shit about Harris because he was homeless, and they don't know that finding his killer is important because no one's told them about the national security issue since it's classified."

"What does this have to do with me or my company?" Richardson said.

"Your company manages a building in Southeast D.C. There's a plumbing supply store on the first floor and there's a camera on the roof of the building that looks down an alley behind the building. Well, James Harris used to spend his nights in that alley. What I'd like to do is see if your camera picked up anything the night he was killed, and I'm hoping you'll let me do so without making me get a subpoena."

"How do I know you're telling the truth about working for Mahoney?"

DeMarco pulled out his badge. He said, "That's the badge that gets me into the Capitol every day. And I'll give you Mahoney's personal cell phone number and you can call him and he'll verify what I've told you."

Richardson studied DeMarco's face for a long moment, then said, "Nah, that's okay. I believe you. What's the day you're interested in?"

DeMarco gave Richardson the date for when Harris was killed and said he needed the video footage from six a.m. that day until six a.m. the following morning.

Richardson said, "I'll have to contact the security company we use. They retain the videos on their servers for thirty days."

"I'm curious," DeMarco said. "Why did you install the camera in the alley?"

"Because the plumbing supply place puts empty wooden pallets out there, and for a while some bum who just liked starting fires kept torching the pallets and we were afraid he was going to burn down the building. We haven't had a problem since we caught the nut, but I didn't see any reason to remove the camera. Anyway, go get a cup of coffee or something and come back in half an hour and by then I'll probably have what you need."

DeMarco found a McDonald's and ordered a cheeseburger and fries. While he was eating, he called Neil. He said, "Were you able to get into Parker's phone records yet?"

"Yeah. I was going to call but got interrupted by a call from Homeland. There's this cyber gang in Belarus and they're . . . aw, never mind. Anyway, yeah, I got his records from my guy at Verizon. There was nothing out of the ordinary about the people he called. You know, people he worked with at the university, his ex-wife, a dry cleaner, a pizza place, and so on. He called Jenny McMillian, and she called and texted him a bunch of times. He sent two text messages the night of the accident. One said, 'Leaving diner.' The other one said, 'Crossing bridge.'"

Which was what DeMarco had suspected.

"Who'd he send the texts to?"

"A burner. No idea who it belongs to."

"Could you locate it?"

"No. Anyway, the last text he sent was to a woman named Lucy, who I think might be his boss. It says that a family emergency had come up and he was taking some time off and he didn't know when he'd return to work."

"When was that text sent?" DeMarco asked.

"The same day the other two were, but a couple hours later. About three in the morning."

DeMarco thought about Parker's last text. It appeared as if Parker had decided immediately after the accident not to go into work, but why send the text at that time of day? That seemed odd, but he didn't know what the significance of the timing was. He'd have to think about that.

After speaking to Neil, DeMarco called Lydia Chang. She answered the phone saying, "Hold on." Then he heard her say, "I have to take this call. I'll be back in a minute."

DeMarco figured she was probably in a meeting and wanted to go somewhere she could talk to him without anyone else hearing.

A moment later she said, "You son of a bitch! I told you not to talk to my daughter."

"Yeah, well, I did. I had to. Get over it." Before she could say anything else, he said, "We need to get together and talk. And as soon as possible. There're some things you need to know."

"Like what?"

"Can you meet me in an hour?"

"Yes. I'll have to cancel a meeting but—"

"Good. I'm in Rosslyn right now. Meet me at the Iwo Jima Memorial. Is that okay?"

"Yes."

DeMarco had picked the memorial because it was less than a mile from Richardson's office. But he wondered if he'd subconsciously picked it because of the veterans involved in this whole mess.

"I'll see you in an hour," DeMarco said.

DeMarco went back to Richardson's office.

Richardson wasn't behind his desk. He'd rolled his wheelchair over to a refrigerator and was taking a Coke from it and DeMarco could see that both his legs had been amputated above the knee.

He said to DeMarco, "Hang on." He rolled back behind his desk and picked up a flash drive and handed it to DeMarco. He said, "The security company sent me an email with twenty-four hours of video attached showing the alley for the time you wanted. I looked at it quickly, fast-forwarded through most of it, and about ten o'clock that night a car goes into the alley and the driver puts a man who I think is your homeless guy into the car. I couldn't see the driver's face, but maybe you can enhance the video in some way."

"Thank you, Mr. Richardson. I really appreciate your help, and I know Congressman Mahoney will too."

Richardson paused before saying, "One night—this was seven, eight years ago—a plane holding four coffins landed at Dover. One of my friends was in one of those coffins. This was after I was injured and I was back here in the States. Anyway, for some reason, Mahoney was there that night. I don't know why he was there, but he was by himself and there weren't a bunch of cameras around, so I know it wasn't a photo op. He never said a word to anyone. He just stood there while they unloaded the coffins and I could see tears in his eyes, and then he went over and put his hand on the flag on one of the coffins and left. You can let him know that I appreciated that."

"I will," DeMarco said, but he was thinking that even after all the years he'd worked for him, Mahoney continued to surprise him.

DeMarco arrived at the Iwo Jima Memorial before Lydia, and looked up at the hundred-ton bronze statue of the six Marines raising the American flag. He knew that the memorial was officially the Marine Corps War Memorial and not the Iwo Jima Memorial, although it was often called that, and that it was dedicated to all the Marines who had given their lives for the country since 1775, when the Marine Corps was founded. He also knew one other sad fact about the memorial.

The most famous of the flag raisers was a Native American named Ira Hayes. Hayes had portrayed himself in a John Wayne movie called *Sands of Iwo Jima*; he was portrayed by Tony Curtis in another movie called *The Outsider*; and had been the subject of a song by Johnny Cash called "The Ballad of Ira Hayes." But Hayes made DeMarco think of James Harris and his friend Bob, because Hayes had died tragically at the young age of thirty-two due to exposure to cold and alcohol poisoning. Thank you for your service, Ira.

He saw Lydia walking toward him. She was dressed in a tailored gray suit, a red blouse, and red high heels and had on sunglasses with large black frames. She looked like a movie star trying not to be recognized. The only other people at the memorial were a couple of tourists, a man and a woman, both very tall and very blond, wearing backpacks and hiking boots. DeMarco suspected they had descended from Vikings because of their appearance—and because their backpacks had Norwegian flag patches on them. They wandered away before Lydia reached him.

She looked simultaneously pissed off and worried. Pissed off because he'd talked to her daughter and worried because of the bind she was in. Before she could rebuke him again for speaking to Jenny, DeMarco said, "Your daughter's boyfriend was a guy named Noah Parker."

"'Was'?" Lydia said.

He ignored the question. "He was one of Jenny's professors."

"You're kidding."

"No. And I have proof that he was involved in setting up the accident."

"What kind of proof?"

"His phone records showed that he sent two text messages on the night of the accident, right before it happened. A friend of mine, who will keep his mouth shut, was able to get Parker's records because he knows the right person at Verizon. Anyway, one text said, 'Leaving diner.' Meaning the diner where Parker and Jenny ate on the night of the accident. The second one said, 'Crossing bridge.' The bridge he was referring to is about a mile from where the accident occurred. The texts were telling the video taker when Jenny would arrive at the place where she hit Harris so the video taker could make sure Harris was standing in the road at the right time. The problem is, Parker sent the texts to a burner phone, and I don't know who owns the phone."

"It was Zhou," Lydia said. "Or someone working for him."

"Maybe," DeMarco said. "But the other problem is that Parker's dead. Someone shot him in the head."

"Oh my God! Who killed him?"

"I don't know. He was probably killed by whoever took the video to make sure he didn't talk, but with him being dead I can't make him tell me who he was working with. But I may be able to find out."

"How?"

"Harris lived on the streets, near a mission in D.C. where they feed and shelter the homeless, and I figured that someone must have picked him up from that area and drove him to the place where the accident occurred. There's no other rational explanation for how he got there. He didn't own a car. So I found the place where he normally spent his nights and it was an alley that's monitored by a security camera. I haven't looked at the video footage myself yet, but another guy looked at it and he told me it shows Harris getting into a car the night he was killed. I'm going to look at the video as soon as I can and see if I can identify the person who picked up Harris, who is most likely the one who made him stand in the road so your daughter could hit him."

Before Lydia could interrupt, he said, "The reason I wanted to see you was to tell you what I've learned but also because you might want to do a couple of things to protect your daughter. But if you do these things, you'll be putting yourself and her in more legal jeopardy because you'll be helping cover up the crime she's committed."

"What are you talking about?"

"The cops can identify the car that was used to kill Harris if they find it because there's a defect on one of the tires. So you might want to think about getting four new tires for Jenny's car. The other thing is, the cops investigating Parker's murder fingerprinted his place to identify possible suspects and they might have gotten your daughter's prints. Do you know if she's ever been fingerprinted?"

"I don't think so. She's never been arrested or applied for a job that required fingerprints. But I'll ask her."

"If she hasn't been fingerprinted, then she's probably okay. But if she has been, then you need to come up with a reason for why she would have been in Parker's house. Like maybe she had to bring him a paper she didn't turn in on time, although it doesn't sound very plausible to me that she'd drive all the way to his place to turn in her homework. Anyway, see if you can come up with something that would explain why her prints would be in his house."

Like she could admit she was screwing him, but DeMarco didn't say that.

"Okay," Lydia said, sounding uncertain.

"The other thing is, the cops might get a warrant to look at Parker's phone records. I don't know if they'll do that, but Jenny also needs to be able to explain why they were calling and texting each other. You can probably make up any story you want as long as it's believable because Parker's dead and can't deny the story. Or Jenny could admit she was having an affair with him—that's not a crime—but the problem with doing that is she'll become the number one person of interest when it comes to his murder. Anyway, Jenny needs to be prepared in case the cops ask about phone calls and texts."

Lydia shook her head. "This is just going from bad to worse. Destroying evidence, lying to the police . . ."

"Yes, it is," DeMarco said. "And then there's the small problem that you're meeting with a Chinese spy. So before you start covering up what she did, you need to think hard about your daughter turning herself in and you telling the Bureau you're being blackmailed."

"I *have* thought hard about it!" Lydia shouted. Then she lowered her voice and said, "But I'm not ready to do that yet. You need to find out who picked up Harris and see if that'll help."

DeMarco almost said, *Hey, I don't work for you, lady*—but didn't.

Instead he said, "That's what I'm going to do next. And I'll let you know what I learn. But you need to talk to your daughter right away— and I mean, like, right after we're done here. She might not know that Parker's dead yet, but I imagine she'll find out pretty soon because the cops are talking to people at the university, and as much as she was in love with him, she's liable to go off the deep end and do something crazy."

18

DeMarco lived in a narrow town house made of white painted brick on P Street in Georgetown that he was still paying the mortgage on and would be for years to come unless he hit the lotto. When his first and only wife divorced him so she could marry, of all people, his closest cousin, she let him keep the house but took most of the furniture, the car he'd owned at the time, and everything he had in savings. He never forgave her or his cousin.

He got a beer from the refrigerator, sat down at the kitchen table, and plugged the flash drive Richardson had given him into his laptop. He fast-forwarded through the video to about ten p.m. when Richardson said the video showed a car driving down the alley.

Harris—DeMarco recognized him from the accident video—was lying down, sleeping or passed out near the blue door in the alley, the door where Purple Heart Bob said Harris spent his nights. At ten thirty a car drove down the alley. The car stopped near Harris and the driver got out. Based on the person's height relative to the roof of the car, the driver wasn't tall enough to be Zhou. DeMarco knew this because he'd seen the photo of Lydia and Zhou together, and Zhou was at least six inches taller than Lydia, who was about five nine, making Zhou about six foot three, and the person driving the car wasn't that tall.

The driver was wearing a dark hooded sweatshirt and black jeans. DeMarco couldn't see the driver's face. Whoever it was went over and talked to Harris for a bit, pulled him to his feet, led him to the car, and put him in the front passenger's seat, but the whole time the driver's back was to the camera or the hood obscured his or her face. And DeMarco was pretty sure the driver was a *her*. Not positive but pretty sure. The person was wearing tight jeans and the shape of the ass and the hips in the jeans was clear.

He got the impression the driver was also aware of the camera; this impression was reinforced not only by the way the person moved to avoid facing the camera but also because the license plate on the car had mud smeared on it, obscuring the numbers. As for the car, it was a dark-colored Honda Accord, one of the most popular cars sold in America.

Now what? He had a video showing Harris's killer, but he had no idea how to identify the person or prove the person was connected to Zhou.

He thought again about what Mike McGuire had told him: that the Chinese most likely wouldn't have set up the accident. The other thought he had was that if this was a Chinese intelligence operation, they probably would have sent more than one person to pick up Harris so they'd be sure they'd be able to control him. And although he suspected that Chinese intelligence agencies employed women, he doubted they'd use a single woman—if it was a woman who'd picked up Harris.

Which brought him to Diane Lake. She was the only other player involved in this mess that he knew of, and she was an ex–army officer and ex-CIA and she probably had the skills and the intelligence to plan a complex operation. Could she have been the one who picked up Harris, staged the accident and videoed it, and then gave the video to Zhou? No, that didn't make any sense. She was the one who'd told Mahoney about Zhou and Lydia, fully expecting that Mahoney would notify the FBI after he'd confirmed she was telling the truth. So why would Lake take a video that could be used to force Lydia to spy for the Chinese and then turn around and tell Mahoney so he could expose Lydia? What would Lake have to gain by doing that?

What he needed to do was see if he could eliminate Lake as a suspect. To do that, he needed to find out how big she was. The person who'd picked up Harris had been about the same height as Harris. He could find out how tall Harris was—the cops had done an autopsy so they'd have that information—and he could get Lake's height off her driver's license. And the person who'd picked up Harris hadn't been fat—hadn't been skinny, either—and if it turned out Lake was an overweight woman or a very thin one, that would eliminate her. He could also find out what kind of car she drove.

He looked at his watch. It was only five p.m. Perry would still be at work. DeMarco called him and said, "Call that detective that investigated the accident and ask her how tall Harris was and how much he weighed. Tell her you need to know so you can arrange a uniform for him for his funeral at Arlington."

"Why?" Perry asked.

"Please, just do it, Perry. I'm trying to figure something out." He didn't want to take the time to explain to Perry why he was looking into Diane Lake when he couldn't explain why Lake would have been involved in setting up the accident.

Next, he called Neil, who he knew would also still be in his office as he practically lived in his office. He said, "Take a peek at Diane Lake's driver's license and tell me how tall she is and how much she weighs. And I need to know what kind of car she drives." Surprisingly, Neil didn't whine about being too busy to help. He must have finished whatever he'd been doing when it came to the cyber gang in Belarus.

DeMarco spent the next hour doing laundry that he'd been neglecting. He thought about vacuuming and said to hell with it. He also called Mookie's phone, but Mookie didn't answer.

Perry called as he was pulling clothes out of the dryer. He said, "Harris was five foot seven and weighed about one ten. The guy was skin and bones."

Neil called twenty minutes later. He said, "Diane Lake is five foot seven and weighs one twenty per her driver's license, which, her being a woman, means she probably weighs more than that because women lie about their weight. She only owns one car, and it's a 2019 Honda."

"What model Honda?"

"An Accord."

DeMarco thanked Neil and hung up.

Well, well, he thought. *So the person who picked up Harris could have been Lake.* He couldn't prove it was her as he couldn't see her face in the video, nor could he positively tie the Accord to her because the license plate number hadn't been readable—but what were the odds that someone else the same size as Lake and driving the same model car she drove would have picked up Harris? And if she had orchestrated the killing of Harris, she was also most likely the person who'd killed Parker.

But *why* would she do it? Why would she take the risk of killing two people? And why would she go to all the trouble of setting up the hit-and-run accident, video the accident, and give the video to Zhou so he could blackmail Lydia—and then turn around and tell Mahoney about Zhou and Lydia? Why would she do that? What could have been her motive?

DeMarco supposed that one possible motive could be that she hated Dutch McMillian and wanted to cause him, his wife, and his daughter a world of grief. But what could possibly make her hate Dutch so much that she'd be willing to kill two people and possibly end up spending the rest of her life in prison?

No, hate didn't seem like the right motive. Although murder was often an exception, most crimes were committed for money. And it made more sense for Lake to have done this if someone had paid her to do it. But it would have to have been a lot of money to get her to kill two people. And who would pay her a lot of money? And *why* would someone pay her a lot of money?

Well, shit. He was giving himself a headache, going in circles.

He cooked a steak for dinner on his rusty barbecue, which was overdue for a replacement, then watched a show on Netflix called *Ripley*, based on the Patricia Highsmith book *The Talented Mr. Ripley*. This wasn't the movie with Matt Damon but starred some creepy actor he'd never heard of named Andrew Scott. And Scott was one of the most convincing sociopaths DeMarco had ever seen on film, a creature without a conscience, motivated only by social status and greed. After two episodes he went to bed hoping he'd dream the answers to the questions he had about Diane Lake.

19

Lieutenant Colonel Stephen Canfield was a lanky, narrow-shouldered guy who wore wire-rimmed glasses. He looked like a fit accountant, not a warrior, although DeMarco's perception may have been influenced by the fact that Canfield worked in the section of the Pentagon that manipulates the numbers the Department of Defense uses to keep its massive budget.

Canfield was Diane Lake's ex-husband.

DeMarco wanted to know more about Lake, like if she might have some personal axe to grind when it came to Dutch McMillian. And, in general, he wanted to know more about her personality. The only thing he currently knew was what Mahoney's friend Mike McGuire had said about her being ambitious and having quit the CIA because she had a higher opinion of herself than the Agency did. What DeMarco wanted to know was if she was capable of cold-blooded murder.

Killing in the heat of the moment is somewhat understandable. An argument escalates to violence, road rage turns into homicide. But killing someone in cold blood is different. Taking a human life intentionally isn't easy, and most people can't bring themselves to do it. They're afraid of going to prison. Some are afraid of going to hell. To kill in cold blood requires one to tamp down any feelings of compassion and fear of the consequences and usually requires a substantial motive. The motive could be revenge or hatred—or money. And what DeMarco wanted to know was if Lake was the sort of person who'd be willing to kill another human being if she was paid enough to do it. He figured one person who might be able to answer that question was her ex-husband.

DeMarco had lied his way into Canfield's office. He said he was a lawyer who worked for Congress—which was true—and that he'd been given an assignment by the Senate Ethics Committee—which was not true. Then he continued with a more elaborate lie.

He said, "A serious allegation has been made against Senator McMillian, the Senate majority leader, and the source of the allegation is your ex-wife who works for Vicount Analytics. I want to ask you some questions about Ms. Lake."

Canfield said, "Okay, but I doubt I can help you. I've never heard of Vicount, and it's been a long time since I've talked to Diane. We didn't stay in touch after we got divorced."

DeMarco said, "Vicount is a company that does opposition research for politicians. And according to Vicount's research—meaning your ex-wife's research—Senator McMillian has done something illegal. I'm not going to get into the specifics of the allegation, but I can tell you that it's false, and what I'm trying to understand is *why* Ms. Lake would make a false accusation against the senator.

"You see, the problem I'm having is your ex is a veteran, a West Point graduate, and there's nothing in her military file—or at least the unclassified, redacted version I saw—to indicate she's ever done anything unethical or illegal."

DeMarco said this having never looked at her file.

"And after she left the army, she was hired by the CIA, and they would have vetted her and wouldn't have hired her if she didn't have a clean slate or if her character was in any way questionable. So, like I said, I'm trying to understand why she would do this and I figured if anyone would know, it would be you since you were married to her."

"How do you know the accusation is false?"

"Because the committee has done enough digging to prove it's baseless."

"I see," Canfield said.

DeMarco said, "Does your ex-wife have some personal reason to dislike Senator McMillian? Did he do something harmful to her?"

"Not that I know of. When we were married, she voted Republican, but I can't ever remember her saying anything about McMillian either positive or negative. Maybe something happened since we divorced."

"If it wasn't a personal reason, do you think she'd do something like this if someone paid her enough?"

Canfield shrugged, which wasn't helpful.

"Well, can you tell me a little about her?" DeMarco said. "I mean about her character, her personality."

Canfield gnawed on the eraser end of a yellow pencil as he thought about the question. Finally he said, "Diane's one of the smartest and most ambitious people I've ever known. But she's also one of those people who blames everyone but herself when things don't go her way. At West Point, her goal was to be number one in our class and she worked her ass off to make that happen. At the time she and I attended the Point, there'd only been one woman who'd ever been the valedictorian, and Diane was determined to be the second one. But, as smart as she is, she isn't *that* smart. She tied for number ten in the class, which is still impressive. I mean, I was fifty-two in a class of nine hundred and fifty, and I don't consider myself a dummy, so graduating number ten is no mean achievement. But Diane couldn't accept that there were people better than her and she was convinced that the only reason she wasn't number one was because some professors screwed her over and were out to get her. She filed a formal complaint against one instructor who gave her a B+ instead of an A in one class, accusing him of being biased because she was a female. The complaint was bullshit and it didn't help her career after she graduated. And when she was posted to South Korea, she didn't get a promotion she thought she deserved and couldn't accept the fact that the officer who got it was better than her and that she was an abrasive asshole who was hard to work with. But when she didn't get the promotion, she claimed that the guy who made the selection didn't give it to her because she refused to sleep with him, which I know was a lie, but she almost ruined his career. But do I think she would do something illegal? The answer is, I doubt it. Her conscience wouldn't bother her, but she wouldn't take the risk of going to jail unless the payoff was enormous." There was a pause before Canfield added, "The truth is, I think Diane's a sociopath."

"A sociopath?" DeMarco said, which made him think of *Ripley*.

Canfield said, "I'm not saying she's some wacko serial killer nut. That's not what I mean. Diane, she's like, oh, Elizabeth Holmes. You know, the Theranos gal and the fake blood tests. Holmes is smart, attractive, and charming, and at the same time she's a lying, manipulative bitch willing to screw people who trusted her and commit fraud to make a fortune. That's the kind of sociopath I'm talking about."

DeMarco said, "Is that why you got divorced?"

"We got divorced because Diane was a pain in the ass to live with and I got tired of her being so bitter and bitching all the time about how the army was screwing her over. And I got tired of her nagging at me about not being more ambitious, like I was somehow dragging her down." Canfield smiled slightly. "And then, well, I had an affair, and when Diane found out about it, she pointed a gun at me and threatened to blow my head off. Frankly, the woman scares the hell out of me, and I'd just as soon not have what I'm telling you get back to her."

"It won't," DeMarco said. "This is totally confidential, and you won't be asked to testify before the committee."

"That's a relief," Canfield said.

"But I need you to keep this conversation to yourself until the committee has completed its work."

———— ◆◆◆ ————

DeMarco made the mistake of leaving the Pentagon through a different door than he'd used to enter it—and he didn't know where he'd parked his car in the enormous parking lot. He'd read somewhere that the Pentagon parking lot would accommodate over eight thousand vehicles and the lot appeared to be full.

As he walked around trying to locate his car, he thought about Diane Lake. He couldn't prove that she'd set up the accident but there were so many things pointing in her direction that he was almost positive she had.

He had the video of the person who'd picked up Harris in the alley and that person could have been a woman and could have been Lake, based on her height and weight.

The person drove the same kind of car as Lake, although a Honda Accord was one of the most common cars on the road.

Lake was very bright, she was ex-CIA, and she had the skills to plan and execute a complicated operation. And according to her ex-husband, she was a sociopath, and if that was true, she might be willing to kill two people if the reward was sufficient.

Lastly, she was the one who got the ball rolling by coming to Mahoney in the first place. Her claim that it was just a coincidence that she happened to see Lydia and Zhou meeting while jogging was plausible, but, considering everything else DeMarco knew, it might not have been a coincidence at all.

But none of the above was proof—not go-to-court, present-it-to-a-jury proof. And on the other side of the ledger, he couldn't prove that Lake had killed Noah Parker and couldn't prove that she'd conspired with him to set up the accident because Parker was dead. He couldn't even prove she had known Noah Parker.

Then there was still the issue of motive. He doubted, based on what her ex had said, that Lake would kill for some political reason, like she was determined to unseat McMillian because she objected to his politics. The only motive that made sense was money. But he was back to the questions: Who would pay her enough to make murder worth the risk? And why would someone pay her that kind of money?

———◆◆◆———

DeMarco wanted to talk to Mahoney, but Mavis informed him that Mahoney wouldn't be available until after nine p.m. He was doing an interview on the *PBS NewsHour*, which would give him the opportunity to lie about his accomplishments and blame the opposition for destroying the country. And if he was asked a question he didn't like, he'd give an answer that had nothing to do with the question. He was a master at doing that. Mavis said if DeMarco needed to see him today, he should meet him at the studio and talk to him after the interview.

DeMarco was trying to decide how he'd spend the day, thinking, *Why not go play a round of golf?* when his phone rang. It was Edna.

She said, "I found Mookie. He's at a place called Sleepy Creek Farm in Berkeley Springs, West Virginia. Berkeley Springs is only about two hours from D.C."

"How'd you find him?"

"I called every big pig farm in West Virginia I could find online. Called more than a dozen of them before I found him. I didn't speak to him—he was working—but when I asked if a guy named Mookie from Kentucky was there, the lady who answered the phone said he was."

"Okay, that's great, Edna," DeMarco said—but was really thinking he'd rather play golf than talk to Mookie. "I've got time to drive over there today, and I'll do that."

DeMarco was halfway to Berkeley Springs—a town with a population of about 750, located in the Appalachian Mountains in northern West Virginia, close to the Maryland border—when his phone rang. He saw it was Lydia Chang calling, probably to find out what he'd learned about the person who'd picked up Harris. She had to be feeling anxious as there were only four days left before she had to meet with Zhou again. He let the call go to voicemail. He didn't have anything new to tell her and he wasn't going to tell her that instead of working on her and her daughter's problems, he was on his way to a pig farm.

Two hours after leaving D.C., his map app guided him through a sixteen-foot-wide metal gate that had a wrought iron sign over it saying *Sleepy Creek Farm*. He drove down a half mile of bumpy dirt road and saw two large aluminum buildings domed like Quonset huts, and near them were metal pens filled with squealing pigs. Or maybe they were hogs. It occurred to him that he didn't know the difference between a pig and a hog—and decided he didn't care. Whatever they were—pigs or hogs—there were at least fifty animals in the pen and three pickup trucks were parked near the buildings and hopefully one of them was Mookie's.

He got out of his car and saw there was mud *everywhere*—in the pens, outside the pens, around the buildings—and DeMarco didn't see a path to the buildings where he wouldn't have to walk through mud. He had on the dark suit he'd worn to see Canfield and black loafers; he wished he had on boots—or hip waders. The sound of pigs squealing was deafening. And plaintive—as if they knew their fate.

Stepping carefully, trying and failing to keep his feet from sinking into the mud, he walked to the closest building, opened a door, and saw more pens and more pigs, some of them piglets. Most of the pigs were near feeding stations, gobbling up whatever was being dispensed. There were two bearded men standing near the pens, talking. They were wearing identical red ball caps and black rubber boots that came up to their knees. They saw DeMarco standing in the doorway in his suit and muddy loafers and one of them said something and they both laughed. One of the men walked over to him. His ball cap had an emblem showing a smiling, dancing pig and said *Sleepy Creek Farm*.

"Can I help you?" he said. "You lost or something?"

"No, I'm not lost. I'm looking for a man named Mookie. I was told he was here helping you butcher hogs."

"He was here but he's gone. He finished the work we had him doing and left a couple of hours ago."

"Well, shit," DeMarco said. "Do you have any idea where he was headed?"

"Nope, never asked and he never said. Why you looking for him?"

DeMarco said, "I'm a lawyer and he witnessed something and I'm trying to get him to testify."

"What did he witness?"

"I can't tell you."

DeMarco walked back to his car, his shoes squishing in the mud, thinking Mookie was going to be the death of him.

He called Edna to let her know that Mookie was in the wind again. "He might be on his way home. Keep an eye out for him."

"I'll do that," relentless Edna said.

20

The PBS studio was in Arlington, and a little before nine p.m. DeMarco parked near it. He could see Mahoney's driver standing by the gas-guzzling, armored Suburban used to haul Mahoney around.

The driver was a short-haired, broad-chested guy in his thirties, wearing a gray suit and dark blue tie, a gun visible in the holster on his belt—and probably intentionally so. Sometimes Mahoney would have just a single Capitol police officer for his protection; other times there might be two, and occasionally there would be a second car containing more bodyguards. DeMarco imagined the number of guards was based on the number of credible death threats Mahoney received from disgruntled citizens.

As DeMarco walked toward the driver, he saw the man move his right hand closer to the holstered pistol, but he didn't put his hand on it.

DeMarco said, "I'm here to see the congressman."

"You DeMarco?"

"Yeah. How'd you know?"

"Mavis called and said you might show up. She does that when she can so I don't accidentally shoot someone."

DeMarco went over and leaned against the Suburban. "What's your name?" he asked the driver.

"George."

"How do you like driving for Mahoney?"

"I like it fine, unless someone tries to kill him," George said. "I got bad feet and driving him around is better than patrolling the Capitol and trying to figure out which tourists are terrorists. And when I'm waiting while he does whatever he does, I play games on my iPad, chess, poker, solitaire, that kind of thing. And I'm learning tourist Italian from an online program. The wife wants to see Rome this summer so I'm learning how to say 'Can I have the check, please,' 'Where's the bathroom?' 'How much does a blowjob cost?'"

DeMarco looked at him and George said, "Just kiddin'. Like I said, I'm taking the wife. How 'bout you, what do you do?"

DeMarco shrugged and said, "I'm just a lawyer who does odd jobs for big shots like Mahoney."

"Huh," George said. "You don't look like a lawyer."

"What's a lawyer look like?" DeMarco asked.

"I don't know, but, uh, *slicker* than you. You look more like a guy who might *need* a lawyer."

Before DeMarco could respond, Mahoney emerged from the building and DeMarco walked up to him and said, "I need to talk to you."

"Yeah, all right, get in the car," Mahoney said, acting as if DeMarco had asked him to donate a kidney.

George held the back door open for Mahoney, then got behind the wheel while DeMarco slid onto the back seat next to Mahoney. Mahoney said to George, "Find someplace for me to get a drink—someplace quiet. You know."

As Mahoney hadn't had a drink in at least an hour, maybe two, he was probably starting to twitch. He usually had a flask on him or in the car, but he must have forgotten it, or it was empty. The driver tapped the map screen on the console and took off and two minutes later pulled into a strip mall that contained a dry cleaner, a tattoo parlor, and a copy shop that were closed and a Vietnamese restaurant that had a bar and was open. Based on the number of cars in front of the place, it didn't look busy.

"This okay?" George asked.

"Yeah," Mahoney said. "Give me the hat."

George handed Mahoney a red Washington Nationals ball cap and Mahoney stripped off his suit jacket and tie, put on the ball cap, and left the car with DeMarco following. The restaurant's bar was so dark you could barely make out the tables. There were only three people in the room: the bartender and two men sitting apart at the bar, nursing drinks, staring up bleary-eyed at a television showing a college softball game.

Mahoney walked over to the table farthest from the bar and before DeMarco could sit down he said, "Go get me a Maker's Mark. A double."

DeMarco did as ordered, got Mahoney's bourbon and a beer for himself, and paid for the drinks. Fucking Mahoney; he knew Mahoney wouldn't reimburse him. He brought the drinks back to the table and Mahoney slugged down half of his in one swallow.

"All right," he said. "What's going on?"

DeMarco told Mahoney everything he'd learned and everything he'd done. He told him about the surveillance video showing someone picking up Harris in the alley and the reasons why he was convinced the person was Lake, even though he couldn't prove it.

"I knew it," Mahoney said. "Goddamnit, I just knew it. My gut told me there was something off about her when she came to me with this thing, and I was right."

DeMarco wasn't really surprised. Mahoney's gut—his instincts—had allowed him to survive politically for forty years to become one of the biggest crocodiles in the swamp.

"But what I can't figure out," DeMarco said, "is why she would do this."

"Well, I can," Mahoney said. "Money."

"Yeah, I know," DeMarco said. "But she's not some mob hitman that would pop a guy for a few thousand bucks. She's not poor. And she's not a career criminal. I think it would take a hell of a lot of money to motivate her to kill two people, but I can't figure out who would be willing to pay her enough to do that."

"A lot of people," Mahoney said. "Individuals and companies in this country spend billions to get people elected. Or unelected. So the money's out there. And if Lake did this, she's most likely working for someone she met through Vicount. Some of Vicount's clients have so much money, they could topple third world governments. Or our government, for that matter. One of their clients owns a Supreme Court justice."

"You think Vicount, the company, would be involved in this?"

"No. The guys who run Vicount—I know 'em both—are willing to dig up dirt on anyone if they're paid enough, but they wouldn't be involved in murder. They're a couple of geeks who spend all day sitting behind their computers and don't have the balls to do anything more than punch a keyboard."

Mahoney sat for a moment, sipping bourbon, then picked up his phone and hit a button. He said, "Perry, get me a number for Jimmy Wong at Vicount."

To DeMarco, he said, "Go get me another drink while I'm waiting to hear back from Perry."

Shit. Mahoney's last drink had cost twelve bucks.

When DeMarco got back to the table, Mahoney was punching Wong's number into his phone. He didn't care that he might be waking Wong up.

The call must have gone to voicemail because Mahoney said, "This is John Mahoney. Call me back. Now."

While waiting, Mahoney drained half his drink, and when he got his return call, he lowered the volume on his phone and put it on speaker mode so DeMarco could hear. No one else in the bar was paying any attention to them.

Mahoney said, "Jimmy, who has Diane Lake been working for recently?"

"Why are you asking about Diane?"

"Because I am. Answer the question. Who's she been working for?"

There was a pause and Jimmy said, "Sir, with all due respect, I can't tell you who our clients are."

"With all due respect, Jimmy, who the fuck do you think you're talking to? I put the word out, you guys won't get another contract from anyone in the Democratic Party. And I might be able to poison you with the Republicans, too, if I put my mind to it."

Another pause. "Diane is no longer working for us," Jimmy said. "She quit a couple of months ago."

"She did?"

"Yes."

Mahoney glared at DeMarco. DeMarco had never bothered to see if Lake was still employed by Vicount; he just assumed she was.

"Well, who was she working for before she quit? Like, in the last six months or so."

"Let me think," Wong said. "There was Gleeson Manufacturing in Cleveland."

"What do they do?" Mahoney asked.

"They make airplane parts for Boeing and some of their parts come from a company in China that Diane was asked to research. She had to fly to China to get the information the client wanted."

"Who else?"

"She did a quick job for the chair of the Republican Party in Kansas, Mike Nichols."

"What was she doing for that asshole?"

"Researching a woman named Lisa Waters. She was running for the state senate."

"Oh, so you're the bastards who torpedoed her."

"Congressman, I—"

"I don't care," Mahoney said. "Who else?"

"Cyrus Offerman. He had us look into—"

"Thanks, Jimmy," Mahoney said, and hung up.

To DeMarco he said, "There you go. Cyrus Offerman. He's crazier than a fucking bedbug and richer than God. And he hates Dutch McMillian. Go get me another drink."

Goddamnit.

When DeMarco returned with Mahoney's third double, Mahoney said, "What do you know about Offerman?"

DeMarco said, "Just that he's a rich guy and a big donor."

Mahoney said, "Cyrus is ninety-something and, like I said, crazier than a fucking loon. He got interested in politics maybe thirty years ago, after he'd already made his fortune. He saw what guys like the Koch brothers were doing, throwing money out there to get what they wanted, and he saw how politicians would come crawling to them on their knees and kiss their asses. Well, Cyrus, he decided he wanted to be that kind of guy and have that kind of influence. It appealed to his ego, and, to be fair, he wanted to do some good. And thirty years ago he was fairly rational, but at ninety something, he's got about half his marbles and he's a vindictive old fart who will go after anyone who pisses him off. And when it comes to Dutch McMillian, when McMillian got those conservatives on the Supreme Court, Cyrus declared war on Dutch. He threw millions—and I mean *millions*—at the guy who ran against Dutch the last time, but of course Dutch still won, which made Cyrus even crazier. So I can see Cyrus paying Lake to go after Dutch and Lake comes up with this screwball plan to get Lydia arrested for spying for the Chinese."

DeMarco said, "The fact that she quit Vicount is also interesting. Maybe she found a better-paying job and that's why she quit. But if Offerman hired her to do something when it comes to McMillian, maybe he's paying her so much that she doesn't need another job." DeMarco shook his head. "But we don't know that Offerman hired her, and we don't have any proof that she did anything illegal."

Mahoney sipped his drink as he sat there thinking. He emptied the glass before he said, "I got a meeting in New York tomorrow afternoon. I think while I'm up there I'll drop in on Cyrus."

Mahoney looked at his watch and said, "You know, Mary Pat's still in Boston and I've got time for one more drink before I head home. I wanna see who wins the game."

Goddamnit, DeMarco thought. He'd already spent almost fifty bucks buying Mahoney drinks and he knew Mahoney didn't care who won the game. He just liked drinking and looking at college girls in tight shorts. DeMarco thought for a second about telling Mahoney that Mookie had eluded him again but he didn't feel like enduring Mahoney's ire, so he had another beer and watched the college girls with him.

21

A man in a black suit and a narrow black tie let Mahoney into Cyrus's apartment. Mahoney thought he might be Cyrus's butler but then the man stuck out his hand and said, "Good morning, Congressman. I'm Paul Waterhouse, Mr. Offerman's executive assistant."

"Yeah, nice to meet you," Mahoney said.

Waterhouse said, "Mr. Offerman will be with you in just a minute. Can I get you a cup of coffee while you're waiting?"

Before Mahoney could say he'd rather have a Bloody Mary, a door opened and a blonde who was more than six feet tall came into the room. She wore a knee-length coat that was unbuttoned and beneath the coat she had on a red string bikini, the bikini top barely containing a pair of D-cup knockers.

She ignored Waterhouse and Mahoney as she buttoned up the coat, then smiled slightly at Mahoney—whose eyes were popping out of his head—and left the apartment.

Waterhouse said, "It appears that Mr. Offerman is available now. Follow me."

Waterhouse led Mahoney into a room where Cyrus was sitting in an armchair, sipping what appeared to be a glass of orange juice. He was wearing a white bathrobe that was partially open displaying his hairless, chicken chest. In the middle of the room was a padded folding table.

———————— ◆◆◆ ————————

Cyrus had probably been five eight or nine when he was younger, but age had shrunk him to the point where—with his bald, liver-spotted head, wrinkled face, and spindly arms and legs—he looked like the creature Gollum in the *Lord of the Rings* movies.

He was currently number 11 on the Forbes 400 list and was worth approximately eighty billion dollars. He made his first million when he was twenty-two. His first billion when he was thirty-four. He'd been a brilliant, ruthless businessman—a genius some said—who never let morality stand in the way of making a profit. Now, after divorcing four wives and siring five children who didn't speak to him, he was ninety-two years old and couldn't remember what he had for breakfast.

Cyrus's ten-thousand-square-foot, ninety-million-dollar penthouse apartment, with its to-die-for view of Central Park, was on Billionaires' Row. Billionaires' Row, over the years, had been home to Jennifer Lopez and Alex Rodriguez, hedge fund managers Daniel Och and Bill Ackman, Michael Dell of Dell computers, and the musician, Sting. Cyrus lived alone in the enormous apartment—well, alone if you didn't count his live-in nurse, his chef, and his executive assistant, who did everything for him but wipe his ass.

———————— ◆◆◆ ————————

Cyrus said to Mahoney, "Did you see that gal who just left?"

"Yeah," Mahoney said.

"She's my masseuse. She's also a former Miss Sweden and I pay her five thousand bucks to give me a massage twice a week. You know why I pay her so much?"

Because she polishes your ancient knob? Mahoney thought but didn't say.

Cyrus cackled and said, "Because she's not only the best masseuse in New York but she goes topless when she works on me."

"Sounds like a bargain to me," Mahoney said, and he meant it.

"So why'd you want to see me? I suppose you want money for something."

"Well, there's a special election in Virginia that could use a little help, but I'm not here about that. I got a meeting here in the city this afternoon, and since I hadn't seen you in a while, I just decided to stop by and see how you were doing. The other reason is, Dutch McMillian is running for reelection in two years and there's a lady we want to run against him. She's a former army helicopter pilot who flew combat missions in Afghanistan. She's smart as a whip and we think she might have a chance of beating him and—"

Mahoney knew the former pilot didn't have a snowball's chance in hell of beating McMillian, but he noticed that while he was talking, Cyrus was smiling. Or smirking, to be exact.

"—and I was wondering if you'd like to meet her. Oh, and she's not bad looking either. I mean, she's no Miss Sweden but she's an attractive lady."

"I don't need to meet her," Cyrus said. "And you don't need to worry about that fucker McMillian. He's about to land in a shit stew."

"What are you talking about?" Mahoney said.

"I can't tell you, but believe me, McMillian's days are numbered."

Back at ground level, before he stepped into his car, Mahoney called DeMarco.

"It's Offerman. He's behind what's going on with Lydia Chang."

22

It all happened because Diane Lake impressed Cyrus Offerman.

At this point of his life, Cyrus didn't care about making money. Why would he at his age and with his fortune? Instead, he now spent his time going after anyone he didn't approve of or who didn't share his political views or who he considered bad for his version of America and democracy—or who simply annoyed him. A lot of people annoyed him. The list included journalists and newscasters and big-mouthed movie stars and, of course, politicians. He supported politicians who agreed with him and did his best to destroy those who didn't. And regardless of which political party a politician belonged to, if the politician offended Cyrus—who was easily offended—he did his best to ensure the politician lost his job.

Diane met Cyrus when he hired Vicount to research an idealistic state senator named Tim Graham, who'd pissed Cyrus off. The senator had gone on a rant on a talk show about how people like George Soros, Sheldon Adelson and his wife, and the Koch brothers undermined democracy by using their vast wealth to keep their pet politicians in power. And Cyrus had no problem with the senator's rant until he included Cyrus. He thought briefly about suing Graham for defamation but figured he'd probably lose the suit, so he decided to make sure he was never elected again.

He called Vicount, and Vicount sent him Diane Lake. The company sent Diane because the senior partners hated to deal with Cyrus—he was crude and abusive and treated them like indentured servants—and because they knew the old man, even at his age, enjoyed the company of pretty women.

Diane had never seen anything like Cyrus's apartment in New York. Not just the size of it—it was eight times bigger than her town house—but the view of the city and the furnishings were incredible. There was spectacular artwork in every room, man-sized statues and paintings in gilded frames on the walls. She didn't know anything about art but suspected that every piece she could see was worth more than she would earn in her lifetime. She couldn't even imagine what it must be like to have the kind of money Cyrus had: enough to purchase the top two floors of a skyscraper, enough to own private jets and helicopters and superyachts, enough to buy politicians.

Diane's first meeting with him was a brief one because his doctor, the best internist in New York City, was going to be there in five minutes to assess and adjust, if necessary, all the medications keeping Cyrus alive.

So Cyrus got right to the point.

He said, "Find something on this son of a bitch, Graham, that can be used to fuck him over."

Diane soon found that the task Cyrus had given her might be impossible.

Tim Graham lived in his ancient, ailing mother's home and took care of her and he lived exclusively on the hundred-and-twenty-thousand-dollar salary the state of New York paid him. Diane could find no evidence that he took bribes or committed insider trading or cheated on his taxes. He never took a campaign contribution that was illegal or came from a questionable source. He volunteered at a Boys & Girls Club in the Bronx and coached soccer and basketball to disadvantaged little kids. He served food to the homeless at a shelter one night a week. She followed him for a couple of days and never saw him approach a hooker or a drug dealer or even spit on the sidewalk. He gave money to almost every bum that stuck his hand out for a handout.

After a week, she went back to Cyrus and took a seat where she could see the park, a view that Cyrus was oblivious to after having seen it for so long. She said, "Mr. Offerman, I'm afraid I haven't been able to find anything that can be used to even damage, much less destroy, Tim Graham."

"Then you tell Wong and Peterman—"

Diane's bosses.

"—that I won't be using their fucking company again."

"Mr. Offerman, I didn't say it couldn't be done. It just can't be done, uh, ethically."

"Fuck ethically," Cyrus said. "What are you talking about?"

"Well, you see, sometimes all it takes is the appearance of guilt for a man to be deemed guilty."

"Quit beatin' about the bush and tell me what you mean."

"Tim Graham is almost forty and has never been married and doesn't have a girlfriend. Or a boyfriend. Some people find that odd. And Graham attended a seminary for a year, planning to become a Catholic priest, and Catholic priests have a certain reputation when it comes to little boys. Graham is a man who spends a lot of time around little boys."

"Ah," Cyrus said. "What's your name again, honey?"

"It's Diane Lake, Mr. Offerman."

"Call me Cyrus."

"Okay. Cyrus, I can give you what you want when it comes to Graham, but the problem is, my bosses won't go along with what I have in mind. They're rather, oh, straitlaced."

"You mean they're a couple of pussies."

"I wouldn't have put it that way, but what I'm saying is that I'm going to have to do this on my own time—I'll take a week off work—but

I expect to be paid. And because I might lose my job, I expect to be paid well."

"How much?"

"A hundred thousand."

She'd pulled the number out of thin air without even thinking about it, fully expecting Cyrus to tell her that there was no way in hell he was going to pay her that much. But he didn't.

He said, "Shit, is that all?"

Which, come to think about it, was an understandable reaction as a hundred thousand dollars was 0.000125% of Cyrus's net worth.

<hr />

A week later there was a photo in the *New York Post* of Tim Graham standing next to a man who was smiling at him and Graham was returning his smile. (Diane had paid the man smiling at Graham to be there and had taken the photo.) In the background was a cluster of ten-year-old boys wearing shorts, kicking a soccer ball around. The man with Graham was identified as a registered sex offender, a pedophile who'd recently been released from prison and wasn't allowed to be within ten miles of ten-year-old boys. The article in the *Post* crucified Graham by doing nothing more than asking questions. What's the senator doing talking to and being friendly with a known pedophile? Don't you find it odd that Graham, who's forty, has never been married? Could it possibly be that this man, who once aspired to the Catholic priesthood, might have something in common with many other disgraced Catholic priests? Graham claimed that the man—the convicted pedophile—had simply stopped and asked him for directions and that he didn't even know who the man was.

Yeah, right, his opponents in the state legislature said.

A couple days after the photo was published, a woman, an addict that Diane had paid, told the reporter who'd written the first article: "He was coachin' my boy, you know, down there at the rec center, until I put a stop to that. I just didn't like the way he touched and looked at my Billy, if you know what I mean."

Oh, yeah, we know what you mean.

The final straw was an unnamed "highly placed source" who worked for the Archdiocese of New York and who said that the reason Graham left the seminary and didn't become a priest had to do with an "impropriety" involving an altar boy, although the source couldn't be more specific due to certain legalities.

And that's all it took when it came to former state senator Tim Graham.

And it was because of how she'd handled Graham that Cyrus called Diane a month later and told her he had another job for her, something much bigger than a state senator.

Cyrus said, "I want you to nail that son of a bitch Dutch McMillian. I've had it with that motherfucker. If you're able to pull it off, I'll pay you whatever you want."

Diane said, "Okay, but I need to figure out how to do it first. McMillian won't be as easy as Graham."

"Well, once you figure it out, come back and see me, honey, and like I said, you can write your own ticket."

23

After thirty years in politics and being the Republican leader of the U.S. Senate, every aspect of McMillian's personal and professional life had already been put under a microscope, and if there'd been anything that could have been used to damage him, the Democrats would have found it and used it years ago. So Diane wasn't going to waste any time researching McMillian. Nor would she spend much time on his wife. Because of who her husband was, Lydia Chang's life had been scrutinized as closely as McMillian's.

She knew from the outset she was going to have to *manufacture* something to harm McMillian, but it couldn't be anything as simple as she'd done with Tim Graham. Innuendo, baseless rumors, and gossip weren't going to harm Dutch. And she had to come up with something *huge*, a 9.0 on the political Richter scale. The thought occurred to her that if McMillian's wife or daughter had committed a crime—an actual crime, one that could be proven—that might cause McMillian the kind of problem that Cyrus wanted him to have. But for the crime to damage McMillian, he would have to be involved in some way; he'd have to be an accessory.

She decided to focus first on McMillian's daughter, Jenny. She was nineteen and more likely than her mother or her father to do something impulsive and stupid. One thought that occurred to her was that maybe she could pin a drug-related crime on the girl. College kids did drugs and maybe she could come up with something along the lines of Jenny not only doing drugs but maybe giving drugs to another college kid, and the kid OD'd. Yeah, she could probably make that happen, but it wouldn't harm Dutch. All Dutch would do was bemoan the fact that his daughter was an addict, and he would stand by her, but he wouldn't be personally tarnished in any way by her actions. No, the daughter and drugs wouldn't do it. She needed something else, something bigger. But she didn't know what.

Although she didn't expect anything to come of it, she decided to spend a few days following Jenny, hoping to come up with an idea. So she called in sick and tailed Jenny around the Georgetown campus and to bars that served underage college kids where she went with her friends. She researched her roommate briefly to see if there might be something there that she could use. The whole time she was watching Jenny, her mind was constantly spinning, trying—and failing—to come up with a viable plan. She was starting to think she might have to switch tactics and take a closer look at Lydia Chang's business dealings.

On the afternoon of the third day, Diane was standing in a hallway, pretending to study a corkboard with flyers pinned to it advertising student meetings and concerts and people offering their services as tutors. She was waiting for Jenny to come out of a classroom, and because the building had multiple exits, she had to wait inside.

One of the flyers on the corkboard caught her eye. It was a photo of a car with the passenger-side door smashed in and the side mirror dangling from its wires. The flyer had been posted by the student who owned the car, saying it had been hit in one of the dorms' parking lots and he was looking for witnesses who could identify the hit-and-run driver. For some reason Diane felt a little mental twitch when she saw the damaged car but didn't know why.

The classroom door opened, and students, mostly girls, began to pour out. But Jenny wasn't among them. Finally, she emerged from the classroom with a man who appeared to be about thirty. Diane figured he had to be the professor who taught the class. And he was *gorgeous*: curly, tousled blond hair, dimples in his cheeks when he smiled. He was dressed a bit shabbily—a worn corduroy jacket, jeans, shoes in need of a shine—but considering what most college professors made, that wasn't surprising.

Jenny was speaking to him earnestly, and as she talked, she looked up at him adoringly. He nodded in response to whatever she was saying, but Diane got the impression he wasn't really listening to her. He glanced at his watch and started walking, Jenny trailing along beside him.

They left the building together, Jenny having to walk fast to keep up with him because his legs were much longer than hers. The girl reminded Diane of puppy following its master. They crossed a street and walked half a block before coming to a small coffee shop. The professor stopped in front of the shop, Jenny still jabbering, him still nodding, then he went into the shop. Jenny stood for a moment after he went inside, looking dejected—like a *lost* puppy—before she finally turned and walked back toward the campus.

Diane didn't bother to follow Jenny. An idea had come to her, inspired by the photo of the damaged car she'd seen on the corkboard. But to make the idea work, there would have to be another player—like the professor that Jenny was so obviously smitten with.

She walked over to the coffee shop and glanced through a window. The professor was sitting with a blonde who couldn't have been more than eighteen or nineteen years old. And where Jenny McMillian was short, practically flat-chested, and almost homely, the blonde was *stunning*: long legs revealed by a short skirt, perfect breasts, pert little nose, luscious lips.

Diane, her instincts tingling, went into the coffee shop, ordered a mocha, and took a seat where she could observe the professor and the girl, who Diane was sure was a student. The professor was clearly trying to charm her. He was completely focused on her, gazing intently into her eyes. He said something witty, and the girl tossed her head back and laughed. At one point the professor looked around the coffee shop to see if anyone was watching—Diane pretended to study her phone—and he put his hand on the girl's tanned, bare thigh.

And Diane thought: *He is* exactly *who I need.*

Diane left the coffee shop and went back to the classroom, got the number of the room and the name of the building it was in, found a class directory online, and an hour later had the name of the professor: Noah Parker.

She then spent a couple of days researching Parker as if he were the target of a Vicount investigation. He taught a creative writing course even though he'd never published a novel. (He'd been working on one for ten years.) She learned that he was practically broke as more than half his salary went to his ex-wife and two kids he never saw. He had no savings, was carrying eight thousand dollars in credit card debt, and lived in a shithole outside of D.C. because the shithole belonged to a dying aunt and the aunt let him live there rent-free. And when the aunt died, he'd be homeless because he wasn't mentioned in her will. She also learned that he'd been reprimanded once by the university for having an inappropriate relationship with a student; the reason he wasn't fired was because he hadn't slept with the girl. He would have slept with her, but another professor saw him and the girl together, acting way too chummy, and reported him. But after seeing him with the leggy blonde in the coffee shop, it was clear that Parker hadn't taken the reprimand seriously and Diane had no doubt that he was planning to, or was already, sleeping with another student.

And as she was researching Parker the other elements of the plan came together: the hit-and-run accident; the Chinese-born mother married to the senator; Zhou Enlai—and little Jenny and the professor.

Yes, it would work if Parker would do it.

But would he? Would he do it if she paid him enough?

The only way to find out was by asking him.

***

She knocked on the door of Parker's shabby house.

He opened the door, saw her standing on his porch, and said, "Yes?"

He was wearing jeans and a T-shirt and needed a shave, but he was still cute as a button.

She said, "My name's Diane. And I have a proposition for you, one that will make you a lot of money."

"What are you talking about?"

"May I come in?"

Parker took a long look at her, his eyes roaming over her body. She may not have been nineteen years old, but she knew men found her attractive.

He said, "Yeah, okay. I'm intrigued."

The interior of the house, as she'd expected, was a mess. Clothes strewn about, unwashed dishes in the sink, the furnishings decades old. On his kitchen table was a stack of paper, most likely stories or essays written by his students that he was supposed to be grading.

"Would you like a drink?" he asked.

"Sure," she said.

"Wine okay?"

She imagined she'd be treated to a glass of Two Buck Chuck but said, "Sounds great."

He poured wine for them, and she could see the little wheels spinning in his pretty head, thinking that after a few drinks he might be able to get her into bed. It was time to nip that idea in the bud and get down to business.

She said, "What I want you to do is seduce one of your students. And don't bother denying you're above such a thing because I know you're not."

"Hey, I wouldn't—"

She raised a hand, cutting off the phony protest. "If you succeed, I'll pay you fifty thousand dollars." Well, Cyrus would pay him; it wouldn't come out of her end.

His mouth dropped open in shock, but he didn't say anything immediately, and she could tell he was now thinking about how much he could use the money. Fifty thousand was about half his annual salary.

"Why do you want me to seduce this woman?"

"She's not a woman. She's a girl. She's nineteen years old. Like I said, one of your students."

"What's her name?"

"Jenny McMillian."

"Jenny? You're kidding."

"Do you know who her father is?"

"No. All I know is that she's an overachiever who's constantly bugging me."

Diane said, "Jenny's the daughter of Senator Dutch McMillian."

"Really," he said. Then the light bulb went on. "Is this, what you want me to do, is it some political thing?"

What a genius. "All you need to know is that if you can get her to go to bed with you, you'll make fifty grand. Actually, I need you to make her fall in love with you. And I'm not going to tell you—not yet, anyway—why I want you to do this because I don't know if you can pull it off. Maybe she won't want to have anything to do with you."

He smirked—the smirk meaning: *As if.*

She said, "Well, will you do it or not?"

He didn't say anything. He finished the wine in his glass and poured himself another.

Finally he said, "You're serious. Fifty thousand."

"Yes, in cash. I'll give you half up front—you'll get the money the day after tomorrow—but you won't get the other half unless you're successful."

"How long do I have to make this happen? I mean, it could take a little time to, you know, romance her."

"I'll give you three weeks. If you haven't gotten her in bed by then, you never will. And, by the way, in case you haven't already figured it out, you can't get caught screwing her, because if you're caught, the university will fire your ass and then you won't be any use to me."

It only took him two weeks.

24

The first thing Diane did after launching Noah Parker at Jenny McMillian like a wire-guided missile was fly to New York to see Cyrus Offerman. She wasn't going to do anything else until she got Cyrus to agree to pay her the amount she wanted. And she needed the cash to pay Parker.

Cyrus met her in a room where there was a padded folding table. He was dressed in a white bathrobe, his knobby chest and his disgusting, gnarled legs visible. He told Diane he was waiting for his masseuse to show up—and Diane couldn't imagine how repulsive touching the old goat must be.

She said, "I've figured out a way to get McMillian. But in order to do it, I'm going to have to commit a couple of crimes, which means that I could end up in jail. And because of that, I expect to be paid a lot."

"How much is a lot?"

"Twenty million."

Cyrus's white, bushy eyebrows elevated in surprise.

Diane said, "After I've done this for you, I want to be set for life."

"And you're sure what you've got in mind will destroy that prick?"

"It will not only destroy *him* but also his wife and his daughter. So are you willing to pay me what I want?"

"Hell yes," Cyrus said. He'd donated five times the amount she wanted to politicians he wanted elected or unelected. Twenty million was a virtual drop in Cyrus's financial bucket.

"So what are you going to do?" Cyrus asked.

"I'm not going to tell you specifically because if I tell you, you'll become an accessory to any crimes I commit. And like I said, I'm going to have to commit some crimes. Serious crimes."

The real reason Diane didn't want to tell him what she was planning was because she was afraid the senile son of a bitch would tell someone and screw everything up. And if he paid her, he would become an accessory no matter what she told him.

"But in general," she said, "what I'm going to do is cause McMillian's daughter to commit a crime and then cause her mother to commit a second crime and McMillian will become tainted by his wife's crime and it will end his career. And you'll know when something happens to McMillian and his family because it will be the only thing they talk about on the news for months after it happens. And I'll give you a heads-up right before it happens so you'll know that I'm the one who caused it."

Cyrus didn't say anything as he mulled over what she'd told him. Finally, he said, "So I'm supposed to just hand over twenty million and trust you." As he was saying this, he reached under the bathrobe and scratched his ancient nuts.

She noticed that he had no objection morally or otherwise to what she was planning; his only concern was paying her and not getting what she promised.

"Yes, but not completely," she said. "I want ten million up front and that's to compensate me for the crimes I'm going to commit and so that I'll have money in the bank in case I need to run. But I don't expect you to pay me the other ten until after I've driven a stake through McMillian's heart. And we both know that if I try to steal from you, you've got the connections to send someone to make me regret it."

"You got that right, honey," Cyrus said, his small dark eyes locked onto hers.

And for the first time he scared her. He might have had one foot in the grave, but with his money, until he was actually *in* the grave, he wasn't a man she wanted for an enemy.

"How long will this take?" he asked.

"I don't know for sure. Maybe a couple of months. But you've had to put up with McMillian for thirty years, so what's two more months?"

Diane just hoped the old bastard didn't die before he paid her the second ten million.

25

After seeing Cyrus, Diane returned to Washington and quit her job at Vicount Analytics. She needed to spend all her time on the McMillian project, and she wouldn't need a job afterward. Not with ten million in the bank and another ten coming. Jimmy Wong was pissed that she quit without giving the company any notice. Well, fuck Jimmy. It wasn't like she was going to ask him for a letter of recommendation.

She then met with Noah and gave him the twenty-five thousand she'd promised him for attempting to seduce Jenny. She told him, "You can't put that money in your bank account. If you do, you might have a problem with the IRS. But the other thing is, you don't want anyone, like anyone in law enforcement, to know you've come into a large amount of cash."

"Why would law enforcement—"

"Do you understand me, Noah? Don't put the money in a bank. Hide it here in your house someplace. And don't go out right away and make a big purchase, like a new car. You can buy yourself some new clothes, but don't buy anything big or pay down your credit card debt right away. When this thing's all over with, I'll show you how to launder the cash through a casino, and then you'll be able to bank it, but not yet."

"Yeah, okay," he said, although he looked confused.

———◆◆◆———

While Noah was seducing and bedding Jenny, Diane went about putting together the other elements of her plan. The plan was complicated—there were multiple parts to it—but not so complicated that she couldn't manage it.

First, she drove around the area where Noah lived and found the perfect place for the accident, the curve on Turkey Foot Road about a mile from his place. That took a couple of days.

She then spent four days hanging around a mission in the poorest part of D.C. that, God bless 'em, provided shelter and hot meals for the homeless. The bums congregating near the mission were as thick as fleas on a mangy dog. She found two candidates, men who appeared to go to the mission every night for a meal but didn't spend the night there as the weather was balmy enough for them to sleep outside like animals.

She never knew, or tried to find out, either man's name. One she called "Army Jacket" because he wore a stained, beat-to-shit old army field jacket. The other was "Redskins Cap" because he wore a Redskins baseball cap, one from back in the day when the Commanders were called the Redskins. The two men had two things in common. First, neither man was very big. They were both short, about five six or seven, and their bodies were so wasted away that they couldn't have weighed more than a hundred and twenty pounds. Their size was important because she might have to muscle them around a bit. Diane was five seven herself and also weighed about one twenty, but she was in good shape, and she was strong, and she wouldn't have a problem if she had to get physical with either of them.

The other thing the two bums had in common was that after decades of drinking and doing drugs, their minds had turned to mush. She knew this after giving them a handout and trying to engage them in a conversation; neither of them was capable of a conversation. So they were perfect. And the reason she picked two of them was in case one of them died or disappeared before she needed them.

The last thing she got was from a street dealer who operated off a corner in a neighborhood in Baltimore that terrified her. She would have felt safer in Mogadishu. So when she went to see the dealer, she took her gun, a Beretta, the kind of gun she'd trained on in the army. The Beretta was unregistered as she'd bought it on a whim at a gun show in Virginia. From the dealer, after a considerable amount of discussion and negotiation—part of which was necessary to convince him she wasn't an undercover cop—she acquired a syringe filled with one hundred percent pure, uncut heroin, for which she paid five times its street value. She was hoping she wouldn't have to use the heroin but wanted it as a backup.

It occurred to her more than once as she was setting things up that the idea of killing someone didn't really bother her. She supposed it should have—but the truth was, it didn't. She wasn't like drone operators she'd known in the army who fell apart mentally and physically when they dropped bombs that killed a few innocent civilians who happened to be standing too close to the target. She knew if she'd been a drone operator she wouldn't have felt any remorse. Did that make her a monster because she could live with taking the life of another human being—because she knew she wouldn't be racked by guilt? She didn't think so. She wasn't a psychopath. She didn't kill for the sake of killing; killing didn't give her any pleasure, sexual or otherwise. She was simply a rational person, able to control her emotions, and only willing to kill if the reward was enough to make it worth the risk. And the amount of money Cyrus was paying her was worth the risk. No, she wasn't worried about the impact killing would have on her psyche; the only thing she was worried about was getting caught.

———◆◆◆———

After she had everything she needed, she sat down with Noah again. By then he'd slept with Jenny three times.

The first thing she did was hand him a bag containing twenty-five thousand dollars in cash, the second half of the fifty thousand she'd promised him.

He looked into the bag, smiled, and said, "Thanks. Now are you going to tell me why you wanted me to sleep with her?"

Diane said, "How would you like to earn another hundred thousand?"

"Jesus! Who do you want me to fuck next? The first lady?"

"No. But you'll have to do something a lot harder and riskier than seducing a naive coed. Which is why you'll be paid so much."

Diane had decided to use both the carrot and the stick when it came to Noah. The hundred thousand was the carrot. Now for the stick.

"But," she said, "if you don't do what I want, then I'm going to rat you out to the university for fucking Jenny McMillian, and then not only won't you get the hundred thousand, but you'll be out of a job and you won't be able to get a job at another university. In fact, you might not be able to get a job with anyone doing anything once Dutch McMillian finds out you screwed his daughter."

"I don't like the way you're talking to me. And I don't like being threatened."

"Tough shit."

"What do you want me to do?"

"You're going to get into a hit-and-run auto accident with Jenny."

"Are you insane?"

After a lot of back-and-forth, a lot of handwringing and handholding and more threats, he agreed to do what she wanted as she knew he would. If he hadn't agreed, she would have been forced to kill him and start over. She had the Beretta in her pocket in case it came to that. But, fortunately, it didn't.

The next day Diane gave Noah half the hundred thousand she'd promised him and told him again to hide it in his house and not make any major purchases. Then she showed him the diner where he was going to take Jenny to dinner and get her drunk. She showed him the road they'd take home and where the accident would occur. She walked him through all the details, told him everything he'd have to do. She told him how he would text her when he left the diner and again when he crossed over the bridge. She told him the most important thing was that he had to convince Jenny to leave the scene of the accident. But she didn't tell him what would happen after the accident.

The odd part was that after she convinced him to help her, he became an enthusiastic participant, helping her work through the details and seeming to enjoy it. It was almost as if he didn't grasp that his actions were going to result in the death of a man. It was like he was working out the plot to a novel he was trying to write. Noah Parker, she concluded, was a bit of a sociopath.

The night of the accident, Diane went to the Good Shepherd Mission and drove around, looking for Redskins Cap or Army Jacket. She didn't see Redskins Cap but there was Army Jacket, lying on the ground in an alley, in the doorway of an abandoned warehouse. She'd learned while she'd been watching them that this was the place where Army Jacket spent his nights. She also knew there was a surveillance camera pointing down the alley—why there'd be a camera there, she had no idea—but she was prepared for the camera. She also figured that the likelihood of anyone looking at the video from the alley camera was minuscule. The cops in Montgomery County weren't going to spend many man-hours on the death of a D.C. bum and it was highly unlikely they'd learn about the alley where the bum slept.

She looked around and didn't see anyone nearby. She drove her car down the alley and stopped next to where Army Jacket was lying. She'd obscured her license plate numbers in case someone did look at the surveillance camera video. She walked up to him, her back to the camera, and kicked one of his feet until he woke up.

She said, "You're going to come with me."

He said, "Wha?"

She said, "Come on, get up." She reached down and pulled him to his feet. "If you come with me, you can have this," and showed him a pint-sized bottle of Hennessy cognac.

"Really?"

"Yeah, really."

"Where we going?"

"I'm going to help you."

"Help?"

"Yeah. Now come along. I'm not going to hurt you. And if you come with me, I'll also give you this." She held up a hundred-dollar bill, and when he reached for it—so slowly, as if he were reaching through a wall of Jell-O—she snatched the bill away. "Like I said, you'll get the money if you come with me."

She took his arm and led the poor brain-damaged dummy over to her car. He didn't resist at all. She doubted he were capable of resisting. She doubted it even occurred to him to resist. As she maneuvered him into the car, she was ever mindful of the surveillance camera. She would have worn a mask, like a Covid mask, but she didn't because she was afraid a mask might alarm him and make him less willing to go with her voluntarily. And, again, she really wasn't worried much about anyone looking at the video from the alley camera, thinking the possibility of that happening was beyond remote.

Inside the car, the odor of him almost knocked her out, and she rolled down all the windows. As they were driving, he sat there sipping cognac, humming a song she recognized but couldn't name, and then fell asleep.

She arrived at the curve on Turkey Foot Road about eleven thirty. She parked her car about seventy-five yards away from the curve on a tractor path that ran between two fields and turned off the lights. She doubted her car would be noticed by anyone driving by. Then she just sat with the sleeping, stinking bum and waited.

Noah was supposed to leave the restaurant with Jenny about midnight and text Diane when he did. When she got Noah's text, she waited fifteen minutes, then woke up Army Jacket and pulled him out of the car. She said, "I want you to come with me. Okay?"

He said, "Where?" She guessed he was asking where they were.

"Just come along," she said.

She grasped his arm and walked him down the short tractor path toward the curve. He shuffled next to her, muttering words she couldn't understand, still clutching the brandy bottle in his hand, not resisting as she tugged him forward.

Two minutes later, Noah texted that he and Jenny had just crossed the bridge, and Diane led Army Jacket to the middle of the road and then took out her gun and pointed it at his head. When he saw the gun, she could tell it scared him, but he seemed more confused than frightened, as if he couldn't process what was happening.

He said, "Why—"

She said, "I want you to stand right where you're at. If you move, I'm going to shoot you. Do you understand."

"No. Why—"

She backed away from him, saying, "Don't you dare fuckin' move. Or I'll kill you. Just stand there. Drink your brandy."

She looked at her watch. All he had to do was stand there for less than a minute, no more than forty seconds.

She lay down in the grass near the side of the road and took out her phone. She was dressed all in black and would be invisible in the darkness. The camera was ready for shooting in low light. She called out, "Don't move or I'll kill you. Don't move."

He didn't. He stood there swaying, the bottle of brandy in his grubby right hand, looking bewildered.

She aimed her phone's camera at him then started the video, and a few seconds later Jenny McMillian hit him with her car.

26

From that point forward, there were things that were out of Diane's control, which she hated.

First, she had to rely on Noah to convince Jenny to leave the scene of the accident whether Army Jacket was alive or not. If Noah couldn't talk her into leaving, then Diane was screwed. But she was pretty sure he would be successful as the girl was young and drunk and traumatized by what had just happened and would probably do what he told her to do, being older than her and an authority figure.

The second thing she couldn't control was the accident killing Army Jacket. If the accident did kill him and if Noah could convince the girl to leave, then everything would be hunky-dory. But if the accident *didn't* kill the bum, then Noah would have to talk her into leaving the scene anyway, telling her that he'd call 911 after they drove away, and make a fake call to 911. And then what Diane would do was inject Army Jacket with the uncut heroin to finish him off. For her plan to work, Jenny McMillian had to be responsible for a hit-and-run *homicide*, not an injury.

As it turned out, things worked perfectly. Jenny killed Army Jacket and Noah easily talked her into leaving.

Part one of her plan was complete.

On to part two.

Diane followed Jenny and Noah from the accident site to Noah's house and then had to wait two and a half hours before Jenny left to drive home. She imagined it took that long for Noah to settle her down. And she wouldn't have been surprised if he'd had sex with the girl.

After Jenny left, Diane put on a pair of latex gloves and knocked on Noah's door. He opened it without asking who was knocking, probably thinking Jenny had returned for some reason. He was wearing boxer shorts and a T-shirt and he was barefoot. Yep, the son of a bitch had slept with her before he sent her on her way.

He said, "Uh, what—"

She walked past him and into the house and said, "Get your phone."

"Why?"

"Just get it."

He got his cell phone from off the table in the kitchen and she said, "Sit down."

He shook his head, puzzled but not concerned, and took a seat in a recliner and she sat across from him.

"So what's going on?" he asked. "Everything worked out just like you wanted."

She said, "I want you to send a text to your boss."

"Now? It's three in the morning."

Diane said, "It doesn't matter. What's your boss's name?"

"Lucy Hamilton."

"Do you call her Lucy or Miss Hamilton or Dean or what?"

"Lucy."

"Okay. Type 'Lucy, something's happened, a family thing, and I'm going to have to take some time off. I'm sorry but it's an emergency and I don't know when I'll be back to work.'"

"Why do you want me to—"

She took out the Beretta and pointed it at his head.

"What are you doing?" he said.

She said, "Type what I told you or I'll kill you." She repeated the text and he typed and when he was done, she said, "Don't send the text. Let me see the phone."

He handed her his phone, and when he did, he said, "Why are you wearing gloves?"

She ignored the question, looked at the words he'd typed, hit the send button, and put his phone in one of her pockets.

"What's going on?" he said. "I've done everything you—"

Still pointing the gun at him, she said, "Where's the cash I gave you?"

Like an idiot, he glanced over at his fireplace, one with fake logs that was propane fueled. He said, "I hid it here in the house like you said. But why are you asking? Are you planning to steal the money from me?"

"Yes," she said. "You won't need it."

She shot him. She shot him in the center of his forehead, just above the bridge of his perfect nose.

She picked up the ejected shell casing and walked over to the fireplace, got down on her knees, and groped behind the fake logs. And there in a plastic bag was the money she'd given him. She didn't bother to count it, but it appeared as if he hadn't spent much of the hundred grand she'd given him. She then spent a few minutes opening and rifling through drawers to make it appear as if someone had searched the house. She saw his wallet sitting on the kitchen table and took the cash from it. She had noticed the first time she came to his place that his mail was delivered through a slot next to the front door, so she didn't have to worry about mail piling up in his mailbox. She closed the blinds on his front window so no one would see a corpse sitting in a chair.

She stood for a moment thinking, trying to decide if there was anything else she needed to do. She wasn't worried about leaving her fingerprints in the house. She was wearing gloves, and the last time she'd been here she'd sat on the couch and hadn't touched anything in the house. She did have a glass of wine that one time, but that had been a while ago and even a slob like him would have washed the wine glass by now.

"You did good," she said to the dead man, and left the house.

27

Diane hadn't lied to Mahoney when she told him she knew Zhou Enlai from her days at the CIA—and she knew Zhou would be perfect. She knew he was bright and ambitious and assumed that he wasn't satisfied being the number two intelligence officer at the embassy; he wanted to be number one. The CIA had been able to put together a dossier on him with information obtained from sources in China and they knew he came from a wealthy family; his father was a Chinese oligarch, although they pretended they didn't have oligarchs in China. His father was also a confidant of Xi Jinping. And she was hoping that because he came from a wealthy, connected family that he'd be willing to act independently. The problem was that Chinese intelligence agencies were no different than American intelligence agencies: they were bureaucracies staffed with ass-covering, cautious bureaucrats who would sometimes take forever to make a decision. She was hoping that Zhou, once he realized the significance of the gift she was about to give him, would take action on his own, without consulting his superiors, because he'd want all the glory and would feel relatively safe because of his family connections. And she was also hoping that he'd act fast. She couldn't collect the other ten million from Cyrus Offerman until Zhou had done his job.

What she needed to do next was present her gift to Zhou. And she wanted to do this in such a manner that he wouldn't be able to identify her. But the first thing she had to do was doctor the video of Jenny killing the bum. As she didn't know how to do this, she had to hire a kid she found online to show her.

Using her phone, she took a video of people walking down a street and had the kid show her how to obscure images in the video and remove audio material. Once he showed her how to do it, she transferred the video of the accident to a flash drive, then blocked out Jenny's face and the license plate on her car and deleted any mention of Jenny's name.

Next, she found an online article in the *Montgomery County Sentinel* that reported that a man named James Harris—so that's who Army Jacket was—had been killed in a hit-and-run accident on Turkey Foot Road and that the Montgomery County Sheriff's office was asking citizens who might have any information to come forward. Harris's body had been found the morning after he was killed, and the article appeared in the paper the next day.

Zhou Enlai lived in a million-dollar condo within walking distance of the Chinese embassy. Diane imagined that the condo had been purchased by his rich daddy as an investment and because he wanted his son to enjoy a nice lifestyle while stationed abroad. Diane wrote a note to Zhou, then put the note, the flash drive of the doctored video, and a paper copy of the *Sentinel* article discussing the accident in a padded mailing envelope addressed to him. She drove to his apartment, and because she was concerned about cameras capturing her image, she put on a Covid mask, large sunglasses, and a baseball cap before approaching the building. She put the envelope in an Amazon drop box near the entrance to the building and a large yellow Post-it note on the entrance door saying he had a package in the drop box.

The note in the envelope said: "I'm willing to sell you the original of the enclosed video, which will allow you to recruit an asset in the American government the likes of which you can't even imagine. Call me at this number—it's a burner phone—and call me from a burner that I can call and text you on."

He called that night. Sounding cheerful, Zhou said, "So. I'm intrigued."

"I'll bet you are," Diane said.

"What's your name?"

"I'm not going to tell you. But I know that you're an intelligence officer stationed at the embassy. You're the number two boy."

She had said that to wound his pride and make it more likely he'd do something to become the number one boy.

"What's the significance of the video?"

"Did you watch it?"

"Yes."

"Well, as you saw, it's a video of a hit-and-run accident, the one reported in the article I sent you. The woman in the video, whose face I've obscured, is the daughter of one of the highest-ranking people in the United States government, and you can use the video to blackmail that person or his wife into providing you information."

"How do I know the video is real? These days, filmmakers can make anything look real."

"I guess it could be a fake, although it's not, but you know the accident really happened because of the newspaper article and you could also call the sheriff's office to verify what the article says."

"And how did you come by this video?"

"I'm the one who took the video. I'm the one who set up the accident. I'm the one who forced that man to stand in the road so the woman would hit him with her car."

"And why would you do that?"

Now came the tricky part. She had to tell Zhou why she had set up the accident but couldn't tell him the reason she had done it was to get a shit-load of money from Cyrus Offerman. But she decided to stick close to the truth without telling the whole truth. She said, "I set up the accident and videoed it because I was supposed to be paid a lot of money for doing so. The original plan was to use the video to hurt the high-ranking individual I mentioned politically. But then the person who hired me refused to pay me what the video is worth, so I decided to find another buyer."

"How much do you want?"

"A million. U.S. dollars, of course."

Zhou laughed and said, "Oh, is that all. I can tell you that there is no way my government will authorize that sort of payment based on what you've told me."

"I'll tell you one more thing. The high-ranking person involved is periodically briefed by the White House national security advisor and the director of national intelligence—and that's the kind of information you would have access to. If you send me a hundred thousand dollars, call it a down payment, then I'll send you the original of the video and explain to you how it can be used. I'll send you a text telling you where to wire the money."

Diane figured that Zhou could personally afford a hundred grand or that the embassy had a slush fund available to intelligence officers for paying sources and agents. He'd easily be able to come up with the money. A hundred thousand dollars was just as trivial to the Chinese government as it was to Cyrus Offerman.

Diane said, "Now, you're probably thinking that once you have the complete video, you'll be able to rip me off and not pay me the other nine hundred thousand. But if you do that and try to use the asset I'm giving you, then I'll rat you and the asset out to the FBI."

What Zhou didn't realize was that she didn't care if he didn't give her the money. The only reason she had asked for the money was that she'd have no credibility if she gave him Jenny McMillian for free.

———◆◆◆———

Twenty-four hours later, a hundred thousand was wired to an offshore account and then Diane immediately rewired it to another offshore account. Neither account was traceable to her.

She called Zhou after she'd banked the money and said, "I'm going to send you a text that contains the unaltered video right now."

She sent the text and heard Zhou's phone ding when he received it. She said, "Go ahead and play it."

She waited a couple of minutes, then said, "The girl in that video is Jenny McMillian, the only daughter of Dutch McMillian, the Republican leader of the United States Senate. And that video is proof that she committed vehicular homicide and fled the scene and she'll go to jail for ten years if the cops see the video. And as I'm sure you've already figured out, because you're a bright fellow, the video can be used to blackmail Dutch McMillian or his wife. Now it's up to you, but I think the one you want to approach is Dutch's wife, Lydia Chang. She's privy to the kind of information her husband gets because he confides in her, and I think, being the girl's mother, she'll be more malleable than the father. But it's up to you."

"Hmm," Zhou said as he thought over everything she'd told him. And she was pretty sure he'd go after Lydia and not Dutch. Dutch was a hard-nosed son of a bitch—he'd throw his daughter to the wolves before he'd become a Chinese agent—and he was also a guy who Zhou would have a hard time approaching because he was constantly surrounded by his own security people.

"So when are you going to send me the other nine hundred thousand?" Diane said.

"Well, not for a little while. As you can imagine, I need to think about all this and see if what you're suggesting is viable. I need to see if McMillian or his wife will be, uh, cooperative."

"Fine," Diane said, "but like I said before, if you use what I've given you and don't pay me, then I'll feed you to the Bureau."

The next day she started following Lydia Chang.

And three days later, when she saw Lydia meet with Zhou in the park in Arlington, she took their photograph.

Now she had only one thing left to do.

She had to tell someone that Zhou and Lydia were meeting.

She had to betray Zhou Enlai.

It would have been nice to get twenty million from Cyrus and another million from the Chinese government, but she knew she'd never get the nine hundred thousand Zhou owed her because she planned to screw Zhou as soon as possible.

All she had to do to collect the remainder of her fee from Cyrus was tell someone that Lydia Chang was meeting with Zhou and then the person she told would tell the FBI—and Dutch McMillian's world would be blown to smithereens. His daughter would be arrested for the hit-and-run accident, and his wife would be arrested for spying for the Chinese. And people would assume that Dutch had known what his wife was doing and that he'd assisted her. And although she doubted that Dutch would be arrested, he would definitely come under suspicion, and he wouldn't be allowed access to classified information until it was proven he was innocent. And there was something else. There were influential folks in the Republican Party who were no longer happy with Dutch and they would push for his ouster from his leadership position after his wife was exposed. And Cyrus would be elated when the shit hit the fan, and she'd collect the other ten million, and then—

Well, she didn't know exactly what she'd do next. What she did know was that her life was going to change drastically and for the better.

The person she picked to destroy Dutch McMillian was John Mahoney.

Mahoney and McMillian had been flinging stones at each other for years, and she figured that Mahoney would jump at the chance to ruin Dutch. She also figured, as she'd told Mahoney, that he would have credibility with the FBI, and the Bureau was more likely to act quickly if it was Mahoney who told them about Zhou and Lydia. But she knew it would take a little time before Mahoney contacted the FBI because he'd first have to have someone verify that Lydia was really meeting with Zhou. Then the FBI would waste a bit more time before it acted. But she figured in less than a couple of weeks Dutch's life would explode.

After she met Mahoney at the restaurant in Virginia and showed him the photo of Zhou and Lydia, she called Cyrus and said, "Watch the news. It's going to happen soon."

28

Diane was pulling clothes from her bedroom closet and tossing them into a large cardboard box. She was getting rid of everything she wouldn't take with her when she started her new life.

After she met with Mahoney, she spent some time thinking about what she was going to do next and decided that she wanted to live someplace where she'd get the most bang for her buck, where she could stretch the twenty million from Cyrus as far as possible, which meant leaving the United States. She settled on Costa Rica.

She'd found a site on the Internet called the Annual Global Retirement Index. The index took into account the cost of living in various countries and evaluated things like taxes, health care systems, government stability, crime, and so on. The number one place on the list was Costa Rica, followed by Portugal and Mexico, and she decided that Costa Rica would be perfect. It was a favorite landing spot for expats, with its lovely beaches and tropical climate.

She'd hired a real estate agent to put her town house on the market—she figured she'd clear about a hundred grand—and today a truck and a couple of lugs from Goodwill would come by and haul off all her furniture except for a few pieces she'd keep to stage the apartment for selling. And they'd take away the clothes she was discarding along with everything else in the place except for a few utensils she'd keep so she'd be able to cook at home until she left. Once she arrived in Costa Rica, she'd go house hunting. She didn't intend to spend more than a million for a home there—she didn't need a mansion—but the house she bought would have an ocean view and a swimming pool. She'd take Spanish lessons so she'd be able to communicate with the natives and was certain she'd have no problem picking up the language: Spanish was nowhere near as hard to learn as Mandarin. She'd also join a country club, one that was expensive enough to keep out the riffraff, and learn to play golf, a game she'd never had time to play before. And she imagined that she'd make friends with the country club set, people in her income bracket who she'd socialize with. Who knows: she might even find a lover. She was so looking forward to her new life, living the way a person with her brains and talent deserved to live.

She'd been raised on army bases, living in the substandard housing provided to enlisted men like her father. She'd gotten an appointment to West Point in part because her family couldn't afford to send her to one of the better universities, like Harvard or Stanford or Yale. But the other thing was, she'd envisioned, with her intelligence and work ethic, rising through the ranks to the four-star level. Becoming one of the Joint Chiefs wasn't out of the question. She knew that the army didn't pay what the private sector did, even at the general officer level, but what came with four stars was a reputation for leadership and competence that followed a general after he or she left the military. Generals retired from the army to sit on corporate boards and run companies. They went into politics and got elected. Most of them became millionaires.

But then the army just screwed her. In order for her to rise to the level she desired, she needed to be posted to a combat zone—that was where the glory was and the opportunity to shine—and Afghanistan was the hottest war zone at the time she graduated from the Point and that was where she wanted to be sent. But the army wouldn't do that for her, and in a way it was her own fault. She'd been encouraged to take Mandarin at West Point because she'd shown an aptitude for learning languages, and she took the courses thinking it would be good to know the language of the country's number one enemy. But the result of learning Mandarin was that, instead of being posted to a combat zone, she was stuck in China-related intelligence units, given shitty postings and shitty assignments. And people, almost all of them men nowhere near as good as she was, were promoted faster.

She realized that after six years she'd never rise to the level she aspired to in the army, so she resigned and switched to the CIA, thinking it would provide a path forward. She'd seen how people like Leon Panetta, Dave Petraeus, and Mike Pompeo—all ex–army men who became CIA directors—had risen to national prominence and figured there was no reason she couldn't do the same. But instead of placing her in a job that would propel her rapidly to the top, she was stuck in a cubicle, watching and analyzing the Chinese, and where her boss took credit for everything she did.

Yes, she'd wasted a decade of her life in service to her country—six years in the army and four with the CIA—and had virtually nothing to show for it. A two-bedroom, cookie-cutter town house. An economy car with a hundred thousand miles on the odometer. A 401(k) that almost guaranteed a penny-pinching retirement. So she gave up on ever becoming someone in the country's national security apparatus and switched to Vicount only because Wong and Peterman paid better than the CIA. They paid her enough to have an upper-middle-class lifestyle— but middle class was still fucking middle class.

Well, finally, thanks to Cyrus Offerman, she was able to reach escape velocity. She wouldn't have the power and fame that she'd always wanted but she'd be rich. *Rich* rich, not middle-class rich.

The only thing keeping her from leaving D.C. and starting her new life was that the news had yet to break that Lydia Chang was spying for the Chinese. Until that happened, she needed to stick around in case she had to do something. She'd met with Mahoney twelve days ago and she couldn't understand why McMillian and his wife weren't the hot topic on every cable news channel. She wondered if the FBI was dragging its big, bureaucratic feet. Maybe she should call Mahoney and ask him why nothing had happened.

She'd just had that thought when her phone rang. It was Cyrus Offerman calling. What did that crazy old goat want?

"Hello," she said.

"When's this thing gonna happen—the thing that's gonna destroy McMillian?"

She said, "I told you it would take a little time. You need to be patient."

"Patience, my ass! John Mahoney came to see me today."

"He did?"

"Yeah. He was trying to get me to cough up some dough to support a candidate they want to run against McMillian, but I told him not to worry about McMillian—that he wasn't going to be a problem."

Oh, fuck. This is what she'd been terrified of: the senile old bastard running his mouth.

"What else did you tell him?" Diane asked. "Did you tell him anything about me?"

"No. I didn't tell him anything else. I just said that McMillian was toast. And you better not make a liar out of me, honey. But this thing, whatever you're doing, needs to get done and get done soon."

"It'll happen; don't worry," Diane said.

"Well, it sure as shit better happen. And if it doesn't, you're gonna give me back the ten I gave you."

"Hey, that wasn't our deal," Diane said.

"You know, honey, people have tried to cheat me before, and when my lawyers can't get 'em, I know other folks who can." Cyrus hung up before Diane could respond.

There was no way she was giving back the ten million Cyrus had given her, no matter what happened with McMillian. That was her money. But she had to find out why Mahoney hadn't told the FBI about Lydia. And why would he make a pitch to Cyrus for a candidate to run against McMillian when she'd given him everything he needed to destroy McMillian?

She had to find out what the hell was going on.

29

DeMarco had two problems. He had to get Zhou off Lydia Chang's back and he had to figure out what to do about Diane Lake. But at least now he knew Lake's motive after Mahoney called him from New York: Cyrus Offerman was most likely paying her an obscene amount of money to hurt McMillian.

He mulled the situation over and called Mike McGuire, Mahoney's retired CIA buddy. He said, "I need some advice."

McGuire owned a home near Middleburg, Virginia.

The house was a two-story Craftsman with two chimneys protruding from the roof, a large front porch, and an attached greenhouse. It sat on ten acres of low, rolling hills surrounded by white-rail wood fences. In a verdant pasture in front of the house were two horses munching grass and next to the house was a red barn—or maybe it was a stable—that was bigger than the house. It was an impressive piece of property.

McGuire let him in then said, "You want a beer?"

"Sure," DeMarco said.

McGuire got the beers and said, "It's nice out. Let's sit outside."

They took seats on two rocking chairs on the porch that looked out at the pasture.

"Nice spread you have here," DeMarco said, but was wondering how McGuire was able to afford it. He may have been ex-CIA, but he was still a retired civil servant, and civil service didn't pay enough to afford a home like this.

Maybe knowing what DeMarco was thinking, McGuire said, "I married into money. Above my station, as they say. This place belonged to my wife's family, and she inherited it."

"Is your wife here?" DeMarco asked. He'd prefer that they speak alone.

"No. She's dead. She died nine months ago, right after I retired."

"I'm sorry," DeMarco said.

McGuire said, "I was gone more than I was home when I was working, and she raised my daughter mostly by herself. I figured when I retired, we'd finally be able to spend time together, and then she goes and gets cancer." McGuire sighed and said, "God's a joker."

They sat silently for a moment, looking out at the pasture. To change the topic, DeMarco said, "Pretty horses."

McGuire shook his head and said, "Those fucking things. I got two granddaughters that are nuts about horses and I bought those animals so I could spend more time with them. But they're costing me a fortune. Fodder, riding lessons, veterinarians, saddles, and all the other shit you gotta buy when you own horses. On top of that, they hate me."

"Your granddaughters hate you?" DeMarco said.

"No, not my granddaughters. The fucking horses. They're fine with my granddaughters—gentle as can be—but every time I come near them, they try to bite me or kick me or whack me with their tails. I keep hoping my granddaughters will lose interest in them so I can sell them to whoever turns horses into glue. Anyway, what can I do for you?"

"Like Mahoney told you, we got a situation where a Chinese intelligence officer who's posted to the embassy in Washington is blackmailing a woman into providing him with information. What I want to know is, what would the CIA do if they became aware of the situation?"

McGuire said, "Well, the first thing the company would think about doing is turning the asset into a double agent and using the asset to feed the Chinese bad information—information that, if the Chinese acted on it, would cause them problems. For example, telling the Chinese that there's a traitor in their house and the Chinese start spending money and manpower trying to find the traitor and they get all paranoid and don't know who to trust. We did that one time with an asset the Taliban had acquired. We used the asset to give them the name of a guy who wasn't really a traitor, but the Taliban ended up cutting the guy's head off, which was what we wanted. The other thing the CIA would think about is seeing if the asset could turn the intelligence officer and get him spying for us."

"Well, that won't work in this case. This asset can't be turned into a double agent."

"Then you burn the asset so she's no good to the Chinese."

"What does that mean?"

"If she holds a job where she's got access to classified information, you get her transferred or fired."

"That also won't work," DeMarco said. He couldn't tell McGuire that Lydia didn't have a job that provided her access to classified information but instead that she was married to the man who had access.

"Then you turn her ass over to the FBI," McGuire said, "and she gets arrested and that's the end of it."

"Can't do that either," DeMarco said.

Well, he could. He could tell the FBI about Lydia Chang and she'd be arrested—or, if not arrested, she wouldn't be meeting with Zhou again—but that wasn't what Mahoney wanted. For that matter, that wasn't what DeMarco wanted, either, knowing now that two people had been killed to blackmail Lydia. He wanted the killer to suffer, not Lydia.

"Are there any other options?" DeMarco asked.

"Yeah, there's one more. You get the State Department to expel the intelligence officer from the country. We expel diplomats all the time who we know or suspect are spies. And you don't need proof that they're spying. At the start of the Ukrainian war, we expelled a dozen Russians working at embassies in this country that we knew or suspected were intelligence officers and European countries expelled almost two hundred of the Russian bastards. Naturally, when we expel some of their guys, they expel some of ours in retaliation, so there will be some blowback."

But DeMarco was thinking that getting Zhou expelled wouldn't work because Mahoney would have to explain that the reason why he wanted him expelled was because he'd gotten his hooks into Lydia Chang—and the whole objective was to get Lydia off the hook without exposing her. But then it occurred to DeMarco that there might be another way to deal with Zhou, but he needed to know more about the man.

DeMarco said, "I'm going to tell you something that Mahoney didn't tell you. The intelligence officer involved in this is a guy named Zhou Enlai. He's supposedly an embassy cultural attaché but he's really the number two spy at the Chinese embassy. Is there any way you could get me more information about him from your pals at Langley? I mean discreetly, without telling anyone why you're asking about him."

"How long has he been at the embassy?"

"I don't know."

"Well, if he was there two years ago, I know a guy I could call. He retired about the same time I did but in the job he had—and if Zhou was around before he retired—he should know something about him."

"Can you call him?"

"You mean now?"

"Yeah."

"Okay. Let me get you another beer and I'll give him a call. Hopefully, he'll still be sober. After he retired, he decided to take up drinking for a hobby."

McGuire brought DeMarco a second Budweiser, then went back inside the house to call his friend. As DeMarco sat there sipping the beer, he watched the horses. They were like a couple of long-necked vacuum cleaners, moving slowly from one green spot to the next, sucking up grass. It seemed like a boring existence, and he imagined they liked it when McGuire's granddaughters came to ride them. But DeMarco was like McGuire when it came to horses. He didn't want anything to do with them.

He'd only ridden a horse once in his life. He'd been dating a woman who wanted to go horseback riding on a beach, so he took her, and DeMarco's horse just sat there, unwilling to move, like its big hooves were stuck in the sand. His date told him he had to show the beast that he was in control and that what he needed to do was kick a twelve-hundred-pound animal with big teeth in the ribs to get it moving—which, frankly, he was afraid to do. And when he finally did kick the horse, the fucking thing took off like Man o' War in the Kentucky Derby, and he clung to the saddle horn, terrified, bouncing up and down on his balls while his date laughed her ass off.

Yeah, he was not a horse fan.

Fifteen minutes passed before McGuire came back and sat in the rocking chair again. He said, "Zhou's a young guy, in his thirties. His family's got money and his dad's tight with Xi Jinping, and according to my buddy, Zhou's living the life of Riley over here. He's married, but his wife's in China, and he's got a hot blond girlfriend who's a yoga instructor. He lives in a nice condo that his daddy paid for, drives a Porsche, attends embassy parties three, four times a week, goes out to dinner at expensive places, and plays tennis at damn near the professional level. One year, when we had two feet of snow here, he took his girlfriend to Jamaica. At the time my buddy retired, they hadn't identified any-one Zhou was running. His job appears to be making connections with people who might be useful and he's probably pretty good at it because he's a charming guy. What he does during the day inside the embassy, we don't know."

DeMarco didn't care what Zhou did inside the embassy. He'd heard enough. He didn't know if what he was thinking would work but he didn't have anything to lose by trying. And it wasn't like he had another option.

30

Lydia called as DeMarco was driving back to D.C. from McGuire's place in Middleburg. He hadn't spoken to her since their meeting at the Iwo Jima Memorial two days ago, and he'd ignored her call when he was on his way to the pig farm in West Virginia.

He said hello and she shrieked: "Why didn't you return my call yesterday? I need to know what's happening."

Lydia was a woman used to getting what she wanted and used to giving orders and was still under the impression that DeMarco was working for her. The last thing he'd told her was that he was trying to figure out who killed Harris—and he was pretty sure he had. But he didn't want to tell Lydia about Diane Lake because he didn't know what Lydia might do. And he didn't want her doing anything about Lake until *he'd* figured out what to do about her.

Lydia said, "A detective from the Montgomery County Sheriff's office came to see Jenny yesterday. Fortunately, I was with her when he showed up. I went to see her after the last time I talked to you, and she'd just heard about Parker's death, and she was practically catatonic. So I made her come home with me so I could keep my eye on her. I'm seriously concerned that she might try to harm herself."

For the first time, DeMarco felt sorry for Jenny. She'd been deeply in love with Parker—he was probably the first big love of her life—and now he was dead. Then there was whatever regret or remorse she was feeling for having killed Harris and the anxiety of being a criminal because she'd fled the scene of the accident. He was glad Lydia, who hadn't struck him as being particularly maternal, had decided to take time off work to care for her.

"Why'd the detective come?" DeMarco asked. "Did they identify her from her fingerprints at Parker's place?"

"No. She's never been fingerprinted. It was like you said. They got Parker's phone records, and the detective interviewed her because he saw a bunch of calls and text messages between Jenny and Parker. And because there were so many, he wanted to know if Jenny might have any information that could lead to Parker's killer, like if he'd been having problems with anyone or had told her that he was afraid for his life or anything like that."

"What did Jenny tell him?"

"I did most of the talking because she couldn't stop crying. I told him that Jenny had been close to Parker, that he'd been a mentor to her, and she was very upset about his death. Regarding all the phone calls, I told him that Parker had been her creative writing teacher and he'd been working on a novel, and that Jenny had been doing research and proofreading for him, and that's why they talked so often and met occasionally out of class."

"Did he buy it?"

"I think so. I looked at text messages Jenny sent him that were still on her phone, and they were, oh, *innocuous*, mostly things like 'I'll see you at six,' or 'Pick me up at the Starbucks,' or 'Call me, please'—that sort of thing. One said, 'Why won't you return my calls?' But nothing that pointed directly to them having an affair."

"Huh," DeMarco said, surprised to hear that, considering how infatuated Jenny had been with Parker. He wondered if Parker had told her to keep text messages and voicemails free of any sort of love talk, maybe spinning some tale about the need to be careful in case the university was ever able to get its hands on their phones. Or maybe Lake had told Parker to tell the girl that. Whatever the case, it appeared as if Jenny had exercised some phone discipline, which was good when it came to hiding her affair with Parker from the cops.

Lydia said, "The other thing is, I got the impression that this detective couldn't imagine a nineteen-year-old college girl having anything to do with Parker's murder, especially not a girl whose father is a senator. Anyway, we told him she had no idea why anyone would want to kill Parker, and he went away happy. I think."

"Good," DeMarco said. "What did you do about the tires on her car?"

"I told the garage repairing it to replace them. And the detective never asked about the car she drove or asked to see it. He was investigating Parker's murder, not the accident. And whoever's investigating the accident hasn't contacted her."

"Then it sounds like she's okay when it comes to Parker's death and the accident."

"No, she's not okay because the video is still out there and I'm not okay because Zhou's still blackmailing me. Did you find out who picked up Harris from the alley?"

DeMarco figured a lie was in order. He said, "I looked at the video like I told you I would, but I couldn't see the person clearly because of the lighting and because it was taken by a cheap camera, so I'm having a tech guy I know see if he can clean it up."

When he said this, he felt a little mental tingle, though he didn't know exactly why. But what he'd said about cleaning up the video had caused it.

"And then what?" Lydia said. "What will you do if you can identify the person? For that matter, what will you do if you can't?"

"I don't know."

"Well, goddamnit, I have to meet with Zhou in three days and I have to tell him something."

"Yeah, I know. And I'm doing the best I can."

"Well, work faster," Lydia said.

DeMarco could have told her what he had in mind when it came to Zhou but decided not to. For one thing, he wasn't sure it would work. The other thing was she might object—and he was going to do what he was planning whether she objected or not.

31

DeMarco needed to talk to Zhou, but he wasn't going to call the embassy and ask to speak to him because some sneaky outfit like the NSA might be monitoring Zhou's phone calls. And he wasn't about to go to the Chinese embassy to see him. He imagined the FBI watched the embassy to see who was going in and out of there, and FBI agents probably followed Chinese intelligence officers periodically—or maybe all the time—and he certainly didn't want to be identified going into the embassy or being seen with Zhou. He figured the best place to meet him was at his apartment.

Zhou had a penthouse apartment in a six-story building about two blocks from the Chinese embassy. From the top floor, he'd have a lovely view of the spires of the National Cathedral. In an alcove near the building's main entrance was a panel with an intercom and doorbells where the residents' names were listed. There was also a camera above the panel so people in the building could see who was ringing their doorbell. He figured ringing Zhou's doorbell should be safe enough because if the FBI was watching the building, they probably wouldn't know who he was or make the effort to find out, and they wouldn't know whose doorbell he was ringing. He hoped.

DeMarco checked his watch. It was almost six, so maybe Zhou would be home. If he wasn't, he'd have to come back later; he hoped the damn guy wasn't planning to spend the night with his mistress. He pressed the doorbell, and a moment later a man answered, saying, "Yes. Who are you?" He spoke English with a slight British accent and DeMarco wondered if he'd gotten part of his education at some place like Oxford.

Looking into the camera, DeMarco said, "My name's DeMarco. I work for John Mahoney. You know, the former Speaker of the House. I need to talk to you."

"Really?"

"Yes."

After a brief pause, Zhou said, "Okay, come on up."

DeMarco noticed that Zhou sounded friendly and not at all apprehensive.

Zhou smiled at DeMarco when he let him into the apartment. He was wearing tuxedo pants with a black stripe down the legs and a heavily starched white shirt with gold cuff links. Around his neck was an untied black bow tie. He had perfect teeth and glossy dark hair and was so good-looking he could have made a fortune as a male model. He said, "I'd offer you a drink, but I don't have a lot of time. I'm going to a function tonight and need to leave in fifteen minutes. But please sit down and tell me what I can do for you."

DeMarco's initial reaction, odd as it was, was that he liked the guy. He was, as McGuire's retired friend had said, a charming devil.

DeMarco took a seat on a couch and Zhou sat across from him, leaned back, and crossed one long leg over the other. He wasn't the least bit nervous.

DeMarco said, "Well, this won't take long. I'm here to tell you that if you don't stop squeezing Lydia Chang for information, Mahoney's going to have your ass expelled from the country."

DeMarco was betting—based on what McGuire had told him about Zhou's lifestyle—that simply the threat of expulsion might be enough to get Zhou to back off. He wouldn't want to lose his cushy job and his condo and his girlfriend, nor would he want to get kicked out of the United States and maybe be posted to someplace in Africa for fucking up.

Zhou raised an eyebrow, pretending to be puzzled, and said, "I don't know what you're talking about?"

"Sure you do. Someone sent you a video of Lydia's daughter killing a man with her car, and you used the video to force Lydia to meet with you and you've been pressing her to give you classified information. You've met with her twice and I've got a photo of you meeting with her in a park in Falls Church. So if you don't stop blackmailing her by threatening to give the video to the cops, the U.S. government is going to boot you out of the country. And if you give the video to the cops, you'll also be booted out of the country."

"So why not have me expelled?" Zhou said. Before DeMarco could answer, Zhou, who was obviously quite bright, said, "I'm guessing the reason is that Mahoney wants to protect Lydia Chang. He doesn't want the fact that she met with me to get out. Why would Mahoney protect her?"

"I honestly don't know. I urged Mahoney to go to the FBI as soon as he learned you were meeting with her, but for some reason he decided not to do that. But why, I don't know. It's always hard to predict what Mahoney might do in any given situation because the last thing Mahoney is is predictable. But if you don't back off—or, like I said, if the video is given to the cops and her daughter is arrested—then he'll do whatever's necessary to get you expelled."

Zhou sat silently for a moment, then shrugged and said, "Okay."

"Okay what?" DeMarco said.

"Okay, I'll leave Lydia alone and keep the video to myself. In the espionage game, you win some, you lose some. Lydia Chang was a gift

I couldn't pass up, but there's obviously no point in continuing to try to use her now that Mahoney knows what's going on. And I don't have any desire to harm her daughter. I was just using what the daughter had done to my advantage."

"Who else in your outfit knows about the video and you squeezing Lydia?"

"No one. I was keeping the operation to myself until I'd gotten something useful from her. I didn't want my boss to interject himself into what I was doing and then try to take credit for it."

"That's good to hear," DeMarco said.

Zhou said, "But I am curious about something, Mr. DeMarco. How did Mahoney know I was meeting with Lydia? I know the FBI follows embassy personnel periodically, but I was very careful to make sure I wasn't followed when I met with her."

"Mahoney knew because a woman who knows you saw you and Lydia in a park in Arlington and this woman told Mahoney, believing that Mahoney would tell the FBI what you were doing. And when I asked Lydia why she was meeting with you, she told me about the video you sent her and that she was being blackmailed. The funny thing is, although I doubt you'll think it's funny, is the woman who told Mahoney about seeing you with Lydia is also the person who made the video. You see what I'm saying here? This woman set things up so that you could blackmail Lydia and then turns around and betrays you by telling Mahoney."

"Really," Zhou said. "Why would she do that?"

"Because a rich man who hates Dutch McMillian gave her a lot of money to put Lydia in a position where she'd be arrested for spying for you, and that in turn would damage her husband because people would believe he was complicit."

"I'll be damned," Zhou said softly.

DeMarco said, "You don't seem particularly upset."

"Oh, I am, actually. I'm quite annoyed that this woman would do this."

And for the first time since meeting him, DeMarco could see there was a serious side to Zhou. A dangerous side.

"Do you know the name of the person who sent you the video?" DeMarco asked.

"I don't. But I know it was a woman because she called me. Are you going to tell me who she is?"

"I don't think so. But I'd like to know what reason she gave for giving you the video, if you're willing to tell me."

DeMarco couldn't believe how calm and civilized this whole discussion was going.

Zhou said, "She told me she'd been hired to damage Dutch McMillian politically but the person who'd hired her wouldn't pay her what the video was worth. So she sold the video to me."

"How much did you pay her?"

"She wants a million, but I've only paid her a hundred thousand so far. I told her I'd pay her the remainder once I was satisfied that Lydia would cooperate. And so far I'm not satisfied because Lydia hasn't told me anything useful. But I did intend to pay her. The odd part is she hasn't contacted me again to ask for the rest of her payment."

"She probably hasn't contacted you because the guy that hired her to make the video is paying her so much, she doesn't need the rest of the money."

Zhou sat back and said, "Well, this is truly fascinating. What do you intend to do next, Mr. DeMarco? I've agreed to leave Lydia alone, but this woman, whoever she is, is still out there and has the original of the video."

"To tell you the truth, I haven't figured that out yet."

"Well, if I can help, let me know. Like I said, I am rather annoyed that she played me the way she did."

32

When Diane called, it sounded as if Zhou was at a party. She could hear a string quartet playing in the background and the low murmur of people talking.

She said, "It's me. Can you talk?"

Diane had decided to call Zhou because she wanted the 900K that he owed her if she could get it. But the main reason she called him was that she was wondering if something had gone wrong when it came to Zhou blackmailing Lydia and maybe that was why there'd been nothing reported about Lydia spying for him.

There was a brief pause before Zhou said, "Yes, just a minute."

A moment later he said, "What can I do for you?" She now heard the sound of traffic and figured he'd stepped outside.

"I want the nine hundred grand you owe me."

Zhou said, "You're an interesting woman. You have a lot of, oh, what's the word? Oh, yes, *chutzpah*. I'm hoping that one of these days I'll have the opportunity to meet you in person."

"Yeah, well, that's not gonna happen. So when are you going to send the rest of the money to my account?"

"I'm not giving you any more money. And if you're smart, you'll return the hundred thousand I've already given you."

"Hey, if you don't pay me, I'll—"

"A man named DeMarco came to see me today."

"Who's he?"

"Someone who works for John Mahoney. He's a thug, or at least he looks like one, but he's a smart thug. Anyway, he knew that you were the one who made the accident video and that I was using it to blackmail Lydia Chang. And he told me that if I didn't leave her alone, the Americans were going to expel me from the country. But that's not the only thing he told me. He told me that you're the one who told Mahoney I was meeting with Lydia in the first place. He said that someone was paying you to harm McMillian and that what you did was betray me, hoping that Lydia would be arrested. After which, I'd certainly be expelled from the country."

Diane was too shocked to respond immediately, and before she could think of something to say, Zhou said, "So, like I said, you'd better return the hundred thousand. If you don't, and if I learn your identity . . . well, there are a couple of men who work for me—very unpleasant men—that I don't think you want to meet."

Zhou hung up and Diane sat there stunned, unable to move. Finally, she got up and walked over to a side table where there were a few bottles of booze and glasses. She started to reach for a bottle, then screamed "Fuck!" and swept all the bottles and glasses off the table. Some of the glasses shattered when they hit a wall; fortunately, the bottles didn't. She took a breath, picked up a bottle of scotch and an unbroken glass, and poured herself a drink and drank it in one swallow. She poured another drink, sat back down, and said out loud: "Okay. Calm down. Think."

Who the hell was this guy DeMarco? And how did he know that she was the one who'd made the video? He might *suspect* she made it, but there was no way he could prove it. Whatever the case, she needed to know what he knew. She needed to figure out if he posed a danger to her.

The one thing she knew for sure was that, despite all her hard work and the risks she'd taken, her plan had blown up in her face. Instead of telling the FBI about Lydia Chang, Mahoney had decided to force Zhou to leave her alone. Why on earth he would do that, she had no idea. And Cyrus Offerman wasn't going to pay her the other ten million he'd promised unless something bad happened to McMillian—and right now it didn't look as if anything would happen to him.

She could send the accident video to the cops, but all that would do was hurt that little twit Jenny McMillian, and it wouldn't damage her father. Maybe she could give the video to some other intelligence outfit, like the Russians. And if the Russians used the video the same way Zhou had, to squeeze Lydia, then she'd find someone other than that fuckin' Mahoney to tell what they were doing. No, it wouldn't work—not a second time. For one thing, it would take time to set something up with the Russians, and she didn't think she had much time if DeMarco knew what she'd done. And to complicate matters, Mahoney seemed to be trying to protect Lydia—which still didn't make sense. Why didn't Mahoney do what he was supposed to do and use Lydia to harm her husband, a man he obviously despised?

She could also imagine that right now DeMarco—she had to learn more about him—could be helping to cover up what Jenny had done, and if the accident video was released, a panel of so-called experts would claim it was AI generated and little Jenny would have a bulletproof alibi for the night Harris was killed. Her car had probably already been repaired to make it look as if it had never been in an accident or it was in a wrecking yard, squashed into a cube. And, of course, Noah Parker was no longer alive to say that Jenny wasn't telling the truth.

No, it was time to quit thinking about using the video to screw McMillian. What she needed to do now was protect herself. She needed to know if DeMarco had really identified her as the video maker and if there was any way he could prove she'd killed two people. And she could only think of one way to do that.

Then, after she dealt with DeMarco, she had to go someplace where no one would find her. But her original plan to move to Costa Rica was no longer viable. When she'd been planning to move there, she'd never intended to change her identity or hide who she was in any way. Why would she? She wasn't a criminal on the run. But now things were different, particularly if DeMarco could prove she'd killed Harris and Parker. Then she *would* be a criminal on the run.

Then there was Cyrus Offerman and the comment he'd made about how he had people other than lawyers who could force her to give back the ten million he'd given her. With his money, he could hire the biggest detective agency in the world to hunt her down and he could probably bribe people in the government to help him, like having the TSA notify him if she got on an airplane. And once he found her . . .

Yeah, she could see herself chained to a chair while some sadist cut off her fingers one at a time with tin snips until she transferred the ten million back to Cyrus. And after she did that, she doubted she'd be given a veteran's funeral at Arlington because no one would find her body. Cyrus wouldn't order her to be tortured and killed himself, of course. People like him—people as rich as he was—didn't commit those sorts of crimes. Financial crimes, yes, but torture and murder, no. All Cyrus would do was express his displeasure to someone, saying how she had stolen ten million from him and he wanted it back. And that's all he'd say. That's all he would *have* to say. But the person he spoke to would know someone who knew someone else, and that person would dispatch a couple of killers who'd never be traced back to Cyrus. Yeah, that's the way it would happen.

So she needed to disappear to a place where she wouldn't be found and as soon as possible, but she probably shouldn't fly anywhere. What she'd do was get a car not registered to her and drive to Texas or Arizona or California and find someone who could create her a new identity. She knew there were people in Mexico and the border states who created identities for illegal immigrants, and she'd find one of them to make her into a new person. And then, instead of moving to Costa Rica as she'd planned, she'd split to a country that didn't have an extradition treaty with the United States—Algeria, Indonesia, Morocco, one of those god-awful places—and live as well as she could off the ten million she'd gotten from Cyrus. It wasn't what she wanted, and she wouldn't be able to live the life she'd envisioned, but she didn't have a choice, thanks to that fucking Mahoney.

Goddamnit, this was the story of her life. No matter how hard she worked, no matter the sacrifices she made, things never turned out the way they should. She was always stymied and never able to reach the goals she aspired to—and it was almost always because of some useless man. It was like she was cursed.

Okay, she told herself. It was time to quit feeling sorry for herself. It was time for action.

She would find out who DeMarco was, find out where he lived, and make the bastard tell her what he knew.

Then kill him.

She really wanted to kill Mahoney—but DeMarco would do.

33

DeMarco didn't know what to do about Diane Lake, but the morning after dealing with Zhou he decided to call Mahoney and Lydia to tell them that Zhou was no longer a problem. He figured they'd be relieved to hear something positive.

Did Mahoney praise him for his good work? Of course not. Instead, Mahoney lied and said, "I'd already figured out the best way to handle Zhou was threatening to expel him."

That was bullshit. DeMarco was positive the idea had never occurred to Mahoney. If it had, he would have told DeMarco to do what he'd already done.

Mahoney concluded the call with: "What you need to do now is get off your ass and figure out what to do about Lake. And why in hell haven't you found Mookie yet?"

Before DeMarco could respond, Mahoney said, "I haven't got any more time for this. I gotta go try to straighten out the damn president, who's about to fuck up a bipartisan bill we've spent months working on. And you: you go do your damn job."

When he called Lydia, he heard her say, "Honey, I have to take this call. I'm sorry. I'll be right back."

He wondered if she'd been sitting with her husband, who still didn't know that she'd been blackmailed by a Chinese spy and that his daughter had killed a man. He also wondered what she'd told Dutch about why her daughter was so distraught but figured, as bright as Lydia was, she'd come up with something plausible.

DeMarco heard a door shut and Lydia said, "What is it?"

"You're off the hook when it comes to Zhou." He told her that he'd met with Zhou and threatened to have him expelled from the country and that he'd agreed to back off and wouldn't be forcing her to meet with him again, nor would he release the video.

"You're sure?"

"Yeah, I'm sure," DeMarco said.

He heard Lydia exhale in relief. She said, "Thank you. Thank you so much."

DeMarco said, "But you still have the problem that the person who made the video is out there and might give it to the police. I'm trying to figure out how to deal with this person, but—"

"Do you know who it is?"

He hesitated, then said, "Yeah, I think so." He didn't think so. He knew. But he was reluctant to tell Lydia Lake's name because he didn't know what she might do. He didn't want her doing something on her own.

She said, "If you know who it is, I can offer him money to destroy the video. That'll end this nightmare."

DeMarco decided not to correct her and tell her that the video taker was a her, not a him. Instead he said, "Even if he agrees to destroy the video, there's no way to be sure that it has been destroyed. A video isn't like the negative of a photo. And if you pay him, what he'll do is blackmail you for the rest of your life. That's what blackmailers do. I need to find a way to make sure that doesn't happen. Look, I have to go now. I'll call you soon."

Lydia was saying something he didn't hear as he disconnected the call.

The good news was that the ball went almost two hundred yards. Well, okay, maybe one eighty. The bad news was it landed fifty yards to the right of the flag on the driving range DeMarco had been aiming at.

His five iron was the most unreliable club he carried in his golf bag. When he didn't hit behind it or top it, the ball, for reasons he couldn't comprehend, sliced to the right almost every time. He'd tried standing closer to the ball. He'd tried adjusting his swing so he didn't come across it. He'd slowed down his backswing. He'd adjusted his grip. He'd done everything humanly possible to hit the fucking five iron straight, and nothing worked. He was thinking about having the clubhead melted down into a lump of cast iron he could attach to a chain and use for a necklace. At least then it would be good for something.

DeMarco knew that what he was supposed to be doing was figuring out what to do about Diane Lake, but because he couldn't come up with a solution, he went to a driving range. Golf ball whacking was therapeutic. It cleared his mind of any other problems he might be having because the only thing he could concentrate on was hitting little white balls. But he'd found in the past when he couldn't solve a problem, the best thing he could do was not think about the problem. Which was why he was whacking golf balls, hoping that his subconscious mind would come up with something.

After hitting fifty balls to no avail insofar as correcting the problem with his five iron, DeMarco walked back to his car, holding the offending club in his hand. As he walked past a trash can, he thought about shoving the demon iron into it.

But, as he'd hoped, the deep, lizard part of his brain had come up with a solution. And what led to the solution was the lie he'd told Lydia about having the video enhanced.

Yeah, he had a solution, though not a great one.

But it was the best one he could think of.

34

DeMarco called Neil and told him what he wanted, but Neil said, "I've never done that. I'm sure I could figure out how to do it, but it would be faster if you got someone with some experience."

"Do you know anyone?" DeMarco said.

"Yeah," Neil said. "The guy's dangerous and he scares the hell out of me, but he'll do it if you pay him enough."

"Who are you talking about?" DeMarco asked, and after Neil told him, DeMarco called Perry and asked if Perry knew the man, and Perry said he did. Then Perry said the same thing Neil had said: that he posed a significant danger to the country and someone needed to come up with the technology to control him and others like him.

The guy's name was Billy Drake, and he didn't look dangerous.

Drake was short and slender and had close-cut dark hair and small black eyes that looked everywhere but at the person he was speaking to. Maybe it was because of what Perry had told him, but DeMarco thought Drake looked like a weasel trying to escape from a cage. His company was called Drake Productions, and he had a studio on an upper floor in a glass tower in Crystal City. From Drake's windows, DeMarco could see the planes taking off and landing at Reagan National. It seemed as if a plane took off or landed every couple of minutes, and DeMarco hoped they paid those air traffic controllers enough to keep them happy.

During political campaigns, if a candidate said or did something stupid or embarrassing, the opposition would try to come out immediately with television ads that took advantage of the gaffe. Like the time one candidate walked up the steps to an airplane with toilet paper clinging to his shoe; in less than twenty-four hours a clever ad was produced to ridicule the candidate and score cheap political points. And one of the people politicians chose to make such ads was Billy Drake because Drake was good and he was fast.

To make the ads, Drake would sometimes use actors or actors doing voice-overs or he would splice together already existing video footage to give what was wanted. But, thanks to computers and artificial intelligence, he could also produce videos showing people saying and doing things that never happened, and he'd made a few videos like that, spreading misinformation at the speed of light that was sometimes impossible to debunk. And that was what made the guy dangerous.

And that was exactly what DeMarco wanted him to do.

DeMarco showed Drake the video of the person picking up James Harris in the alley. The person, who DeMarco was convinced was Diane Lake, had on a hoodie and her face was never visible. So DeMarco showed Drake a photo of Lake and told him to stick her face in the video.

The photo of Lake had come from Neil, who'd taken it from Lake's driver's license. DeMarco thought Lake was a pretty woman—short blond hair, blue eyes, nice cheekbones, full lips—but he also thought she looked hard in the photo, like someone you wouldn't want to mess with. Maybe that was because of what he knew about her.

DeMarco said to Drake, "I want just a bit of her profile to be visible— just a slice—but enough so she's identifiable. Can you do that?"

He figured Drake would be able to develop a profile from the full-face driver's license photo, and apparently he was right, as Drake said, "Not a problem."

Drake didn't ask why DeMarco wanted him to doctor the video, nor did he ask for money. The reason he didn't ask why was because he didn't care. The reason he didn't ask for money was because Perry had called Drake and said the DNC would use him to make half a dozen fifteen-second ads for the candidate Mahoney had paid Reverend Roland Calhoun to endorse the day Lake came to him about Lydia Chang. But if Drake didn't do what DeMarco wanted and didn't do it for free, Perry told Drake the DNC would hire one of Drake's competitors to make the Virginia ads. Perry didn't want a money trail from Drake to Mahoney's coffers for what DeMarco wanted him to do.

Drake said it wouldn't take long for him to produce a video—just an hour or two—but he couldn't work on it until later that evening because he had three projects in front of DeMarco's. He told DeMarco to come back at eight p.m.

———————◆———————

At eight, DeMarco returned to Drake's studio and Drake transferred the video he'd produced to DeMarco's phone. DeMarco looked at the altered video—and there was Lake helping Harris to his feet that night and her face was barely visible, but there was no doubt it was her.

Like Neil and Perry had said, Drake was a dangerous man. But he was good.

———————◆———————

In a perfect world, Diane Lake would be arrested for killing Harris and Noah Parker, but it wasn't a perfect world. However, the doctored video of Lake picking up Harris in the alley, along with the video that Lake had produced showing Harris being killed, might be enough to convict Lake for killing Harris—but that would mean exposing Jenny McMillian and her mother. So what DeMarco planned to do in the imperfect world he inhabited was *neutralize* Lake, not have her arrested. He would tell her that if she used the video of Jenny killing Harris, then he'd use the video of her kidnapping Harris. So Lake would get away with killing two people but Jenny would get away with what she'd done—which was only fair as it hadn't been her fault—and her mother would never be exposed for meeting with Zhou.

The fact that Lake had killed Noah Parker didn't particularly bother DeMarco because he knew Parker had conspired with Lake to set up Jenny.

But Harris's death did bother him.

And he couldn't figure out a way to make Lake pay for that.

It wasn't a perfect world.

35

Thanks to having worked for Vicount, Diane knew several congressional staffers—people like Perry Wallace, Mahoney's chief of staff. But she couldn't call Wallace to find out about DeMarco. The person she called was Kevin Sullivan.

Kevin Sullivan was a senior aide to a powerful congressman from Ohio and she'd met Kevin, who was married, at a political gathering at the Mayflower Hotel. Diane was there to recruit clients for Vicount. After way too many drinks they ended up in bed together, but she hadn't gone to bed with Kevin because she was trying to use him in any way. Her only reason was that she was in the mood and Kevin was a stud. But the fact that he was married—Diane had to pay for the room that night so it wouldn't show up on his credit card—gave her a bit of an edge when it came to asking him for a favor.

She said, "Kevin, it's Diane Lake. Remember me?"

There was a long pause. She had no doubt he remembered her. The pause was most likely due to him worrying that she might be calling to take advantage of the fact that he was a married man who'd slept with her, which was exactly what she was doing.

"Of course I remember you, Diane. How are you?"

"I'm fine. The reason I'm calling is I'm trying to get some information on a guy who I think works for John Mahoney, but I'm not sure."

"Oh," Kevin said, sounding relieved that that was all she wanted. "What's his name?"

"DeMarco. I don't have a first name. I looked at a staff directory and I didn't see a DeMarco listed as being a member of Mahoney's staff, but I was told he works for Mahoney. So I'm confused and was hoping you could help."

"Yeah, I know who he is, although I've never met him. And he's not officially a member of Mahoney's staff. He's got an office the size of a phone booth in the subbasement of the Capitol and he's supposedly an independent lawyer who's available to House members on an ad hoc basis."

"What does that mean?"

"It means that if some member needs a lawyer, he's available. But something happened several years ago and DeMarco was arrested for something he didn't do, and because of that, the media put a spotlight on him. Until then, I don't think anyone on Capitol Hill knew who he was. But the media claimed he was Mahoney's fixer, although Mahoney and DeMarco both denied that. So make of that what you will. And there's one other thing about him that's interesting. According to the press, DeMarco's father was a hit man for the mob up in New York before they put all the New York Mafia types in jail. His father's dead and there's no evidence that DeMarco was ever connected to any mob outfit, but I gotta tell you, the guy looks like he could be a New York wiseguy. So that's about all I know about him. But, knowing Mahoney, my gut tells me that DeMarco really is some kind of fixer because Mahoney's an asshole who would need a fixer, all the shit he's pulled over the years."

"Huh," Diane said. "Do you know his first name?"

"No, but google DeMarco and Lyle Canton."

"Who's that?"

"You'll see."

"Well, okay, thanks, Kevin. I appreciate it."

"Not a problem," Kevin said. "Don't hesitate to call if there's anything else I can do."

Meaning: *Please, please don't call me again.*

Diane went online again and plugged "DeMarco" and "Lyle Canton" into the search engine and saw that DeMarco's first name was Joseph and learned why the media had become interested in him. Seven years ago, he'd been arrested for killing Canton, who was the House minority whip at the time. He was later released when it was determined that the real killer had been a Capitol cop. One article speculated that he worked for Mahoney, but Mahoney denied this, as did DeMarco. She also found a photo of DeMarco on the day he was arraigned. In the photo, he was wearing an orange jail jumpsuit and hadn't shaved in a couple of days and was glowering at the camera. And she could see what Kevin meant about him looking like a New York wiseguy: big nose, slicked-back dark hair, cleft in a blunt chin. He was a hard-looking SOB, although not a bad-looking SOB.

She searched a bit longer and found the SOB's address.

Diane spent the rest of the day getting ready to run.

She packed a small suitcase, one a bit bigger than an airplane carry-on bag. She was going to have to travel light. In addition to her clothes, she put the hundred thousand she'd given to and taken back from Noah Parker into the suitcase along with an extra clip for her Beretta.

It infuriated her that she was going to have to leave behind most of the nice clothes she'd been planning to take with her to Costa Rica.

She spent the afternoon online emptying her bank accounts, cashing out everything in her 401(k), and transferring the money to the same account where she'd hidden the ten million she'd gotten from Cyrus Offerman. She lost over fifteen grand closing down her 401(k) because of the price of some of the stocks she'd been forced to sell. She contacted the real estate agent she was using to sell her town house. She told the agent that she'd be traveling and might not be reachable, then Docusigned the papers giving the agent authority to sell the town house without her approval and an account number to send the money to.

After she finished packing and taking care of all the financial stuff, she took a nap. She'd go to DeMarco's place after it was dark out, and she wanted to be fresh when she did. Once she'd taken care of him, she'd buy a car from someone on Craigslist or Facebook who would take cash and drive to the Mexican border. She couldn't use her car because the cops might be able to locate her if she did. She'd leave her car on the street with the keys in it and hope that some lowlife would steal it and the cops would waste their time trying to catch the thief. It pissed her off that she didn't have time to sell her car, just like it pissed her off that she had taken a bath closing out her 401(k). Everything that was happening pissed her off—and she was going to take out her fury on that fucking DeMarco.

She woke up at eight, took a shower, and microwaved a meal for dinner. It was now nine and would be dark when she got to DeMarco's place in Georgetown. She was about to grab her suitcase and head out the door when her doorbell rang.

Who the hell could that be?

She picked up the Beretta and went to the door and looked through the peephole.

What the fuck!

It was DeMarco. What in the hell was he doing there?

He rang the bell again.

She thought for a moment about pretending she wasn't home, then decided not to. She'd been planning to go to his place and deal with him there, but this might work out just as well.

She called out: "Who is it?"

He said, "My name's Joe DeMarco. I work for John Mahoney. Open the door, please."

She put the gun in the back waistband of her jeans and opened the door.

She said, "What can I do for you?"

"Can I come in?" DeMarco said.

36

DeMarco took a seat on the couch in Lake's rather barren living room. He saw a suitcase near the door and wondered if she was planning to take a trip. She sat across from him in an armchair and he noticed she didn't lean back. She was on the edge of the chair, both feet on the floor, as if she wanted to be able to move quickly if she had to.

"So what can I do for you?" Lake said.

DeMarco said, "Just to save some time, and so I don't have to listen to you tell me a pack of lies, I'm going to show you something."

He reached into his suit jacket, and when he did, he saw Lake start to put her hand behind her back. He wondered if she was reaching for a gun, which would not be good. She relaxed once she saw he was only taking out his phone. He tapped the phone and handed it to her. "Hit play," he said.

Lake took the phone, tapped it as instructed, and watched herself as she guided James Harris into her car. When she saw her profile, her first reaction was: *That's not possible.* There was no way the camera in the alley had gotten a view of her face.

She said, "Where did you get this?"

"Can I have my phone back?" DeMarco said.

She handed him the phone and he said, "You know where I got it. From the surveillance camera in the alley where you picked up Harris before you drove him to Maryland so Jenny McMillian could kill him. And I've seen the video you gave to Zhou Enlai that he used to force Lydia Chang to spy for him."

"I don't know what you're talking about. The only thing I did was tell Mahoney about Lydia meeting with Zhou. That video you showed me is a fake."

"Diane, I told you I didn't want to waste time listening to you lie to me. The video isn't a fake. I got it from the company that installed the surveillance camera in the alley. And it shows what it shows: you picking up Harris the night he was killed. And I know the reason you staged the accident was because Cyrus Offerman paid you to hurt Dutch McMillian."

"Hey, I'm telling you—"

DeMarco raised a hand. "Now, what I could do is take that video to the cops and that video, combined with the video of Jenny hitting Harris, might be enough to convict you of murder. The two videos combined make it clear you kidnapped the poor guy and then made him stand in the road so Jenny would run over him, and *you'd* be convicted for killing Harris, not Jenny. But if I took the videos to the cops, there'd be a trial, and I'm afraid that the story of how the accident video was used to force Lydia to spy for the Chinese would get out. It would get out because someone would ask the question: Why did you video the accident? And I don't want that question to be asked or answered. So what I'm saying is—and as much as I hate to do it—I'm willing to let you get away with killing Harris and Parker as long as you don't cause problems for Lydia Chang and her daughter. You just crawl back into the hole you crawled out of, and everyone will pretend this whole thing never happened. But. *But.* If the video of Jenny gets out there—and it doesn't matter if it comes from you or Zhou—then I'll show the cops the video of you kidnapping Harris and you'll go to jail."

Lake didn't say anything immediately but she looked like she was about to explode, her pale blue eyes bulging, her face turning red, her lips compressing into an angry slash. Then she stood up quickly, put her arm behind her back, and pulled out a gun. She pointed it at DeMarco's head and said, "You smug son of a bitch. I'm going to blow your fucking head off."

DeMarco didn't move. He sat there pretending to be calm, although in reality he was terrified. The woman looked insane with rage. He said, "Diane, did you think I'd come here without telling other people I was coming? I know you're a killer. I know you killed Parker. So did you think I'd be dumb enough to come here without telling anyone and without giving the information I've got to someone else?"

Lake said, "Yeah, I think maybe you might be that dumb. Or that arrogant. But it doesn't matter. You're a dead man."

The truth was he hadn't told anyone. He'd called both Perry and Mahoney before going to Lake's place, but neither had answered his call and he hadn't left a voicemail.

———◆———

Diane was so angry, she almost pulled the trigger. This bastard had cost her ten million dollars.

But then it occurred to her if she killed him in her town house, her neighbors might hear the gunshot. Her town house shared a common wall with the town houses adjacent to hers. And she wanted to make him tell her everything he knew and everyone he'd talked to. And she wanted to force him to admit the video of her kidnapping Harris was a fake. Goddamnit, she *knew* it was fake. What she'd like to do was duct-tape him to a chair and poke an ice pick into his ears to make him talk, but to tape him to a chair she'd have to get close to him and he might be able to get the gun away from her. He was a pretty big guy—way bigger than she was. So the only way to torture him would be to shoot him a few times in places that wouldn't kill him, like in the kneecaps, until he told her what she wanted to know. But, again, she couldn't do that in her house as her nosy neighbors might hear the shots.

Okay. She'd take him someplace and deal with him—someplace where nobody would hear his screams and where his body wouldn't be found right away. Once his body was found, and because he worked for Mahoney, the FBI would be coming after her in force and she wanted to be far from D.C. before they started hunting for her. She figured there was no reason to come back to the town house—she was already packed—and she didn't want to come back because she suspected that DeMarco might have told someone that he was coming to see her tonight and whoever he'd told might call the cops if they didn't hear back from him. So she wouldn't come back home after she'd dealt with him. And first thing in the morning she'd buy a new car and drive south.

She said, "Where's your car?"

"What?"

"I said where's your car?" She'd use his car, and after she'd dealt with him, she'd dump the car miles away from the body.

"It's out front," he said, "parked on the street, a little ways down the block."

"Get up. We're going to take a ride."

He didn't move.

"You don't do what I tell you," she said, "I'm going to kill you. I don't have anything to lose at this point." Actually, she had a lot to lose, but she wanted him to think she was so desperate she would do anything. "Now, get the fuck up."

He got up. She motioned with her head and said, "Grab that suitcase."

He hesitated, then walked over and picked up the suitcase.

She said, "You try flinging that at me, I'll shoot you. Now let's go. Walk out the door."

Moving slowly, he went to the door and opened it, then stood on her porch. She saw his head moving, probably looking to see if there was anyone on the street he could call out to. She prodded him in the back with the barrel of her gun and said, "Go. Down the steps. Walk to your car."

When she was on the porch, she looked around the way he had. It was nearly dark, and she didn't see anyone on the street. The people in the other town houses might see her with him, but all they'd see was her behind a guy holding a suitcase. They wouldn't see the gun in her hand because she'd hold it down by the side of her leg. They might think he was an Uber driver.

She said, "You call out to anyone, I'll shoot you. You try to run, I'll shoot you. You try anything, I'll shoot you."

He walked down the steps, carrying the suitcase, and turned left when they reached the sidewalk in front of the row of town houses. He walked about fifty yards and stopped next to a Toyota Camry. His car was parked with the driver's side against the curb.

She said, "This your car?"

"Yeah."

"Put the suitcase in the trunk."

"There's no room for it. My golf clubs are in the trunk."

She said, "Then put it on the back seat."

He opened the rear driver's-side door and put the suitcase behind the driver's seat. She said, "No, push it across the seat. I'm going sit in the back, right behind you."

She didn't want to sit in the front, next to him, because he might try to take the gun from her.

She said, "And if you try something, like try to get in a wreck or honk the horn if you see a cop, I'm going to shoot you in the head."

He leaned into the car again and pushed the suitcase across the seat, then straightened up and stood next to the open door.

"Leave the back door open and get behind the wheel," she said.

He hesitated.

She said, "Get in the fuckin' car or I'll shoot you right here. I'm getting tired of having to tell you everything twice."

———◆◆◆———

As DeMarco stood next to the open back door, his left arm was at his side. Barely moving his arm, he used his thumb to push down a small, black button that was on the side of the door, the part of the door that couldn't be seen when it was closed.

He got behind the wheel and Diane slipped into the back seat, sitting directly behind him as she'd said.

"Start the engine and pull away from the curb."

"Where are we going?"

"Poplar Point."

"I don't know where that is."

"It's by Anacostia Park, on the Anacostia side of the Frederick Douglass Bridge."

Poplar Point was a hundred acres of undeveloped land on the bank of the Anacostia River, across from the Washington Navy Yard. The land had originally been marshland, and sediment dredged from the river was dumped on it to make it suitable for building, but the only buildings currently on it were a couple of small structures owned by the National Park Service. It was in a poor neighborhood, not used much in the daylight hours except by dog walkers and people who liked to walk along the river, and at ten o'clock at night, it was unlikely anyone would be there unless they had a desire to get mugged. It was about fifteen minutes from Diane's place and a perfect place to shoot DeMarco a few times to make him talk and then shoot him in the head and dump his body in the river.

"You know how to get to the bridge?"

"Yeah," DeMarco said.

DeMarco knew that she was going to kill him.

Ruining her plan for McMillian had driven her over the edge. She was no longer rational—if she'd ever been.

He said, "You're making a mistake. Like I told you, I don't want to use the video of you kidnapping Harris because, to convict you for killing him, the video of Harris being killed would have to be shown. So right now you can get away with killing two people. But if you kill me, you'll be caught for that. Mahoney will make sure you're caught."

"Shut up and drive."

A beeping noise came from the dashboard.

He said, "You gotta buckle your seat belt or that thing's going to beep the whole way."

He heard her buckle the seat belt.

He said, "You made a mistake when you kidnapped Harris and got captured on a camera. And you've probably made mistakes tonight. There're probably cameras on the block where you live—there're cameras everywhere these days—and one of them probably caught you making me get into the car. And when Mahoney doesn't hear from me—"

She hit him in the head above his right ear with the barrel of the gun, and DeMarco yelled, "Jesus!"

"I didn't make a mistake when I picked up Harris. That video is a fake. Now, shut up and drive."

He reached up to feel the side of his head where the vicious bitch had hit him. It was tender but she hadn't drawn blood.

Ten minutes later DeMarco crossed over the Frederick Douglass Bridge. To his left he could see the lights of downtown D.C. and the lighted dome of the U.S. Capitol. As they got off the bridge, she said, "Go to your left, along the riverfront." A few minutes later she said, "Now take a right."

DeMarco did as she directed and ahead of him was an open space, the onetime marsh that was now called Poplar Point. The glow from the city across the river provided some illumination, although not much, and he didn't see anyone around. He drove a little farther on the road next to the river until Lake said, "Stop here."

He stopped the car and looked around. There was no one nearby; they were alone. He unlatched his seat belt and put his hand on the door handle but didn't move.

She said, "I'm going to get out first and then you'll get out."

He heard her unlatch her seat belt, and when she pulled on the door handle, she said, "Hey—"

DeMarco opened his door and dove out of the car, landing face down. She fired at him as he was moving, and the bullet just missed his head and hit the front windshield.

He scrambled to his feet and started running, running as fast as he could, toward the river, praying he wouldn't trip. As he was running, he heard her yell—he couldn't understand what she was saying—and then she fired again and he heard glass breaking, and he knew it was her shooting out the back-seat window next to where she was seated. She shot out the window because she couldn't open the back door. Then she fired half a dozen shots at him, squeezing the trigger as fast she could. One of her shots hit the ground in front of him, but he figured that the chances of her hitting him were small. For one thing, it was dark and he was a moving target. But the other thing was, she was right-handed, and in order to shoot at him, she would have to use her left hand to shoot through the shattered window next to where she was seated or would have to lean awkwardly out the window to shoot with her right hand.

But what she couldn't do was open the door from inside the car to get out and shoot at him.

The button that DeMarco had pushed down when he'd been standing next to the rear door was the child safety lock, the lock that prevents the back doors from opening to make sure a kid doesn't fall out when you're driving. With the safety lock engaged, the back door on Lake's side of the car could only be opened from the outside, but she probably wouldn't realize that right away.

DeMarco didn't know how long it would take for her to get out of the car—but he knew it wouldn't take long, and he didn't have time to find a hiding place. He had only one option. He ran to the river and down the bank, plunged into the Anacostia, and started swimming away from the shore. He knew she'd have a hard time seeing him in the water at night, and his plan was to swim toward the middle of the river, where he'd tread water and wait for her to leave. He'd left his keys in the ignition, and he figured that after firing half a dozen shots at him that someone might have heard, she wouldn't hang around long and would drive away.

The problem, he soon discovered, was that the river was moving a lot faster than he'd expected. The Anacostia flows into the Potomac and the Potomac flows into the Chesapeake Bay, and both rivers experience tidal surges. And it looked as if there was an outbound tidal surge occurring right now and he was moving downstream at a pretty good clip.

"You motherfucker!" Diane yelled.

She saw she hadn't hit him and needed to get out of the car to kill him. She didn't know why the door on her side didn't open and she decided to try the other door. She leaned over the suitcase on the back seat next to her and pulled on the handle of the passenger-side rear door. Fortunately, that door, unlike the rear door on the driver's side, opened. She didn't know what he'd done to prevent the other door from opening—maybe he'd pushed a button located on the steering column—but whatever he'd done hadn't affected the other door. Once she had the door open, she pushed the suitcase out of the car and got out and took off after him.

As she was running toward the river, she heard a splash. That was probably him going into the water. She reached the river's edge a few seconds later but couldn't see him. He had dark hair and had been wearing a dark suit and he was invisible in the river. Or he'd ducked under the water and was holding his breath as the river carried him downstream.

She started shooting into the river. She knew the likelihood of hitting him was small, but she didn't care. She was shooting because she was furious, and she didn't stop firing until the clip was empty.

She stood a minute breathing heavily, looking at the river, so frustrated she wanted to scream. But she had to get out of the area. Someone might have heard all the shots and could be calling the cops. She returned to DeMarco's car, picked up the suitcase she'd shoved off the back seat, and put it back on the seat. She had another clip for the gun in the suitcase and thought for a second about getting it, then decided not to. She needed to get going.

Diane got behind the wheel and started the car. Fortunately, the sneaky bastard hadn't had time to grab the keys before he escaped. She noticed the car was a mess. The back-seat window on the driver's side was gone and the front windshield had a hole in it. If she got stopped by a cop, she'd have a hard time explaining the condition of the car, particularly the hole in the windshield that looked exactly like what it was: a bullet hole. So she better not get stopped.

As she was driving away from the river, she asked herself: *What will DeMarco do next?*

She doubted that any of her bullets had hit him, and she doubted that he would drown. Not the way her luck had been running lately. But what would he do if and when he managed to get out of the river? If his phone was still working, he might call the cops and report that she'd tried to kill him and stolen his car, and the cops would start looking for the car.

But *would* he call the cops? And the answer to that question was: *Maybe not.*

He'd said that he didn't want her arrested because he didn't want the hit-and-run video with Jenny McMillian to be seen. And if he told the cops she'd tried to kill him, he'd have to explain *why* she wanted to kill him, which could open up the whole can of worms about Jenny killing the bum and her mother spying for the Chinese. So there was a good chance he wouldn't call the cops and she could get away.

Okay. She'd stick to her original plan: she'd get out of D.C., get a clean car, then head toward the Mexican border. It was almost eleven p.m. and she probably wouldn't be able to find someone to sell her a car tonight, so she'd have to wait until the morning to find someone. But she didn't want to drive too far in a stolen car with a broken window in case a cop stopped her. What she'd do was drive to Manassas, which was an hour from D.C. and where it was unlikely the cops would be looking for DeMarco's car. They weren't going to put out a nationwide alert for a stolen car. Then, in the morning, she'd look for people selling cars on Craigslist near Manassas, contact one of them, buy a new car, and dump DeMarco's vehicle.

Before she got on the beltway to leave the city, she stopped at an unoccupied bus stop and put her cell phone on the bench. She was hoping someone would steal the phone and if the cops tried to use the phone to track her, they'd waste their time tracking whoever had the phone. She still had the burner phone she'd used to communicate with Zhou if she needed a phone.

As she drove to Manassas, she thought: *How in the hell did it ever come to this?* Instead of starting a new life in Costa Rica with twenty million in the bank she was now on the run, headed for the Mexican border, and had no idea what she was going to do after that.

She should have shot DeMarco the moment he stepped into her house.

37

When Lake started firing at him in the river, DeMarco dove and held his breath for as long as he could before resurfacing—and then realized he had another problem. He could see the Frederick Douglass Bridge was less than a mile away. And the way the river was running, he was likely to bash his head on one of the bridge support structures and needed to swim to shore before he did.

His suit jacket was weighing him down. The only thing in the jacket he needed was his phone, so as he was drifting downstream, he took the phone out of the inside pocket of the jacket and shoved it into a pants pocket and stripped off the jacket. He thought for a second about pulling off his shoes but decided not to. He pulled hard with his arms to get to the shore; it was a lot more difficult than he'd expected. He was a golfer, not a swimmer, and riding around in a golf cart probably didn't qualify as aerobic exercise. As he was swimming, the water sometimes getting into his mouth and nose, he couldn't help but think of stories he'd read about the Anacostia being one of the most polluted rivers in the country. Ten long minutes later, he could feel the bottom and straggled to the shore and collapsed in the mud on the bank of the river. Yeah, he definitely needed to get in better shape.

He was on the Anacostia side of the river, the same side he'd been on when he'd plunged in, but figured he was almost a mile from the place where he'd entered the water. He looked around and didn't see any car lights or anyone on the grassy field of Anacostia Park. He doubted Lake was still in the park after firing a dozen shots at him. Although, as crazy as she was, she could be. The damn woman had come within an inch of shooting him in the head when he dove out of the car. He was lucky to be alive.

He pulled out his cell phone. He needed to call someone to come pick him up. He'd read somewhere that his iPhone should work if it was submerged in less than ten feet of water, and he was sure he hadn't gone down ten feet. But the phone was dead. It was a waterlogged chunk of black plastic.

On the other side of the park, beyond the 295 overpass, he could see the lights of the Anacostia neighborhood. He started walking in that direction, his head swiveling, looking for Lake. It appeared as if the crazy bitch had taken off. What really pissed him off was that she'd not only stolen his car but also his golf clubs which were in the trunk. He wanted his clubs back, even the damned five iron. He needed that car found.

After walking six blocks or so, he came to a residential neighborhood, and not a prosperous one. He could see run-down single-family dwellings and identical two-story brick buildings that looked as if they might be part of a housing project.

It was only eleven at night and it was a warm evening and there were people walking the streets and cars going by. He needed to see if someone would let him use their cell phone. The first people he encountered were two Black teenagers sitting on the front steps of a house with boarded-up windows that looked abandoned. They were both wearing sleeveless T-shirts and shorts. One of them had on yellow Timberland boots that DeMarco thought looked odd with shorts. The other wore red Air Jordan high-tops. They were both tall and muscular and looked like athletes and were drinking tall cans of Colt 45.

He walked toward them, his hair matted down, his clothes sopping wet, his white shirt covered with mud from the riverbank. He said, "Hi."

Yellow Boots said, "You lost or something?"

"Not exactly," DeMarco said. "I fell in the river and—"

"Fell in the river!" the kid said, laughing. "How the fuck you manage to do that?"

"It's a long story. But my car was stolen and my phone doesn't work. Can I borrow your phone? I need to call someone to get a ride."

The kids looked at each other and Air Jordans said, "Yeah, okay" and handed DeMarco a cell phone. He asked, "Was your car jacked or something?"

"Yeah, you could say that."

He figured it would take forever to get a cab, and that was assuming a cab would venture into this neighborhood close to midnight. He called Perry.

Perry answered sounding alert. DeMarco wondered if he could still be at the Capitol.

He said, "I need you to come pick me up." Speaking quietly so the boys didn't overhear him, he added, "Diane Lake just tried to kill me and stole my car."

"What?"

"I'll tell you about it later. But right now I'm in Anacostia and I need a ride."

"Oh, uh—"

To the boys he said, "What's the address here?"

Air Jordans told him, and he repeated the address to Perry. "Hurry up, Perry."

He handed the phone back to the kid who'd loaned it to him and said, "Thanks. My friend should be here in the next half hour."

"Ain't you gonna call the cops and tell 'em about your car?" Yellow Boots said.

"Not yet."

"Huh," the kid said. He knew DeMarco not calling the cops was odd; that was what a straight citizen would do.

But DeMarco figured he'd wait awhile before reporting his car stolen— he didn't want the cops asking why it had been stolen in Anacostia—and hopefully Lake would have abandoned it by the time he reported it and it would be found. And if it wasn't found, his insurance company would eventually reimburse him. It wasn't his car he was worried about. It was his golf clubs. He doubted the insurance weasels would pay the couple thousand bucks it would take to buy and get fitted for new clubs, and a new golf bag, and all the stuff in his bag, like his range finder. Fucking Lake.

"You mind if I sit down?" DeMarco said to the boys.

"Nah, grab a step," Air Jordans said. "You want a beer?"

He looked at the kid and said, "You know, a beer would really hit the spot right now."

38

As he was driving DeMarco home, Perry said, "You're lucky you didn't get mugged in that neighborhood."

"You've been hanging around Mahoney too long," DeMarco said. "You need to have a little faith in people."

He told Perry about his encounter with Lake and how he had ended up in the river and without a car. When he finished, Perry said, "Jesus Christ. So what are you going to do about her?"

"I don't know," DeMarco said. "I hadn't planned on doing anything. I want her to pay for killing Harris, but I couldn't figure out a way to do that without exposing Lydia and her daughter. And I figured if I offered to let her get away with the killings, that would be the end of it. But then she goes and tries to kill me. She's insane. And she could still send the video of Jenny killing Harris to the cops even though it won't do her any good, but she might do it because she's a twisted, vindictive bitch. I figure right now she's probably on the run since she tried to kill me and thinks I might have called the cops. But who knows what she's thinking and what she might do. If I could figure out some way to take her off the board, I would, but I can't think of one."

"Mahoney might not be satisfied with that."

"Yeah, well, I'll cross the Mahoney bridge when I come to it."

He sat silently as Perry wound his way through the city to DeMarco's home in Georgetown. Even after having lived in D.C. for so long, DeMarco still loved the way the monuments looked at night.

He said to Perry, "Do you think what they say about putting a water-logged phone in a bowl of rice will work?"

"Beats me," Perry said. "I've never had to try it."

After Perry dropped him off, DeMarco put his phone in a bowl of Uncle Ben's, then stripped off the clothes polluted by the Anacostia River, took a long, hot shower, and went to bed.

The next morning he plucked his phone out of the rice bowl to see if it had recovered. It hadn't. It was still dead. So he took a cab to a Best Buy, bought a new phone, and had the Best Buy geeks transfer the data stored in the cloud to the new phone. When he asked the geeks why putting his old phone in a bowl of rice hadn't worked, they said because the rice thing was bullshit.

His first call on his new phone was to the cops, to report his car being stolen. When the cop he spoke to asked where it had been stolen from, he said from the street in front of his home in Georgetown. The cop, sounding bored and disinterested, asked DeMarco for the license plate number and the make and model and color of the car. He concluded the call with "Well, we'll put it on the list and we'll let you know if we find it"—making DeMarco wonder how long the list was. From the cop's tone, he doubted it would ever be found.

His next call was to his insurance provider to let them know about his car. When he asked if his policy would cover his golf clubs, which had been in the trunk, the lady said, "Based on what I see here, it doesn't look like it, but I'll ask my boss." When he asked how much he'd be given to replace the car if it wasn't found and the lady told him, he closed his eyes and prayed that God would rain fire and brimstone down upon Diane Lake.

39

Diane arrived in Manassas, parked DeMarco's car behind a building where it couldn't be seen from the road, and then tried to sleep, but she couldn't. She couldn't stop thinking about how everything had gone wrong. And because she hadn't been able to question DeMarco, she wasn't able to confirm the video showing her face was a fake, even though she was ninety-nine percent certain it was. Nor did she know if he had any evidence that she'd murdered Parker. And she still had no idea why Mahoney hadn't done what he should have and told the FBI about Lydia Chang.

At five thirty in the morning, she found a Starbucks that was open, used the restroom to brush her teeth and wash her face, then got a cup of coffee and went online to find a car. At eight she called a number she'd found on Craigslist for someone who lived in the Manassas area selling a 2019 Subaru Outback for twelve thousand dollars. Based on what she saw online, the price was fair and the Outback was a decent car, and it would probably get her to the Mexican border without a problem.

A man answered the phone when she called. In the background she could hear kids jabbering. She asked if the Outback was still for sale, he said it was, and she said, "Give me your address and I'll be right over."

He said, "I've got to get to work now. You'll have to come by this evening."

She said, "I'll give you twelve five in cash if you sell it to me this morning. If you won't, I'll find someone else."

After a pause, he said, "Yeah, okay. As long as you can get here quick."

She said, "I'm in downtown Manassas. Give me your address and I'll be right over."

———◆◆◆———

She drove past the seller's house and saw the Subaru sitting in the driveway. It was dark blue and didn't have any dents that she could see. It looked like a soccer mom's car. It wouldn't stand out. She drove around the block and parked DeMarco's car on a side street. She opened the suitcase on the back seat and took out twelve thousand five hundred, closed the suitcase, and removed it from the car. She left the keys in DeMarco's car, hoping someone would steal it—or set it on fire.

A little girl who was maybe seven, with pigtails tied with pink ribbons, answered the door when she rang the bell. Diane said, "I'm here to see your dad about his car."

The girl turned her head and screamed "Daddy!" so loud it hurt Diane's ears.

When the man saw her suitcase, he asked how she'd gotten to his house, and she said a friend had dropped her off. Five minutes later she was on her way. The map app on her phone said it would take her thirty hours to drive to El Paso and she figured she'd take three days to get there.

She stopped the first day on the outskirts of Nashville and drove around looking for a motel that would take cash. She couldn't use her credit cards anymore. When she saw a place with a neon sign that said MO EL with the T burned-out, she stopped. The hot water in the shower was tepid, and when she pulled back the sheets, she checked for bedbugs, not knowing if bedbugs were large enough to be visible in the inadequate lighting in the room.

She fell asleep thinking, *A woman as rich as I am shouldn't have to live like this.*

That fuckin' Mahoney. Why didn't he do what he should have done?

40

DeMarco rented a car and drove to Middleburg to see Mike McGuire. He could have called McGuire but, considering what he wanted to ask him, he was paranoid about some entity, like the NSA, monitoring his phone calls—although he had no idea why the NSA would do that. Which made him think of Mookie. He wondered if Mookie had returned home yet but didn't really care.

The horses were still in the pasture munching grass. McGuire didn't answer the door, but DeMarco noticed the barn doors were open. He walked over.

The barn had a dirt floor covered partly with straw. There were stalls for horses, and bridles and saddles on hooks on the walls, and bales of what DeMarco assumed was hay for the horses. An orange Kubota tractor with a bucket on the front for clearing snow in the winter and a backhoe on the rear took up some of the space. McGuire had his back to DeMarco. He was wearing a white T-shirt that was damp with sweat and knee-high rubber boots and was shoveling horse shit into a wheelbarrow.

DeMarco said, "Hey, Mike."

McGuire turned and saw him. He said, "I wonder if they make a drug that will constipate a horse for about a week. There's gotta be something out there."

Before DeMarco could respond, he said, "What brings you back here?"

"I wanted to ask you a question."

Last night DeMarco had spent a lot of time thinking about how to make Diane Lake pay for what she'd done. And he'd come up with an answer, but one that could land him and Mahoney in considerable hot water—and maybe even jail. But there was something he needed to know before he discussed the idea with Mahoney.

McGuire said, "Well, I've shoveled enough horse shit for one day. Let's go have a beer."

They took seats again on the rocking chairs on McGuire's front porch. A fly, attracted by the aroma, was buzzing around McGuire's rubber boots. Pointing at the horses with the neck of the beer bottle in his hand, McGuire said, "I've thought about attaching lightning rods to their backs and letting God turn them into four-legged chunks of charcoal. I swear, if it wasn't for my granddaughters . . . Anyway, what's the question?"

"How much damage could Diane Lake do if she defected?"

"Defected? To who?"

"The Chinese."

"You want to tell me why you're asking?"

DeMarco told him.

McGuire looked at him for a beat and said, "Never figured you for such a hard-nosed bastard. Anyway, to answer your question, she couldn't do a whole lot of damage. She was an analyst at the CIA but she wasn't a supervisor, so she could talk about the stuff she was analyzing and in general how it was acquired, whether it came from human sources or nonhuman sources like satellites and phone intercepts or computer hacking. But she wouldn't know the names of any human sources or even exactly how the information was acquired. We keep things pretty compartmentalized at the CIA, and she probably spent half her time looking at stuff that's online to find out what's going on over there. She could talk about how the CIA is organized and who works in senior positions, but she wouldn't know anything about people in the field or agents they're running. And she's been gone a couple of years, so whatever information she has wouldn't be current. So I guess the bottom line is she could provide them some insight into operational matters but not much, and probably not much that isn't already known by the Chinese. And if she did tell them anything, she could be arrested for treason and the Agency would make sure she spent about a million years in jail."

At that moment a car pulled into McGuire's driveway. A pretty dark-haired woman was driving. The back doors flew open and two little girls, about nine and ten, came barreling out of the car and ran to the porch screaming, "Grandpa!"

And DeMarco could see why McGuire put up with the horses.

41

After meeting with McGuire, DeMarco called Mahoney's office in the Capitol and told Mavis that he needed to speak to the man in charge. Mavis informed him that Mahoney wasn't available as he'd flown up to Boston that morning to meet some of his constituents, the people he was supposed to be representing.

Mahoney did this every three or four months. In the morning he'd hold an open house at his office in Boston and talk to the common folk who would line up and bitch to him about everything under the sun. Oddly, Mahoney actually liked meeting with the ordinary citizens, and they could tell he liked it, which was one reason he was reelected every two years. In the afternoon, however, he'd meet with the Boston big shots who gave him large amounts of money to ensure they remained big shots. Mavis said that he would be back that night and that his flight was landing at Reagan National at about nine.

DeMarco needed to tell Mahoney about his idea for dealing with Diane Lake, and he needed Mahoney's help to do what he wanted, so he drove to the Watergate complex at nine and parked in a no parking zone where he'd be able to see Mahoney's car when he arrived. At ten, the SUV transporting Mahoney pulled up to the building, and Mahoney's driver-bodyguard opened the back door for Mahoney and he got out of the car. The driver wasn't George, the one DeMarco had met at the PBS studio, but a different guy. DeMarco stepped out of his rental car and yelled, "Congressman!"—and the driver whipped around, reaching for the gun in his holster as he did. Fortunately, before the trigger-happy son of a bitch could shoot him, Mahoney said, "He's okay." To DeMarco he said, "What do you want?"

"I need to talk to you."

"Can't it wait until tomorrow?"

"No."

"Well, shit," Mahoney said.

———◆◆◆———

In his condo, Mahoney dropped his briefcase on the floor, shrugged off his suit jacket, dumped it on a chair, and immediately walked over to the liquor cabinet. DeMarco had been close enough to him to smell his breath in the elevator and knew the last thing Mahoney needed was another drink.

Mahoney splashed bourbon into a glass, dropped heavily into a chair, and made a *Get on with it* hand gesture.

DeMarco told him about the doctored video and how he'd confronted Lake in her apartment, figuring that would be the end of things, but then she decided to kill him. When he told Mahoney how he had gotten away from her, Mahoney, the insensitive bastard, laughed and said, "You jumped in the river!"

"She was shooting at me," DeMarco said. "She could have killed me."

Mahoney laughed again and said, "I wish I could have seen that."

DeMarco didn't bother to tell him about his stolen car that contained his golf clubs as he knew Mahoney wouldn't care.

DeMarco said, "Right now she's on the run. I don't know where she's headed or what she'll do next. Maybe she won't do anything next. But I want her to pay for what she did, and in way where she won't release the video of Jenny McMillian killing that poor guy."

"You figured out a way to do that?" Mahoney asked.

"Yeah, maybe. But I need something to give Zhou—something that sounds classified but really isn't—something the Chinese would want to know about. Can you think of anything that might fit the bill? Like, something you might have heard in an intelligence briefing or a hearing?"

"Why do you need something like that? What are you planning?"

DeMarco told him.

Mahoney said, "Huh." DeMarco couldn't tell if the "huh" meant he approved or was impressed. He was silent for a moment, then shook his big head. "I'll see if I can come up with something tomorrow. Right now I'm too tired to think and I need to get to bed."

But he didn't get out of the chair and just sat there sipping bourbon, and DeMarco wondered if he might end up spending the night in the chair after he passed out. He could tell Mahoney's wife was still gone because the apartment was a mess and smelled of cigar smoke. Mary Pat was going to kill him.

As DeMarco was leaving, he said, "I'm curious about something. Why didn't you just give Lydia to the FBI when this whole thing started?"

"I probably would have," Mahoney said, "but then you told me how they'd used Lydia's daughter to blackmail her. Politics is a shitty business and people do a lot of shitty things, but you don't do that."

"Do what?"

"Go after someone's kid."

42

Mahoney arrived at the Capitol the next morning, hungover and tired as he'd slept poorly. He was barely listening as Mavis told him what was on his schedule.

After Mavis left, he closed his eyes and just sat there. Maybe a Bloody Mary—hair of the dog—would help. He needed an eye-opener before making his first call of the day, which was to the governor of Massachusetts, who wanted to whine about needing more federal funding for some bridge that had collapsed. His eyes were still closed when Mavis opened the door and said, "You need to be at the SCIF on the Senate side in twenty minutes. The president just ordered that the gang be briefed by the CIA director and the national security advisor."

SCIF stands for Sensitive Compartmented Information Facility, and is a space designed to prevent bad actors from eavesdropping electronically on information being discussed in there, and people attending meetings in these spaces are not allowed to bring in personal computers or cell phones or smart watches. Some security experts have argued that not even hearing aids should be permitted, but considering the average age of senior politicians, that was deemed impractical. And typically, if the president called for an impromptu meeting of the Gang of Eight, it meant that he was about to authorize the military to drop a bomb on a terrorist or he'd decided—usually so he could spread the blame—to have the leaders of Congress briefed on some emergent and urgent national security threat.

By the time Mahoney arrived at the SCIF, the rest of the gang were all there, seated around a large conference table. Also present was the director of the CIA, the president's national security advisor, and an army colonel. Dutch McMillian glanced up at Mahoney as he entered the room and acknowledged him with a cool nod—and Mahoney wondered if he'd ever have the chance to tell the arrogant prick how he'd bailed his wife and daughter out of the jam they'd been in. It just killed him that he couldn't do that—not with what DeMarco had in mind.

The CIA director told the assembled politicians that they'd located a warlord named Abshir Mohamed Bali who, at that moment, was sitting in a farmhouse he'd confiscated near a fire-ravaged sugarcane field in Somalia. Bali commanded a group called the Army of the Righteous God and he'd been running around for the last three years kidnapping young girls and slaughtering villagers for no good reason other than he was an evil bastard who wanted to cause as much chaos as he could and get rich selling the girls. The CIA director, a woman who Mahoney thought looked tougher than shoe leather, explained how the agency had found Bali and why she was a hundred percent certain he was in the farmhouse. The army colonel passed around a map showing Bali's location and told how a drone being operated out of the Manda Bay Airfield in Kenya would drop a Hellfire missile on his head. The president's national security advisor said that the president wasn't asking for the gang's permission—he was just informing them—and added that the drone was already in place and the operator was waiting for the green light, which the president planned to give in about five minutes. None of the politicians objected and they knew the government of Somalia wouldn't object because there was no government. The only politician who asked a question was the Democrat on the House Intelligence Committee. She asked how sure the CIA was that no innocent civilians would be killed, and the director waggled a hand and said about ninety percent. Close enough for government work.

The meeting was essentially over at that point, but Dutch McMillian asked if there was anything else going on that the CIA director would care to share with them. The politicians rarely got a chance to sit down with her in an informal setting, meaning other than when she was called to testify under oath before the intelligence committees. And the director didn't trust the politicians farther than she could spit a warthog, but she needed the bastards to maintain her budget. She also liked to impress upon them how effective she was—better than any swinging dick who'd ever held the job—and so she told them about a few things her spies were working on.

She said her people were watching one group of bumblers plotting a coup to overthrow the Mongolian government, as if anyone gave a shit about Mongolia. They were also helping the Pakistanis locate a nuclear warhead that had gone missing and monitoring a financial crisis looming in Iran. The last one she tossed out there in case any of the politicians had stocks they wanted to dump. Then she laughed and said, "Oh, and there's one other funny thing that's happening and at this point we've just decided to let it play out."

And when she told them what the funny thing was, Mahoney, who'd been half-asleep, perked up.

43

Ralph Tate pulled aside the living room curtains and peeked out the window.

He turned to his seventy-five-year-old wife, who was cackling about something Whoopi Goldberg was saying on *The View*. He said, "That car's still out there."

Without looking at him, his wife said, "So call the police if it bothers you so much."

The car had been there for two days. He'd walked around it once and saw the back-seat window on the passenger side had been broken and there was a hole in the windshield that could have been made by a small rock, but he thought it might be a bullet hole. He figured the car had been stolen and abandoned but wasn't sure because of his next-door neighbor.

The long-haired bastard had moved in a couple of years ago and he was a lazy slob who didn't take care of his yard. Ralph had asked him once what he did for a living, and he said he was a "tech guy"—whatever that meant—and he worked from home. Ralph suspected that he was a criminal, although he didn't know what kind of criminal. All he knew was that the people who visited him all looked like trash—tattoos everywhere, women dressed like hookers, scrawny, fidgety guys who had to be dopers—and Ralph thought that maybe one of them was staying there and that's who owned the car. Well, he wasn't going to have it parked outside his house forever.

He told his wife, "I'm gonna ask the shitbag if he knows whose car that is." His wife knew who he meant when he said *the shitbag*. But all she did was wave a hand him, meaning he should quit bothering her while she was watching the gossipy twits on *The View*.

He rang the shitbag's doorbell. He came to the door wearing nothing but dirty white boxer shorts, his big gut hanging over the boxers, his hair tied in a fruity ponytail. He was rubbing his eyes like Ralph had woken him up, and Ralph could smell what he was pretty sure was the odor of marijuana coming from inside the house.

He said, "What's up?"

Ralph pointed and said, "You know who owns that car?"

"No."

"It's been sitting there for two days."

"Hadn't noticed." A phone started ringing. He said, "Sorry, I'm expecting a call. I gotta get that," and closed the door. Ralph figured it was probably one of his dope suppliers calling.

Ralph walked over to the abandoned car. He pulled on the driver's-side door handle and the door opened. The key was in the ignition. He stood a moment and walked around to the other side of the car and opened the passenger-side door, hesitated, then opened the glove compartment. The glove compartment had the usual collection of junk, but lying right on top was the car's registration and another little card that had insurance information. Those documents said the car belonged to a Joseph DeMarco who lived in D.C. He didn't see a phone number on either document but then noticed a receipt from an auto parts store. DeMarco had gotten a new battery two years ago and had kept the receipt because the battery was covered by a warranty. And there was his phone number.

What he should do was just call the cops, but Ralph was curious, and he called the number on the receipt. The call went to voicemail, so he left a message saying: *"My name's Ralph Tate and there's a car that I think belongs to you parked in front of my house and I wondered if your car was stolen. My number is—"*

DeMarco let the call go to voicemail because he didn't recognize the number and figured it was a spam call. But when he listened to the message, he immediately called Tate back and Tate answered.

He said, "Mr. Tate, this is Joe DeMarco. You say my car's parked in front of your house?"

"Yeah, been here for two days. A side window's broken and there's a hole in the windshield, but otherwise it looks okay."

"Thank God," DeMarco said. "I really appreciate you calling me. Where are you located?"

"In Manassas."

"Manassas?" Why had Lake abandoned the car in Manassas? But then, who cared?

"Yeah," Tate said.

"Could you text me your address?"

"Yeah, I suppose I could do that."

DeMarco said, "I gotta figure out a way to get from D.C. to Manassas but I'll be down there today to pick it up."

"You don't want me to call the cops?"

"No, don't do that. They'll probably tow it and I'll have to pay to get it back. And I've already reported it stolen to the cops in D.C. I'll come down today to get it."

"Okay, I'll text you the address."

DeMarco hung up and checked the Uber app on his phone and saw it would cost about seventy bucks for a ride from D.C. to Manassas. That wasn't too bad. His phone dinged with a text message. It was Tate's address. He started to type the address into the Uber app when the phone rang. It was Mahoney's office.

He answered and Mavis said, "He wants to see you."

"Now?"

"In half an hour. He'll be at Michael Thomas Custom Clothiers. That's on Thirteenth Street Northwest."

"Why there?"

"Because he's getting fitted for a new tuxedo and he doesn't have any other time available."

"Yeah, well, I gotta—"

Mavis hung up.

Goddamnit. He called Tate back and said, "Mr. Tate, I may not to be able to pick up my car today. Something's come up at work—something important. But I'll be down as soon as I can, like, probably tomorrow. And I was wondering if you could do me a favor. My golf clubs are in the trunk. Would you mind taking them out and putting them someplace, like in your garage? I'd really hate to have those clubs stolen."

"I don't know," Tate said. "I got a bad back."

"I'd really appreciate it."

"Yeah, okay, I'll see if I can get the shitbag to help me."

"The shitbag?" DeMarco said.

When DeMarco arrived at the clothing store, Mahoney was standing in front of a mirror, wearing a tuxedo, and the tailor, a small, bald-headed man, was on his knees, making chalk marks on the cuffs of the pants. So much for Mahoney's weight loss plan.

Mahoney saw DeMarco in the mirror. He said, "Wait for me outside, by the car."

DeMarco walked back out and over to Mahoney's SUV. His driver was standing outside the vehicle, looking at his phone. This time it was George, the same driver he'd met at the PBS studio.

George saw DeMarco and said, "You again."

"Yeah," DeMarco said. "How're the Italian lessons going?"

George shook his head. "One of my wife's bigmouth girlfriends took a trip to Africa and raved about seeing Mount Kilimanjaro and all the lions and shit, and now she wants to go there instead of Italy. I mean, Jesus, *Africa*. I can just see myself catching Ebola or malaria or getting bitten by a fuckin' tsetse fly."

Twenty minutes later Mahoney emerged from the clothing store. He told DeMarco to get in the car and for George to wait outside.

Inside the car, Mahoney reached into his pocket, took out a small silver flask, and took a swig. He said, "I got something that'll probably work. But it's classified."

"Then that's not good," DeMarco said.

"Nah, I think it's okay to use it. It won't cause us a problem."

"'Us'?" DeMarco said. "You mean you and me?"

"No. I mean the United States. And a lot of people were in the room where I heard it, so it can't be traced specifically to me. But if you get caught for passing it on, you'll be in a shitload of trouble, and I'll deny I ever told you anything."

That Mahoney would throw him to the wolves was no surprise.

"So what is it?" DeMarco asked.

Mahoney told him.

44

DeMarco needed to talk to Zhou but didn't have a phone number for him, and if he'd had one he wouldn't have used it. He didn't want there to be any record of him talking to Zhou. He could go to the Chinese embassy to see Zhou—like an ordinary U.S. citizen going there to get a visa or information—but he didn't want to do that either. He didn't know if American intelligence agencies took photos of people going in and out of the embassy, but he wouldn't be surprised if they did. A third option was to go to Zhou's condo and ring his doorbell as he had before, but he doubted Zhou was at home during the workday and he didn't want to take the chance, however unlikely, of federal agents seeing him at Zhou's place. He'd already taken that risk once and he didn't want to do it again. Having to act like a spy was a pain in the ass.

Unable to think of any other way to talk to Zhou, he bought two pay-as-you-go phones, placed one of the phones in a small box, put Zhou's name on the box, and paid a courier service to deliver the package to the Chinese embassy. In the box, along with the phone, was a message that read: *This is from the guy who told you about the video taker. I've got some information that I think you and your government will want. And keep in mind who I work for. Call me at the number in the phone's contact list.*

DeMarco didn't put his name on the message in case Zhou decided to pass it on to someone. But he'd referred to who he worked for hoping that Zhou would think he'd acquired something from Mahoney that would be of interest to the Chinese—which was exactly what he'd done.

———◆———

Less than an hour later, DeMarco's new burner phone rang. He answered it saying: "No names. And I don't want to discuss anything on the phone. We need to meet someplace. You choose the place, and make sure you're not followed there."

"Okay," Zhou said, sounding cheerful. The guy obviously enjoyed his work, which, as he'd indicated in their last conversation, was like a game to him.

After a brief pause, Zhou said, "Why don't we meet at the place in Falls Church where I met the lady."

He meant the park in Falls Church where he'd met Lydia Chang. The last time he'd met with Zhou, DeMarco had told him that he had a photograph of him with Lydia in the park.

"That's fine," DeMarco said.

"I'll see you there in an hour and a half," Zhou said.

It wouldn't take Zhou that long to drive to the park, so DeMarco assumed he'd use the time to make sure he wasn't tailed. Or at least he hoped that was the case.

———◆———

DeMarco arrived at the park first and took a seat on the same bench where Lydia Chang had sat with Zhou, near the statue of the guy sitting on a horse, waving a sword. DeMarco thought for a moment about going over to see if the statue was one honoring a Confederate general that the state of Virginia hadn't gotten around to destroying but then decided he didn't care.

Zhou arrived five minutes later. He was dressed casually in jeans and a polo shirt. He walked toward DeMarco in long, athletic strides, smiling. He sat down next to DeMarco and said, "So, Mr. DeMarco, we meet again."

"Yeah," DeMarco said.

"And you have something that I assume you'd like to sell me."

That's what DeMarco had thought Zhou would assume: that DeMarco, after learning that Zhou had been willing to pay Diane Lake a million dollars for information he could use to blackmail Lydia Chang, had decided to become a Chinese asset and sell him information he'd obtained working for Mahoney.

DeMarco said, "Nope, don't have anything to sell you. But I'm willing to give you what I have in exchange for you doing something I want—something that I think will also appeal to you."

"What are you talking about?"

DeMarco said, "I want you to offer the person who sent you the hit-and-run video a job."

Zhou laughed. "A job? That woman betrayed me."

"Yeah, I know," DeMarco said. "But let me tell you a few things about her. Her name is Diane Lake and she used to work for the CIA."

DeMarco then told Zhou everything Lake had done and why she'd done it and about Lake's background. He told him how Lake had been working for Cyrus Offerman because Cyrus was a rich, old nut who hated Dutch McMillian. He told him how Lake had killed James Harris and Noah Parker and how she'd tried to kill him. He concluded by telling Zhou what he'd like him to do. Or what *he* would do when it came to Lake if he were Zhou.

When he finished, Zhou said, "So you want me to kidnap an American citizen?"

"Not kidnap. You won't have to kidnap her. Right now she's on the run. She's probably trying to get out of the country. So you won't have to kidnap her. And you'll end up with a former CIA analyst who might be useful to you."

"I doubt it," Zhou said. "From what you've told me about her, I doubt she'd have much information that we don't already have, and her information wouldn't be current."

"Which is why I'm willing to give you something that *is* current and that will be useful to you if you do what I want."

"And what is this information?"

"Not yet," DeMarco said. "For one thing, I don't know if you can find Lake or contact her."

"I have the number of the phone she called me on—the one she used to send me the video. If she still has that phone, I can call her. If she's dumped the phone, then I'm not sure we can find her if she doesn't want to be found. For example, if she's no longer using her credit cards. Or if she's using a different name to book flights or cross borders. And since I don't know anything about the information you're willing to give me, I'm not sure putting in the effort to find her is worth it."

"Yeah, well, I'm not willing to give you the information until she's accepted the job. Tell you what," DeMarco said. "Let's take it a step at a time. You try to locate her and if you succeed, make the offer and see what she says. If you can't locate her, well, then I guess the bitch gets away with murder. And keep in mind how she planned to screw you, so I'd think you might be willing to expend some energy trying to find her."

"All right," Zhou said. "We'll do it your way."

Zhou got up from the bench and started to walk away, then turned back and said, "I have to admit that your idea is very appealing, considering the way she used me. You're an interesting man, Mr. DeMarco. I like the way you think."

45

Diane arrived in El Paso exhausted. She'd spent the previous night in Texarkana, drove eleven hours to reach El Paso, and then spent another hour driving around to find another shitty motel that would take cash. Since she didn't know how long it would take to find someone to make her a new identity, she rented the crummy room for a week. The next morning she went to a coffee shop and used her laptop to go online. She'd deleted her email account so no one could send her an email and trace her that way.

She'd had a thought for how to find someone to make her an ID. She could have hung around in sleazy bars near the border crossing and let it be known she was looking for a forger who could provide what she needed. The problem with that tactic was she could be steered to an undercover cop and get arrested, or she could be steered to someone who didn't even make fake IDs and would rip her off. So what she'd decided to do was contact someone who'd *already* been arrested for making false IDs and see if that person would take the risk of making her one or point her to someone who could.

After two hours of online searching, she found an El Paso citizen named Hector Hernandez who'd been arrested four years ago for selling fake birth certificates to people sneaking across the border. He'd been sentenced to five years in prison but was paroled after serving three and was roaming free again. She found an address for Hector in El Paso but couldn't find a phone number.

She drove to the address and found herself on a block where every person she saw was Hispanic and where every house had bars on the lower-floor windows and the screen doors. There were cars parked on cinder blocks on front lawns and bare-chested guys with tattoos covering every visible inch of their bodies sitting on lawn chairs, drinking beer at ten in the morning. At Hector's house, in the front yard, were two fat little brown boys sitting in an inflatable swimming pool barely large enough to contain them, laughing and splashing water on each other and jabbering in Spanish.

Diane walked up to the boys, praying they spoke English, and said, "Does Hector Hernandez live here?"

One of the boys, in unaccented English, said "Yeah, he's in the house."

Diane rang the bell and a man who must have weighed two hundred and fifty pounds, wearing a white T-shirt, cargo shorts, and flip-flops, came to the door.

Diane said, "Mr. Hernandez?"

"Yeah," he said. "What can I do for you?"

"I have a business proposal for you. I'll give you a hundred dollars just for talking to me."

"A hundred?" Hector said.

"Yeah." Diane pulled a roll of bills out of a pocket and showed it to him. She wanted him to see that she had money and figured that a man who'd just gotten out of prison a few months ago and was home during the day was most likely unemployed. "Can I come in?"

Hector let her into the house, and she found herself in a living room that seemed cramped because the maroon sofa and matching armchairs were too big for the space. On one wall was a picture of a crucified Christ, blood on His face from the crown of thorns and blood on His torso from where He'd been stabbed with the centurion's lance. She thought the picture was gruesome and couldn't imagine why anyone would put it in their living room. From the kitchen came the smell of something wonderful cooking.

Hector said, "Give me the money."

Diane peeled five twenties off the roll and handed them to him and he gestured for her to take a seat.

Diane sat and said, "Are we alone?"

"Yeah, my wife's working. What do you want?"

"I saw you were arrested a few years ago for making fake IDs. I want you to make me one. I need a passport or the documents that I can use to get a passport. You know, driver's license, birth certificate, that sort of thing."

Hector started shaking his head while she was still speaking.

"I'm willing to pay ten thousand if the documents are perfect."

He hesitated but then said, "I don't do that no more. I get caught again, they'll put me away for twenty years."

"What if I made it fifteen thousand?"

Hector hesitated again—she could tell he was desperate for money—but then he said, "No. I want to see my sons grow up."

"Okay, good for you," Diane said. "But I'll bet you know people who are still in the business."

"Maybe," he said.

"I'll give you a thousand if you can put me in contact with one of them, but it's gotta be someone good, not some hack. And I need the documents fast."

"I'll have to make some calls," Hector said.

"You got a piece of paper? I'll give you a number where you can reach me."

Hector went to the kitchen and came back with a pink Post-it note and a pen and handed them to Diane and she wrote down the number of the burner phone she'd used to communicate with Zhou.

"If I don't hear back from you by nine tonight, I'll find someone on my own," Diane said.

"How will I get the thousand from you?" Hector asked. "I'm not going to give you a name and then I never see you again."

Diane nodded. "You come up with a name, I'll tell you a place to meet me near where I'm staying. Then I'll call and talk to the guy, or whoever it is, and if he tells me he'll do it, I'll pay you. There's no way I'm coming back here at night with a thousand dollars in my pocket."

———◆◆◆———

Hector didn't call that night.

Son of a bitch!

46

After a bad night's sleep on the saggy bed in her motel room, Diane went to the same Starbucks where she'd had coffee and breakfast the previous day and started another online search to find another criminal like Hector.

After three hours of searching, she'd only found one, a document forger who'd been released a year ago, but he lived in Brownsville, a twelve-hour drive from El Paso. Shit! The state of Texas was so damn big, it was mind-boggling.

She wondered why Hector hadn't called. She was sure he needed the money, so maybe he hadn't been able to locate any of his old buddies still in the business or maybe they didn't answer his calls and he was waiting to hear back from them. She'd give Hector the rest of the day to get back to her before deciding to drive to Brownsville. In the meantime, she'd keep looking online. What else could she do?

Her phone rang. She didn't look to see who was calling; it had to be Hector. She punched the accept button before the phone rang a second time and said, "Hello."

"Ms. Lake," the caller said, "it's Zhou Enlai."

She was so stunned, she couldn't speak for an instant. She said, "How did you get my name?" She'd never told him her name.

He said, "I work for an intelligence service and that's what we do: acquire intelligence."

"What do you want?"

She wondered if he could be tracing her location as they were speaking. And she remembered what he'd said the last time she talked to him. He'd ended the conversation with: "If I learn your identity . . . well, there are a couple of men who work for me—very unpleasant men—that I don't think you want to meet." She needed to dump the burner phone and get the hell out of El Paso.

Zhou said, "I've got a proposition for you."

"A proposition?"

"Yes. Although I'm still quite annoyed by how you tried to trick me, when I spoke to some of my colleagues about you, they were impressed, as I was, by the lengths you were willing to go to cause Dutch McMillian a problem. And after I got your name—"

How the hell did he get her name?

"—I learned you were former CIA and spoke Mandarin. Well, my superiors decided, over my objections, that we should offer you a job."

"A job? A job doing what?"

"Working for us."

"You mean for Chinese intelligence?"

"Yes. We have very few female Caucasian operatives, and even fewer who are as smart and attractive as you are. I've seen a photograph of you. A woman like you would be able to blend in in some of our adversaries' countries. Maybe not in the United States, where you could be arrested, but in the UK or Australia or Europe. And we know you've killed people, which shows how far you're willing to go to get what you want."

"You want me to become an assassin for the Chinese government?"

"I sincerely doubt you'd be used in that capacity. But like I said, your willingness to kill shows you have potential. Anyway, if you're interested, we'll fly you to China, where the first thing that will happen is that you'll be debriefed regarding your prior employment at the CIA. After that, there would be some training you'd have to go through, although I wouldn't think it would be more than a couple of months in your case."

"What would I be paid? I'm not going to work for you guys for free."

"I don't know. I didn't ask because I wasn't in favor of hiring you. But I imagine we'd be very generous with you because you're somewhat unique, and part of your compensation would be a nice apartment or house where you could live when you weren't on an assignment."

"And where would that be?"

"Again, I don't know. I hadn't given that any thought. Where would you like to live?"

"Hong Kong, not Beijing."

"Well, I suppose that's negotiable."

"I gotta think about this," Diane said.

"Fine, think about it," Zhou said. "And, frankly, I don't care what you decide. But if you do accept the offer, we'll charter a jet to fly you from El Paso to Beijing so you won't have to worry about going through customs."

The son of a bitch had traced the call!

"I have to think about this," Diane said again, and hung up.

She did *not* want to work for the Chinese government. She didn't want to become a Chinese spy. She could see herself being given an assignment where her job would be to acquire an intelligence asset by seducing some official in the UK or Australia or God knows where. Or she could be inserted into some country where her mission would be to get a job with a government agency that handled classified material and where she could be stuck for years. And she didn't want to live in China in between missions, although Hong Kong wouldn't be too bad, as the former British colony was more cosmopolitan than the Chinese mainland.

As for what they paid her, she doubted it would be very much. She'd basically become a Chinese civil servant, just as she'd been a civil servant when she'd worked for the CIA, and the pay scale for civil servants sucked. On the other hand, she had ten million in the bank, so whatever they paid her wasn't that important.

If she took Zhou's offer, that would solve the problem of how to escape from the United States without using her own passport. And if she was in China and employed by the Chinese government, she'd be protected from Cyrus Offerman and U.S. law enforcement if they came after her.

And it might even be possible for her to start a new life as she planned. She'd waste a few months in China being debriefed and trained but then would most likely be given an assignment outside of China, and that would give her another opportunity to acquire a new identity. And then, and maybe with a little plastic surgery to improve her chances, she'd escape from her Chinese handlers and live off the ten million she'd taken from Cyrus.

If she didn't take Zhou's offer, she still had to find someone who could make her a new identity, which was turning out to be a harder problem to solve than she'd imagined. She could be spending weeks, not days, in Texas or Arizona, living in crummy motels until she found a forger. And she needed to leave El Paso immediately. It didn't sound as if Zhou planned to harm her, but she knew she couldn't trust the sneaky bastard.

So what should she do? Take the job offer or run?

47

While waiting to hear back from Zhou, DeMarco Ubered to Manassas to retrieve his car. Before going to Ralph Tate's house, he had the driver stop at a store and bought a hundred-dollar Visa gift card.

He saw his car was parked in front of Tate's house and walked over and looked at it. It appeared to be okay, other than the shattered back-seat window and the bullet hole in the windshield, the hole reminding him of how close Lake had come to killing him.

He rang Tate's doorbell. The man who answered was in his seventies, short and thin. He reminded DeMarco of a bantam rooster. He said, "You DeMarco?"

"Yep," DeMarco said.

When he saw his golf clubs in Tate's garage, he had to stop himself from hugging his golf bag, which would have looked weird.

He gave Tate the Visa gift card and said, "That's to show my appreciation for calling me about the car. Take yourself out for a nice dinner."

As he was driving back to D.C., Zhou called him on the burner. He said, "She decided to accept the offer. She's in El Paso and—"

"She was probably planning to sneak across the border."

"Probably. Anyway, I told her I'm sending a plane for her tomorrow, but I'll cancel the plane if the information you say you have for me isn't worthwhile."

"Where do you want to meet? I'm not going to give you the information over the phone."

"I guess the same place where we met before."

"I can be there in an hour," DeMarco said.

DeMarco again arrived at the park in Falls Church first. Zhou got there ten minutes later. He was wearing tennis whites: white shorts and a white polo shirt.

He sat down on the bench next to DeMarco and said, "I hope this won't take long. I'm playing in a mixed doubles match in forty-five minutes. My partner and I are going to kick ass. She played for Duke in college."

"Do you ever work?" DeMarco said, wondering when the guy found time to work between embassy parties, seeing his mistress, and playing tennis.

Zhou said, "I'm working right now. So what is the information you have for me?"

"Your boss is having an affair with a woman named Lena Templeton."

This was the information that Mahoney had passed on to DeMarco.

"I already know that," Zhou said. "The fool is having some sort of midlife crisis and cheating on his wife with a bimbo twenty years younger than he is, but so what? If that's all you've got—"

"Lena Templeton is a Russian intelligence officer. Her real name is Anna Ivanova."

"You're shitting me!"

"Nope. Don't know if your boss is providing her intelligence or not; I just know what she is."

"How did you come by this information?"

"My boss. He learned about it in an intelligence briefing given by the director of the CIA."

Zhou didn't respond, but DeMarco could guess what he was thinking.

DeMarco said, "I would think that this would be an opportunity for you to shine. You prove your boss is a Russian asset, or you just say he is, and he flies back to China and gets a bullet in the head, and you become the number one guy at the embassy. And on top of that, you get Diane Lake."

Zhou rose from the bench. He said, "A plane will pick up Lake tomorrow in El Paso."

DeMarco said, "Have you figured out what you're going to do with her?"

"Oh, yes," Zhou said, a small smile on his face. It was not a pleasant smile.

Zhou stuck out his hand and said, "It's been a pleasure, Mr. DeMarco."

———◆◆◆———

After Zhou left, DeMarco sat for a minute, then called Lydia Chang.

He said, "You don't have to worry about the video of your daughter hitting Harris getting out. Everything's been taken care of. You and she can relax."

"What did you do? How do you know it's been taken care of?"

"Because I do. But I can't tell you what I did or how I know. You'll just have to trust me."

She didn't say anything for a moment—trusting him wasn't something that would come easily for Lydia—but then she let out a breath and said, "Okay. And thank you, DeMarco. I will always be in your debt. But I still don't understand why Mahoney had you help me."

"He told me it was because someone went after your kid and that was unacceptable. So tell your husband to quit busting Mahoney's balls every time he's in front of a camera." Before Lydia could respond, he said, "I'm kidding. I know that'll never happen."

On the way to a body shop to get the windows in his car replaced, DeMarco called Mahoney. Surprisingly, Mahoney answered his cell phone.

DeMarco said, "I don't want to get into any of the details on a cell phone, but it's over. I'll tell you more the next time I see you."

"That's good," Mahoney said. "Now take care of Mookie. I want that done."

Before DeMarco could tell him that Mookie was still in the wind, Mahoney hung up.

48

DeMarco's phone rang at six thirty the next morning. Who could be calling at such an ungodly hour? DeMarco wasn't an early riser—never had been—and on top of that he had a slight headache, no doubt caused by the three-martini steak dinner he'd had the night before to celebrate the demise of Diane Lake.

The phone kept ringing. It wouldn't stop. He reached for it, knocked it off the nightstand, then had to get out of bed to retrieve it from under the bed. By the time he had it in his hand, the caller had hung up.

He looked at the phone, barely able to see it as his eyes wouldn't fully open, and saw it was Edna who'd called. The damn woman probably had a rooster that woke her up at sunrise and it never occurred to her that normal people didn't get up when she did. She'd left a voicemail. It said: "*Mookie's home.*"

DeMarco called her back and croaked: "I'll get down there as fast as I can. But sometime today."

"Well, hurry up," Edna said. "Before he takes off again."

DeMarco made a pot of coffee, took a shower as it was brewing, and, while drinking the first cup, took out his phone to see when the next flight was from D.C. to Huntington, West Virginia. Goddamnit, the last thing he wanted to do was spend four hours on planes and in airports to get to Huntington and then another hour and a half driving through the Kentucky hills to Salyersville. And then he thought that maybe if he whined enough someone would come to his rescue.

He didn't bother to call Mahoney. He knew Mahoney would still be sleeping and wouldn't answer the phone, nor would Mahoney give a damn about how much time he'd have to spend traveling. He called Perry, who answered on the first ring, sounding as alert as Edna. He was probably already in his office. What was wrong with these people?

DeMarco said, "I need a plane."

"A plane?"

"Yeah, Mookie's back home. If I fly commercial, it'll take me all day to get to Salyersville and he could be gone by the time I get there. Mahoney must know some rich guy who has a private plane here in D.C. that he could talk into taking me to Huntington. There's no airport near Salyersville—there's nothing near fucking Salyersville—but if someone could fly me to Huntington, that'll save me maybe three hours, and I'll still have to drive more than an hour to Mookie's place."

Perry didn't say anything. He didn't speak for so long that DeMarco said, "Perry, are you there?"

"Shut up," Perry said. "I'm thinking."

The phone was silent for thirty more seconds before Perry said, "I'm going to get Jack Ferguson's pilot to take you to Huntington."

"Ferguson? Are you kidding?"

Jack Ferguson was the House majority whip. He was a Republican.

"No, I'm not kidding," Perry said. "Ferguson hates Maggie Bower as much as Mahoney does. She's been nothing but a headache for him ever since she got here. And he knows if she's gone, she'll be replaced by another Republican, but one he can work with. There's no way a Democrat will take her seat. Anyway, Ferguson has a Cessna at National. He uses it sometimes to fly back to his district but mostly to fly down to see his girlfriend in Roanoke on weekends."

"Ferguson has a girlfriend?" Ferguson was sixty-eight years old.

"Yeah. Everyone here in Washington, you maybe being the only exception, knows about her. But, fortunately, his wife doesn't yet. I'm gonna tell Ferguson about Mookie. And I'm going to ask him to line up the right reporter to talk to Mookie. It would be better if the story was broken by Fox or Newsmax because I'm damn sure none of Maggie's constituents will believe Rachel Maddow and her pals on MSNBC."

"You really think Ferguson will let me use his plane?"

"I know he will," Perry said. "The damn woman tried to get him booted out of his position. You just make sure Mookie's telling the truth and will talk to the media."

Perry, creator of political miracles, called DeMarco back half an hour later. He said, "Get your ass over to National. When you get there, call a guy named Buddy. He's Ferguson's pilot. I'll text you his number. Buddy'll drop you off in Huntington."

Buddy turned out to be a thin guy in his forties with wavy blond hair and an Errol Flynn mustache. He was a nonstop talker and DeMarco learned that he'd flown Apache attack helicopters in Iraq, that he'd been sober for ten years, and that he had three ex-wives and he still slept with all of them occasionally. While Buddy was talking, DeMarco sat next to him, his eyes mostly closed, his teeth clenched, his hands clenched, every part of him clenched. He hated flying in small planes, and every time the plane hit some turbulence, he had to stop himself from squealing like a girl.

———◆◆◆———

DeMarco pulled up in front of Mookie's trailer on Mash Fork Creek. He noticed the water was a muddy brown color and moving fast and not that far below the bank. He wondered if Mookie and his neighbors had a bunch of sandbags handy.

A man he assumed was Mookie was sitting in one of the green plastic lawn chairs in front of the Airstream, sharpening knives on a foot-powered grinding wheel. The knife he was sharpening had a twelve-inch blade and on the ground near his feet were half a dozen more knives, the tools of Mookie's trade.

DeMarco got out of his rental car. Mookie looked at him but kept on sharpening the knife.

There were two chocolate brown springer spaniels in Mookie's dog kennel, which had been empty the last time DeMarco had been there, and the spaniels started barking as DeMarco walked toward Mookie.

Mookie said softly, "You girls, be quiet." And, amazingly, the dogs stopped barking.

Mookie was wearing a sleeveless blue T-shirt that said UK WILDCATS, knee-length nylon basketball shorts, and flip-flops that had to be a size 15. DeMarco doubted that Mookie had ever played for the University of Kentucky—Edna's son said he hadn't graduated from high school—but he looked tall enough to have played for the Wildcats; he was at least six foot seven. He had long, muscular arms and short dark hair he probably cut himself, and his face was long and gaunt, with hollow cheekbones and dark circles under his dark eyes. He looked somewhat like another Kentucky boy named Lincoln but without the beard.

DeMarco said, "My name's DeMarco."

Mookie said, "You the one who told Herbie that bullshit about an aunt of mine leaving me something in her will?"

"Yep, that's me. I lied to Herbie. I want to talk to you about Maggie Bower and the story you told Bobby Cooper."

"How do you know what I told Bobby?"

"Because Bobby told his mother, and she told me. So is the story true? Did she really shoot her dog?"

If Bower had shot a dog, she'd committed political suicide. People in general loved dogs and people in rural areas tended to have more dogs than city dwellers and the dogs were often working animals that their owners didn't think of as pets. They were family. They were coworkers. DeMarco had seen flood rescue operations on television in places like Magoffin County where people would sit on their roofs with their dogs, shivering with cold, the rain pouring down, and refusing to move unless their dogs were saved with them. He'd seen dogs being pulled up into helicopters, their owners insisting that the dogs be airlifted to safety even if they had to wait for a ride if the helicopter was full. People were nuts about their dogs. And a couple of years ago, a governor in a western state who was thought to be vice presidential material had been dumb enough to write in her memoir about how she'd shot her dog—and folks stopped talking about her becoming anyone's vice president. And Mahoney—and Jack Ferguson—knew that most of Maggie Bower's constituents wouldn't stand for her killing a dog.

If the story was true.

Mookie said, "Yeah, it's true. But why do you care?"

"Because what she did was reprehensible," DeMarco said.

Mookie, a sly look in his eye, said, "You're trying to fuck her over politically, ain't you?" Mookie wasn't stupid.

DeMarco thought for a second about claiming to be a card-carrying member of the ASPCA and that this had nothing to do with politics but then decided not to as he remembered Bobby Cooper quoting Mookie saying that he'd never vote for that bitch again.

"Yep," DeMarco said. "And not just me. The person who helped me get here today is Jack Ferguson. You know who he is?"

"Nope, never heard of him."

"He's the majority whip in the House of Representatives."

"Whip? What's he whip?"

Well, maybe Mookie *was* a little bit stupid.

"*Whip* is his job title," DeMarco said, "and what he does in his position is whip up votes, which is why they call him the whip. He's the third-highest-ranking guy in the Republican Party in the House."

"Huh," Mookie said.

"So what happened with the dog?" DeMarco asked. "Bobby Cooper said you were working for Bower, butchering hogs for her, when it happened."

Mookie shook his head. "It was just awful. I can't get it out of my head. I swear to God, I have nightmares about it."

"So what happened?" DeMarco asked again.

"I was dressing out this hog and she decides to walk over to see how it was going. She was talking on her phone, and she had these two German shepherds with her—beautiful dogs—and one of them kept barking while she was talking, and she kept yelling at it to shut up. The dog was just a puppy. I heard afterward it was only, like, eleven months old. Anyway, she's talkin' on the phone and the puppy's barking to get her attention, and she tries to swat it on the head to get it to stop, and the dog nips her hand. Nipped her pretty good. Drew blood. Well, she screams and whips out her gun—"

DeMarco knew, as it had been reported frequently on the news, that when Bower was not on Capitol Hill and she was anyplace where she was allowed to carry a weapon, she carried one: a shiny .357 revolver in a holster on her hip.

"—and says, 'That's the last fuckin' time you're gonna do that,' and shot the puppy in the head. I'm sure the first shot killed it, but she shot it a second time when it was on the ground. Then she must have realized what she'd done because her eyes got all big and she said to me, 'That animal was untrainable. It was vicious. And that's the third time it's bit me.' Then she told one of her guys to bury the dog and left. I could tell she was pretty shaken up."

"So someone else saw her shoot the dog?" DeMarco said.

"Yeah. Two people. One of them was one of her congress people, one of her aides or something. He was with her. A city boy, dressed like you."

DeMarco was wearing a golf shirt, khaki Dockers pants, and Top-Siders, an outfit he thought of as both town and country. Maybe it was because he had on Top-Siders and not work boots covered with pig shit that Mookie had pegged him as a city dweller.

"The other guy was Clint Edwards," Mookie said. "Clint manages her farm for her when she's in D.C. He was as shocked as I was about what happened. And just as sick about it too. He was the one who buried the dog."

"Would you be willing to tell a reporter what you saw?" Before Mookie could answer, DeMarco said, "She works for Fox, and maybe Fox would be willing to pay you for the story."

"Yeah, I'll talk to her," Mookie said. "What that woman did was just pure evil. She's crazy. And they don't have to pay me, but I won't say no to a bit of money."

DeMarco took out his cell phone and, with Mookie watching, punched in a number. He said, "This is Joe DeMarco. I believe Congressman Ferguson told you I'd be calling."

He was speaking to a reporter named Jennifer Adams. She worked for the Fox affiliate in Lexington. Perry had called DeMarco while he was driving from Huntington to Salyersville and given him Adams's name and number and said that Jack Ferguson had already given her a heads-up on the story and that if DeMarco was convinced that Mookie was telling the truth, he should call her.

DeMarco said, "I'm with Moo—Mr. Morehouse right now and he confirmed the story. How soon can you get here?"

"I'll be in Salyersville in ten minutes. I left Lexington right after the congressman talked to me. What's Mr. Morehouse's address?"

DeMarco told her.

DeMarco hung up and said to Mookie, "The reporter will be here soon."

Mookie nodded. "You think I oughta go change?"

DeMarco shrugged. "That's up to you. But I imagine they can just film you from the neck up."

DeMarco said, "I'm going to take off now. Just tell the reporter what you told me and be sure to tell her about the other witnesses."

"I will. Her aide probably won't talk, but I'll bet Clint Edwards will back me up. He won't lie."

DeMarco said, "Well, thank you for doing what you're doing." DeMarco turned to leave, then turned back and said, "Can I ask you one thing?"

"What's that?"

"Why do they call you Mookie?"

"Because of my sister."

"Your sister?"

"She's two years younger than me. When I was about four, she was two, and my mom and my dad and my brothers all called me Markie— you know, short for *Marcus*. Well, Cindy couldn't say *Markie*. She said *Mookie*. And it just stuck. I been Mookie since I was four years old."

49

––◆◆◆––

A pale sun was just creeping over the horizon as she made the half-mile walk to the factory. All she could see was scorched, reddish-brown dirt in all directions. There was no vegetation, no wildlife, no mountain ranges, just a flat landscape strewn with rocks under a pink-and-gray dawn sky. She imagined that this was what the surface of Mars looked like, but it wasn't Mars. It was the Gobi Desert.

She was wearing a thin denim jacket over an outfit like hospital scrubs—dirty beige cotton pants held up by a drawstring and a soiled beige long-sleeved shirt. On her feet were slip-on, once-white tennis shoes, no socks. It was about twenty degrees outside and she was freezing, but once she got to the factory, she'd sweat like a mule all day because they maintained the temperature in the building at about eighty degrees. The temperature had nothing to do with the workers' comfort. It was dictated by the requirements for processing the cotton and the heat generated by the machines.

She was walking with forty-nine other women, her roommates, her barrack mates. They walked side by side, in twos. No one was talking. Talking was forbidden. If you talked, one of the guards accompanying the group would hit you with the bamboo batons they carried. The blows were painful but intentionally not disabling. A disabled worker wasn't useful.

The short woman walking next to her, a Uyghur, was coughing continually, as if she had tuberculosis. The Uyghur looked like she was about sixty but was probably twenty years younger. And she stank—she stank to high heaven—as did Diane. They were allowed a three-minute shower every four days and it had been three days since her last one. And her hair felt greasy and thin, plastered to her itchy scalp because the harsh bars of soap in the shower room were what she now used for shampoo. She had no idea what she looked like as there were no mirrors in the barracks, but she could feel the gauntness of her face and the roughness of her skin. Like the Uyghur woman walking next to her, she imagined she also looked old beyond her years.

The factory was a textile factory, one where cotton was turned into fabric. It was located in Xinjiang, a region in northwestern China, which bordered the Gobi Desert and was one of the largest cotton-producing areas in the country. It was also the home to the largest population of Uyghurs in China. The Uyghurs were a Muslim Turkic minority, and the Chinese government had decided to eradicate their culture. Millions of Uyghurs had been harassed for practicing their religion or speaking their own language or committing any other act deemed socially or politically unacceptable. The most egregious offenders were interned in "reeducation" camps, which were forced-labor camps, to get them to see the error of their ways. The Chinese government denied that it was persecuting the Uyghurs. It denied that the reeducation camps even existed.

Diane suspected there were about two hundred inmates at the camp—and not all of them were Uyghurs. About a quarter of the camp's population were Han Chinese, the most dominant ethnic group in China. She didn't know the reason the Han were there—she didn't speak to any of them—but suspected they were people who'd made the mistake of criticizing the government or participating in a protest or posting something considered anti-government on the Internet. But they weren't criminals. If they were criminals, they'd either be dead or be in a real prison. But whoever they were and whatever they'd done, the Chinese government considered them a threat to a smoothly functioning society, and they needed to be "reeducated" like the Uyghurs.

She was the only American in the camp and the only non-Chinese person. She'd been at the camp for about three months and lived in a two-story barracks with the women she was marching to work with. When she first got to the camp, she thought about escaping. It was surrounded by a chain-link fence and the gates were locked at night but there was no concertina wire on top of the fence and no watchtowers manned with armed guards. The doors to the barracks where she slept were also locked at night, but she imagined that if she put her mind to it, she could escape by going out of one of the ground floor windows in the restroom. And she could probably evade the two guards who had the night duty and patrolled the grounds infrequently, and then scale the fence, which was only about eight feet tall. But then what? Then what would she do? Disappear into the Gobi Desert? Walk two hundred miles to Mongolia, the only other country close to the desert? She had no money, no identification, no means of transportation other than her feet and just the clothes on her back. The only way to escape the hell on earth she inhabited was to commit suicide, something four inmates had done since she'd been there. Two had hung themselves in the shower; the other two had slashed their wrists with sharp objects stolen from the factory.

But she wasn't ready to take that way out yet.

But maybe soon.

She couldn't go on living the way she was for much longer.

Zhou had told her to be at the private jet terminal at El Paso International Airport at nine a.m. for the flight to China. When she walked into the terminal holding her suitcase, a pretty Chinese woman dressed in a blue suit like a stewardess's walked up to her. The woman smiled and said in perfect English, "Ms. Lake, it's good to see you. Thank you for arriving on time. My name is Chen Li. I'll escort you to the plane."

"Do we have to go through customs?" Diane asked.

"No," Chen said. "Everything's been arranged. The plane will be taking off in about fifteen minutes."

She followed Chen out of the terminal and they were met by a man driving a golf cart who took them to a sleek white Learjet on the tarmac. The golf cart driver stored her suitcase in the plane's cargo hold and she and Chen walked up the steps to enter the plane. The plane had eight plush leather seats that could recline into a horizontal position for sleeping. At the rear of the plane was a galley. The pilot and co-pilot, both Chinese men, were in their seats. They glanced at her when she entered the plane but didn't say anything.

After she'd settled into a window seat, Chen said, "We'll be making a refueling stop in Hawaii and spend the night there." She smiled and added, "Which will make the long trip less arduous for you and will give me and the pilots some time to do a little shopping. We'll all be staying at the Hilton on Waikiki." Diane had stayed at the hotel before. It was lovely and she was looking forward to a walk on the beach after an expensive dinner paid for by the Chinese government.

Chen said, "Tomorrow morning we'll leave at about eight for the flight to Beijing. Now, would you like some coffee and a croissant? Or I can prepare you an omelet if you'd prefer."

Diane said, "You know what I'd really like? A mimosa. Can you make me one of those?" She felt like celebrating.

"Of course," Chen said.

While the plane was taxiing to the runway, Chen served her the mimosa. It was delightful, the orange juice freshly squeezed, mixed with an excellent champagne. The plane took off and she looked down at the sprawling cities of El Paso and Ciudad Juárez as she sipped her drink. She was so happy to be leaving Texas; she hated Texas. She wasn't, however, looking forward to the time she'd have to spend in China, but all she could do was hope that her debriefing and training wouldn't take more than a couple of months as Zhou had said. Whatever the case, she'd do her best to impress her Chinese bosses to better ensure that she'd be quickly assigned to some job outside of China. She prayed her first assignment would be someplace pleasant in Europe where she would be able to . . .

And that was the last thing she remembered.

———◆◆◆———

She woke up. Her head was throbbing. It took her a moment to realize that she was naked. Why was she naked? Who had undressed her? She was lying on a cot with a thin mattress covered by a brown wool blanket. She looked around and saw she was in a small room, no more than six feet square. There were no windows. In one corner was a metal toilet that didn't have a toilet seat. The door to the room was a solid piece of unpainted steel. She was in a cell, a prison cell. Why was she in a cell?

She stood up but became dizzy and almost fell and collapsed back onto the cot. The mimosa she'd been given had obviously contained a drug that had rendered her unconscious for a long time—at least twenty hours if she was in China—and she was still experiencing its side effects. She waited a minute and tried standing again. This time she was able to maintain her balance and she walked over to the door. She saw immediately that she couldn't open the door because it didn't have a doorknob on her side of it. She stood for a moment, not knowing what to do, then went over to the toilet. She looked around to see if there were cameras in the room, and didn't see any. Not that cameras would have stopped her from urinating as her bladder was about to burst and if there were invisible cameras, whoever was watching had already seen her unclothed. Which made her wonder if she'd been raped. It didn't feel like she had been.

She got up off the toilet—the concrete floor cold on her bare feet—and noticed then that on one end of the cot were clothes: an orange, short-sleeved pullover shirt and orange pants with a drawstring to hold them up. There was no underwear. On the floor were slip-on white tennis shoes. After a moment, her mind still not working right, she put on the clothes. The pants were too long.

She sat for almost an hour, terrified and bewildered, getting up once to pound on the steel door, but no one came. She couldn't understand why she was being treated like a prisoner. Zhou had said that the Chinese government wanted her. So why was she being treated this way? Was Zhou getting his revenge for her betraying him? Or maybe he was just doing this to show who was in control, to make sure she understood her place. But there was no need to do that. She was willing to do whatever the Chinese wanted. She needed a chance to explain that a mistake had been made—she was sure it was a mistake, some sort of communication snafu—and whoever was holding her had to contact Zhou.

The door finally opened. A woman was standing there, dressed in green military fatigues and wearing a small green cap; the cap had a red star patch on it. On the woman's shirt sleeves was the insignia of a Chinese army major. She appeared to be about fifty and had short black hair, a round face, and a flat nose. Her eyes were black and devoid of emotion. She was a couple of inches shorter than Diane but outweighed her by about thirty pounds, and she looked strong. Standing behind the major were two male soldiers wearing Chinese army uniforms bearing the insignia of corporals. The major stepped aside and in Mandarin she said to the male soldiers, "Take her."

Before Diane could react, they yanked her off the cot. She said, "Wait a minute." They didn't. They hauled her out of the room and marched her down a hallway where she could see other doors like the door to the cell she'd been in. In Mandarin, she said, "What are you doing? I'm here voluntarily. I came to work for your government."

They turned a corner, walking so fast they were mostly dragging her, and finally stopped outside another steel door. The major opened the door and walked into the room first. Inside the room was a small metal table and two metal folding chairs. On the table was a manila file folder and a yellow legal pad and a couple of pens. On one wall, near the ceiling, was a surveillance camera. A red light was blinking on the camera, indicating that it was functioning. The major sat down in the chair facing the door and the two male soldiers walked Diane into the room, shoved her down into the other chair, and left the room, closing the door behind them.

Diane said, "What's going on? Why am I being treated like this? I was recruited by Zhou Enlai and he—"

The woman slapped her. She slapped her so hard she fell out of the chair. While she was on the floor, the woman walked around the table, kicked her in the back with a heavy steel-toed shoe, then reached down and cuffed her on the head. In Mandarin she said, "You don't speak unless you're asked a question. Now get up and sit down."

Diane got off the floor and sat down again. She could feel blood in her mouth. The woman had cut her lip when she hit her.

She said, "Look—"

The woman slapped her again, again knocking her to the floor. She had large, calloused hands—hands as hard as Ping-Pong paddles. She walked around the table, kicked her again, then grabbed her by the hair and hauled her up and sat her down in the chair. She was incredibly strong. But Diane was furious at being struck and she almost attacked the woman—then restrained herself. She knew if she attacked her, she'd be seen on the camera and the two male soldiers would come and she'd probably be beaten more severely.

So she sat there and didn't speak as the major studied her face with her dispassionate dark eyes, waiting to see if Diane would say anything, waiting to see if she had gotten the message and understood her situation. After a few seconds passed, she opened the manila folder on the table, looked at a page briefly, and said, "We will begin with your time in the United States Army. What was your first posting after leaving West Point? What unit were you assigned to? What were your specific duties? Who was your commanding officer? And so forth. And do not try to lie to me. We've seen an unclassified version of your military record, so we know in general what you did, and I'll know if you're lying."

Diane said, "I won't lie. I'll tell you anything you want to know."

And she would. She would show the major she was more than happy to cooperate. That she was *eager* to cooperate. Then, after a bit, she'd bring up Zhou Enlai again and the promises he'd made to her. But not right away. She didn't want to be slapped and kicked again. One of her ribs felt tender and she wondered if it was cracked.

After four hours, the major stood up and opened the door and called out, "Take her back to her room. Feed her." The two corporals came in and escorted Diane back to her cell. A few minutes later, one of them brought her a bottle of water and a bowl of cold white rice containing small pieces of fish and green onions and carrots. No utensils were provided, so she ate with her fingers. After she ate, she lay down on the cot to think. She had to convince the sadistic major that she wasn't the enemy. She had to develop some rapport with her. And maybe, after she showed her willingness to cooperate, she could convince her to call Zhou and speak to him about her. Or let her call Zhou.

Ten minutes after she'd finished eating, she was taken back to the room and the debriefing continued. The major had her recount in painstaking detail her first army posting. She took a few notes as Diane was speaking but she wasn't writing down what Diane was saying. The conversation was almost certainly being recorded, and she was most likely making notes on follow-up questions. The woman was completely humorless and didn't digress in any way from the topic of Diane's military service, nor did she allow Diane a chance to make the conversation more cordial. After four hours, the major stood up abruptly and left the room, and Diane was returned to her cell. Dinner that night was another bowl of cold white rice and fish and a bottle of water. Diane cried herself to sleep.

The following morning she was taken back to the interrogation room. The major said, "I want to go back over the computer equipment in the facility where you were first posted."

Diane said, "Of course. Anything you want. But before we begin, you need to understand that a mistake has been made. I came to China voluntarily at the request of Zhou Enlai, who is posted to the Chinese embassy in Washington, D.C. If you would just call him—"

The major said, "If you mention that name again, you will be beaten. You will be beaten severely. Now, as I said, you will discuss—"

———— ◆◆◆ ————

The debriefing took two months, covering her career in the army and the CIA, the longest time spent on her four years at the CIA. She was never asked about her employment with Vicount Analytics. She met with the major six days a week. On the seventh day—she didn't know if it was Sunday or not—she was allowed to spend two hours outside walking around in a small courtyard. She had no idea where she was but assumed she was in Beijing or some other large city. She could hear city sounds—traffic and horns honking—and see commercial jets flying overhead. The rest of her time was spent in her cell alone. She was given nothing to read or otherwise occupy her mind. Her diet consisted of mostly white rice, fish, and vegetables, although occasionally she would be given a hard-boiled egg and small pieces of fruit. She imagined her diet was the minimum needed to keep her alive and healthy, but she lost at least five pounds and was constantly hungry.

And she slowly began to go insane. She started talking out loud to herself in her cell at night. She couldn't stop thinking about how Mahoney and DeMarco and Zhou had destroyed her life. But she still had hope.

She thought that maybe, after Zhou had gotten his revenge on her by treating her as a prisoner, he would do what he'd originally promised and allow her to work for Chinese intelligence. He had to know, as he'd said to her, that she had the potential to be useful to the Chinese, and at some point she figured they would use her. And she still had the ten million dollars she'd gotten from Cyrus Offerman in an account in Panama.

And then she didn't.

<hr />

On what turned out to be the last day she spent at the prison, she was taken from her cell and brought to a different room, not the interrogation room where she'd been questioned by the major. In the room was a short, slender Chinese man in his sixties wearing wire-rimmed glasses; he was dressed in a blue suit, a white shirt, and a narrow blue tie. He was sitting at a table and on the table was a laptop, a silver MacBook Air. It was *her* laptop. She could tell because of a white stick-on label on the lid that had her name and phone number on it. The laptop had been in her suitcase along with approximately eighty thousand dollars in cash, the money that she'd used to pay Noah Parker minus what she'd spent on a new car and paying for food and lodging. She figured that the cash was long gone.

Also in the room were two muscular young men wearing white T-shirts and army fatigue pants and combat boots. They were standing next to a stainless steel table, like an autopsy table, that had channels on the sides for blood to run into. Beneath the table were two large containers of water, like the big bottles used for office water coolers.

And Diane thought: *Oh, shit.*

The man with the glasses gestured for her to take a seat at the table where he was sitting. Speaking in English, he said, "It took us a little while to get around the password protection on your computer and your old email account, but we eventually did." He smiled slightly and said, "A young man who works for Apple in Cupertino, California, assisted us. Anyway, we know you gave your real estate agent the authority to sell your town house in Alexandria and she did. You made a profit of sixty-two thousand dollars after fees and taxes, and the money was deposited into a Wells Fargo bank account per your instructions."

He spun her laptop around so she could see the screen and saw it was at the home page for Wells Fargo Bank. He said, "You will transfer the money to an account number I will provide."

When she just sat there, he said, "Ms. Lake, you're going to do what I want eventually"—he gestured at the young men and the table—"so please do what I told you."

She did. She typed in her username and password and transferred the money to an account number he had written down on a Post-it note.

As she did this, she was thinking: *Fine, so I lose sixty-two grand*, but there was no way he could have gotten into the encrypted programs she'd used to set up the account where she'd parked the ten million from Cyrus Offerman.

"Thank you," the man said when she finished. "Now, we know that Mr. Offerman paid you a lot of money to harm Senator McMillian. You are going to transfer that money to the same account number I just gave you."

She said, "You're wrong. Cyrus didn't pay me because I failed. As I'm sure Zhou told you my job was to damage her husband politically. However, that never happened thanks to a guy named DeMarco who works for Congressman John Mahoney. And so Cyrus never paid me what he promised he would. The only money he gave me was a hundred thousand in cash that I used to pay Noah Parker to seduce McMillian's daughter and set up the hit-and-run accident. And that money's gone because Parker hid it and I couldn't find it after I killed him. And Zhou gave me a hundred thousand dollars also, as I'm sure you know, and most of that was in my suitcase. I only spent about twenty thousand of it to get to El Paso."

The man shook his head as if he was disappointed and gestured to the two young men.

They dragged her over to the steel table, slammed her down on it, and restrained her with cargo straps. Then they placed a burlap cloth over her face, and while one of the men held her head in a viselike grip, the other poured water over the burlap and into her mouth and nose. She knew about waterboarding but had only seen it being done in movies. She'd never seen it done in person and had never experienced it. The sensation was like being drowned, a drowning that wouldn't end. She passed out once and was quickly revived, and the drowning continued. She bruised both of her heels as she pounded them on the table. And they kept on drowning her.

She was able to resist for all of twenty minutes—twenty minutes that seemed like an eternity. She didn't know it, but holding out for twenty minutes actually impressed her torturers.

When she said she would do whatever she was told, she was taken off the table and given a towel to wipe her face and sat down again at the table. The little man with glasses gestured at the laptop, and ten minutes later, as he watched, she transferred over ten million dollars—which included the amount that had been in her 401(k)—to an account she assumed belonged the Chinese government. She was now completely broke; she literally didn't have a penny to her name.

When she finished, she said, "What are you going to do now? Kill me?"

"No," the man said. "There is a possibility you could still be of use to us, but you need, oh, how can I put it? An attitude adjustment."

She was taken from the prison, her hair and clothes still damp, and placed in the back of a black unmarked van with a windowless cargo box. Manacles bolted to the floor of the van were placed on her ankles. The only other person in the van was a Chinese soldier armed with a wooden riot baton. The van stopped four times to pick up two Han women and three Han men. The guard told them not to talk as soon as they were placed in the van, and when one man started to say something, the guard hit him hard enough with the baton to knock him unconscious.

The van didn't stop again on a ride that seemed as if it would never end. They were given a single bottle of water but no food and there were no bathroom breaks. Diane wet herself, as did most of the others, and the van stunk of urine and sweat—and another odor that she suspected was the odor of desperation. About twenty-four hours after leaving the prison, the van stopped at the reeducation camp in the Gobi Desert. The day she arrived the temperature was over 100 degrees Fahrenheit. Winter temperatures in the desert have been recorded as low as minus-40 degrees.

———◆———

As Diane walked back to the barracks at the end of the twelve-hour workday, it was dark and cold out, the sweat on her clothes freezing to her skin as soon as she stepped outside. She trudged along, exhausted as always, but looking forward to the meal she'd be given, as she hadn't had anything to eat since that morning. Then she would sleep. She loved to sleep. It was the only time she could stop thinking about what DeMarco and Zhou had done to her, and if she ever escaped, she'd kill them both.

The road to the camp from the factory was mostly unlit, with only a couple of streetlights to provide illumination. But the gate to the camp had bright lights on both sides. And as the group approached the gate she looked up and saw a gleaming black Mercedes and a tall man with sleek dark hair standing next to it, his back to her. He was wearing an expensive brown leather bomber jacket and matching gloves.

It was Zhou Enlai. He'd come for her. He hadn't abandoned her. Her horrible ordeal was finally over.

She broke away from the group and ran toward him. She heard one of the guards shriek, and he ran after her, yelling at her to get back in line. She ignored the guard and kept running, calling out, "Mr. Zhou, Mr. Zhou! I'm here!"

When she was about twenty yards from him, the man turned to face her.

It wasn't Zhou.

She dropped to her knees, then put her head on the ground and started sobbing.

She didn't even feel the blows from the guard's bamboo baton as he struck her repeatedly on the back and shoulders.